Broken Soul

BOOK ONE

CONTENT WARNING: This book contains graphic and violent scenes, including rape, physical violence, emotional violence, animal abuse and psychological turmoil. Please don't take this warning lightly. The contents are brutal at times. I don't want anyone to be harmed from the words I've written.

If you or someone you know needs help, please know you're worth it! National Abuse Hotline **800-799-SAFE**

Acknowledgements

This wouldn't have been possible without so many people who helped me along the way. Thank you to my beta readers, Shelly, Vivian, and Aleaha. Also, a big thanks to Leanne for making such an awesome cover and to my Mom, for financing it! Again, thank you to Aleaha for putting up with all my texts and the countless conversations regarding this book in all its stages.

Thanks to my husband for helping when technology tries to best me!

I am glad and proud to be part of a great community, with amazing people willing to answer even the most unusual questions. Thank you to everyone who answered any questions I had about making this dream a reality.

Without all of you, I couldn't have gotten this far, so thank you!

Prologue

I open the door to the apartment that I share with my high school friend, Jason. It isn't much, just what two college students can afford on part-time incomes, but it's the only place where I can relax and that makes up for the lack of space.

Having a roommate does that too. Jason is one of the best people I've met. Protective, caring, considerate. He's always trying to look out for me, trying to make sure I keep good company, warning me off potentially bad romantic partners. He means well but I want to make my own mistakes and live a little.

He often leaves a light on for me for when I get home late and today is no exception. I smile at the consideration and toss my keys on the end table, where my purse follows.

Tonight was a bust. My date was so interested in himself that I might as well have been a wall. Sometimes, I wonder if it's me. Am I too boring to engage with? Am I just not interesting enough? I want to be talked *to,* not talked *at.*

Shaking off the insecurity and uncertainty, I head into the little kitchenette in our shared living space. It isn't much but it serves our needs. Between the plain, white refrigerator and the kitchen sink, that's prone to leaking, sits the stove with a microwave above it.

I open the fridge door, reach in for the milk and set it on the crappy, Formica countertop. I stand on my tiptoes to reach the cupboard for a cup, when a weight presses into my back, making my heart stop and my breath catch before I remember that it's only me and Jason here.

"You scared the shit out of me, Jason," I huff, laughing lightly. I push to relieve the pressure and get out from the tight space to create some room between us.

But the weight of his body presses harder against my back, making the counter dig into my pelvis.

This is the third time this week he's done this. Is the bubble of my personal space getting smaller or is he just ignoring it altogether? The discomfort makes the blood turn cold in my veins.

"Jason," I say in a light, but firm, tone. "Back up. You're hurting me." I wait a beat for him to immediately back off and apologize, as he always does.

What I don't expect is his hand creeping up my scalp. His fingers are in my hair, gripping and tugging at the roots. He yanks my head to an uncomfortable angle and presses harder against my back. My skin crawls.

Is this his version of a very sick joke?

My hands reflexively go to his. I catch his fingers, fisted in my hair, and try to relieve the pressure, squirming, trying, failing, to get away from him.

He's bigger than me, stronger, and I've never felt threatened by that—until now.

"You think you can go out and fuck anyone you want and come back to me like it's nothing?" Jason spits at me, voice fierce and full of rage, ringing in my ear. "Your sweet ass and cunt are mine, you little whore!"

What is he talking about? Panic turns my blood to ice for a moment before I'm filled with adrenaline, my heart racing like a shot just went off. What the fuck is going on?

"Jason, what are you talking about? I haven't been with anyone!" It feels ridiculous to confess that to him. "We aren't dating. We're roommates!"

He snaps at that, his rage erupting and taking me with it.

"Fuck you!" he shouts, pushing away from the counter and pulling me with him. He swings us around, me by my hair, while my hands desperately try to break free from his grip.

I stumble and try to catch my footing, falling to my knees just beside the end table that holds my phone and I strain towards it. My hair is being yanked from the roots as he pulls me one way and I lean the other. *"Get off me!"*

"You're mine, you bitch! All fucking mine."

I fly onto the couch with a rough shove and scramble to get up before he can get his hands on me again.

His full weight lands on me, knocking the breath from my burning lungs. He grabs and turns me, forcing my back against his front. His grip on my hair loosens as the sharp contortion of his knee stabs into my ass, restraining, controlling, imprisoning.

I don't know when I started crying but tears wet my hair, making the strands plaster to my face. I try to push off the couch but all that does is trap me when Jason moves his knee onto my back. That's when hysteria kicks in and I start fighting like an animal.

His hands are on my pants, ripping them off my hips, but he can't seem to decide if he wants me or himself naked first. All I hear is the clink of his belt buckle coming undone and the roar of blood rushing in my ears. My vision blurs, panic and tears creating a fog where all I can do is feel when the one thing I don't want to do is *fucking feel!*

No, no, no, no, no! This cannot be happening to me.

6

It can't.

This isn't Jason! Jason is normal, maybe a little overprotective, maybe a little too conscious of guys around me. But he's never crossed any lines before.

"*No! Jason! Stop!*" I scream when I feel my jeans being pulled roughly down to my knees. His fist lands heavy on the back of my head, making my already-blackening vision fill with stars. My sense of awareness distorts until I can't differentiate between one moment and the next. My head pounds in agony as he jostles me, ripping my underwear off and positioning himself between my legs.

It feels like my insides are being ripped out and all that exists is pain as he thrusts inside me, assaulting me. With my eyes closed, I whimper through clenched teeth. Every time I try to shift under him and relieve the burn between my thighs, he punches me again, my vision darkening a little more with each blow until I feel like I'm one strike away from blacking out. But I don't fucking black out.

Wrapping his hand around the back of my neck, Jason drops his weight on me, jerking my body and making my thighs scrape on the rough fabric of the couch cushions. I try, one last time, to lift my head so it's easier to breathe but his hand tightens on my neck, cutting off my air supply even more.

I stop moving because I can't escape. He's got me. I can do nothing but lay here. Can do nothing but wait for him to be finished with me. It takes an eternity of agony, of teetering on the edge of unconsciousness that I wish I could drop off of. With his final thrust and a groan, he presses his weight into me and stays, making my already ragged breath cease for a few beats. My sobs shake us both until he pushes up from me, still keeping me trapped.

His hold on my body is pointless. Even if he didn't have me pinned, I wouldn't move. I can't. I'm numb. Paralyzed. My thoughts keep hitting a cement wall, falling before they can fully form. I can't feel now. My mind has shut down and *finally* won't let me feel. A hysterical thought builds: *too little, too late?*

His hand moves from my neck to the back of my head, lightly petting in what I'm sure he thinks is a loving touch. His lips meet my cheek in a gentle kiss and his hot breath makes my stomach roll. "That was perfect, Nora. Thank you for giving that to me," the sick fuck whispers in my ear.

He pulls me up and leads me to our shared bathroom. The pain from just standing steals my breath for a moment before hitting the same cement wall my thoughts keep bouncing off of.

"Sit." He points to the toilet with his order while drawing me a bath.

Cold porcelain hits the back of my thighs. My eyes fall to them. My legs and pelvic bone are turning black and blue. Blood streaks the bruising skin, evidence of my broken hymen, mixed with his seed, because he didn't use protection. Humiliation, fear and shock settle in me, those things my only companion now. They're suffocating me.

I'm running on autopilot, doing as he says. I don't hear his voice, the protective wall keeping me from that much at least, but my lips form answers to questions I pay no attention to.

He grabs the hem of my shirt and pulls it up over my head. Unsnaps my bra and slides the straps down my arms. Takes my jeans off.

Only then do I realize that the entire time I was walking, my jeans were still around my knees. Where is my shirt? I have no

8

idea where my shirt is and for some reason, that makes the tears build anew.

Gently taking my shoulders in his hands, he pulls me to standing and helps me climb into the tub. I hiss when the warm water hits my pussy and freeze, hovering above it and preventing contact with my abused flesh.

"No, Nora, all the way in. It will help with the soreness." He pushes me into the water, with no regard for what I want, or how I feel.

I'd scoff if I could feel anything but numb inside. Why I expect him to start caring now after what he just did to me, I'm not sure, but the feeling of him forcing me down into the water kills the last vestiges of hope I held.

I slide down and a cry escapes when the water touches the backs of my thighs and ass but I keep going. Not wanting to find out what more he can do to me if I don't. What felt like lukewarm water on my feet and lower legs, now feels scalding where the abuse is the worst. My ass hits the bottom of the tub and my body weight lands on my pelvis area. The pain is excruciating. I clench my eyes shut as tight as I can and try to hold myself together. My head continues to throb, but I'm just biding my time until I get a chance to escape.

That's the only thought that computes, running through my head on a loop.

His hands glide over my body with a gentleness that he shouldn't be able to possess, washing me like I'm made of glass. My head just can't reconcile the brutal assault from earlier with his now almost reverent touch. How they can be from the same person is not in my realm of comprehension at this moment.

When his hand moves between my legs to wash me, I clamp them together to halt his progress as a whimper escapes through my tightly pressed lips.

Jason shakes his head, smiling with a devilish gleam in his eyes. "Tsk, tsk, Nora. I've already been inside you. I'm leaking out of you. Now is not the time for shyness." Jason uses his other hand to pry my legs apart and cups my pussy. "Whose is this?" He tightens his grip, waiting for my answer. The smile falls from his face with my silence; the gleam shifts to malice.

I stare blankly at the wall in front of me, humiliation and dread choking me as his unwelcome touch distresses my stinging wounds.

How did my life get to this? I was so happy this morning, filled with nervous anticipation for my date, and now, here I sit, violated. What comes next? Where does this end?

When he roughly shoves two fingers inside me, I cry out from the pain that flares up.

"Whose is this?!" He roars in my face, words heaving out in anger, his face red with rage.

"Yours," I whisper. I'll say whatever he wants me to right now.

I just want this to stop.

Jason's fingers pump in and out of me, making his point, and I tighten my jaw as he lowers himself to my level. He stares at the side of my face while I keep staring at the wall. "Don't ever try and stop me from touching this"—his nails dig into my ass, his fingers curling inside me to the point of pain—"*ever* again. It's mine and that means I can do what I want with it. If I want to touch it, I will. If I want to carve it up so no one will ever want you, I fucking will." I must look appropriately subdued because he withdraws his hand from between my legs. "Stand up, Nora," he commands, steel in his eyes and voice.

I do as he says, as quickly and quietly as I can. He's a timebomb just waiting to go off and I want to avoid the explosion. But my body is in so much pain that my speed suffers and I choke out a garbled cry. I keep stealing glances at him, waiting for him to erupt, when he leans over to pull the plug from the drain.

I stand in the tub, watching as the pink-tinged water swirls down the drain, washing over my toes.

The water swishes through the tub, streaming into the drain.

Water that was clear until I stepped in.

Water mixed with my blood.

My blood.

Something inside me snaps. My mind screams at me to do something, yells that this could be my chance, my *only* chance.

I don't know how my hands got on his back. I hear a grunt of pain but when did my knee connect with his torso?

I'm already halfway out of the bathroom and to my phone before he can recover and before I can think. I can *see* my phone.

But I don't even come close to touching it.

He tackles me from behind. We crash into the floor. His weight on my naked body knocks the breath from my lungs and pain shoots up like acid from the points of impact and my wrists and knees scream in protest.

My head bounces off the linoleum flooring, temporarily disorienting me. If I didn't already have a concussion, I definitely have one now.

My face is suddenly pressed into the flooring and I feel like he's going to crush my skull right here.

"That was incredibly stupid, Nora. You can't get away from me." He pulls me by my hair onto my knees. His hand glides from my arm to my hand and he twists it around my back until it feels like it's going to pop out of the socket. I lean to try and release some of the pressure and regret it immediately when I feel his hard-on pressing into my ass again. My deranged roommate forces me over to the back of the couch and bends me over it. "Don't move, my little whore. If you're good, I might just let you have a break," Jason whispers into my ear as he lines his dick up with my opening again. I cringe and nod my assent.

He slams into me, drawing out a cry from my throat. I'm already swollen and abused from the repeated violation and he feels so much bigger like this. His hands on my hips yank me back as he slams into me. I try to steady myself with my hands on the couch cushions but his violent, frenzied thrusts make my grip slip. Every jolt is fucking agony. When he's done yet again, he pulls me up and leads me to his room. My arms and legs feel like jelly and my legs give out halfway there. I fall on my hands and knees, my head hanging low, my hair a mess. I can hardly see from my swollen eyes.

The tears still streaming down my face mix with my blood and mucus. I'm sure I'm a sight to behold but I don't give two fucks right now. I guess it's too much to ask that he gets disgusted by the sight of me.

Jason yanks me up, half supporting my weight as I stumble behind him.

He kicks the door closed as my body crashes on the bed with a hard push from him. He climbs up behind me, laying down next to me. The only obstacle between my only way of escape is the person I want to escape from. *Fucking perfect.*

My body is screaming at me to rest, my mind screaming to run, but the pain radiating from everywhere, the agony in my mind, makes both possibilities unfeasible. Hoping that I've pleased him enough to cover my body, I go against everything inside me and turn my face towards his.

I clear my throat to get my voice to cooperate. "Can I get a shirt and some pants to cover up?" I implore. My hopes are dashed quickly when he starts shaking his head before I've even finished my sentence.

"No, Nora. I want full access to your body at all times. Now get some rest. I'm sure I'll want you again before too long." His additional blow lands hard on my psyche. I'm not sure how I'll survive anything like that again. Still, I try one more time so I might gain some ground, even if only in my head.

"I only ask because it's a bit cold in here and I can't sleep when I'm cold." There, that sounded reasonable and logical. What I don't consider is that Jason is not either of those things. Quicker than I like, he's on top of me again, using his weight to double the fear his words don't need help doing.

"I said no, Nora. But if you want to keep fighting me, we might be fucking again sooner rather than later." His lips come against my ear as he pushes his pelvis into me. "You make me hard when you fight back." The proof of that statement presses into my thigh.

I shake my head, hoping that he'll lay back down, hoping he'll give me a reprieve, even if it is only a short one. I'm raw, physically and emotionally.

My brain vetoes any attempt I might make to speak, hesitant and afraid of being the recipient of more of his unwanted attentions. He just looks down on me until he finds whatever he's looking for and then lays down next to me again, with his hand cupping my sex, his leg thrown over both of mine, pinning them down. His other arm gets shoved under my neck, further tangling my knotted hair. My entire body is tensed up, frozen. I'm stuck physically and mentally, until Jason finally falls asleep.

His breaths even out in sleep and my brain goes into overdrive. I catalogue all the possible escape routes in the apartment and from within his grip. My mind runs in circles as my body slowly releases the coiled tension.

I wake to Jason's unwelcome touch, his fingers pinching my nipples. When did I fall asleep? I gasp out in pain and push his hand away, to no avail. He's prepared for it and pins both my wrists above my head.

"Good morning, sugar," he says, moving over me. "Are you ready for me again?" Before my brain can even formulate a mental 'no,' his hot, sloppy kiss is on my neck and everything inside me shuts off.

Some moments, I feel the pain more than others; some moments, I feel nothing at all. I don't look outside. The sun sets without my knowledge, rises the same way, but time no longer exists in the normal sense of the word. I measure things by pain now. Nothing else exists. I don't know how long he's had me for and have nothing left inside me that can muster up the desire to care. All I know is that he *has* had me.

And it feels like I no longer have myself.

∞∞∞∞

I place the plate of sandwiches in front of Jason and another in front of my seat. He pats the couch next him and I sit, the picture of obedience and domestic bliss.

He thinks that I've become compliant and, so, he has become complacent. I'm biding my time, waiting until I can get the fuck out of here and never look back.

He's forced himself into me more times than I can count, beaten me more than he's violated me. My head is in a constant state of pain. I've likely had a persistent concussion for as long as he's had me. My pussy's raw and perpetually swollen. The damage is concentrated to his favorite target areas but the rest of me isn't doing much better. I'm covered in black, blue and purple. My arms, my wrists, legs, hips.

My lip's split and the wound gets no chance to heal. It seeps blood with every harsh kiss. When my anger erupted and I called his dick tiny, he proved me wrong by shoving it in my mouth as a lesson.

I only regained the faculty to plan my escape three meals ago. Every time he averts his attention, I place any potential weapon out of his reach and, hopefully, out of where he may think to look.

We eat in silence.

Silence has become my default setting. Unless he directly asks me a question that requires a response, I keep my lips sealed. I learned that lesson quickly after the first morning. I had thought things were as bad as they could get after that first night. I see now that I was being naïve.

Jason's been in every part of me, defiled every orifice, infected my mind. I've done things I never knew could be done and everything I'll never do again. No man will get that right or opportunity ever again.

Jason gives me his plate without sparing me a glance. I'm expected to take care of the kitchen and clean any mess. I've been naked since the first night and each day more bruises paint my skin.

No more.

I move to the kitchen mechanically and clear away the ingredients of our lunch, putting the meat and cheese back into the fridge. As I close the door, Jason comes up behind me and spins me around.

"On your hands and knees. Expose that cunt to me," he growls out.

This, I've come to find, is his favorite position.

I comply and tilt my ass into the air, hoping and praying that he won't take my ass again. He doesn't take the time to make sure I'm properly lubricated when he does. Not that he does when he fucks my pussy either. The pain is unbearable either way but my ass is still raw. I'll gladly have him in any other place.

"That's my good whore." He sneers at me as he kneels behind me. He lines up with my pussy and my head almost drops in relief. As usual, I'm dry as desert dust, as if I'd get wet by this sick fuck and, as expected, he doesn't give a fuck. Sometimes, it pisses him off that he can't turn me on. Others, like now, he doesn't give it a second thought.

My knees dig and scrape with his every thrust and I already dread the bruises. I can feel my skin cutting open against the kitchen floor, my autonomy stolen, and at that thought, I snap.

My will spills out in full force.

I lift my torso up and twist my body until he slips out. My left fist connects with the right side of his previously-unmarred face. I've never hit anyone like that before and while I haven't the first clue what I'm doing, I'm happy to return the favor. Jason is quick to recover and an evil grin comes across his face, like he's been missing the fight and the struggle. He hauls me up to my feet, bending me back over the counter so my spine hits the edge and cuts into me.

I wrap my legs around him and use my stomach muscles to push him back to relieve some pressure. All it does is make it easier for him to lift up and slam me back into the counter. I cry out and pain disorients me. While I waste those precious few seconds, he flips me over and smashes my breasts into the cold surface.

But my arms are free and I scramble to find anything I can grab to help me finally get out of this. My eyes zero in on the knife-block and I try to reach for it but the tips of my fingers just graze the edge. I use my other hand to scoot myself up. I try again to reach out as Jason tries to get his dick back inside me. I struggle to keep him distracted from what I'm doing with my hands and I've almost got it when he impales me again. My resolve steels over and I grab the first knife my fingers wrap around.

I swing behind me with all my might and feel the blade connect with flesh. Jason rears back and I bolt with the knife still in my hand. I stumble around the counter and catch myself on the wall, moving toward the front door of the apartment. I don't know where he is or how badly he's hurt but I hope it hurts worse than he's fucking destroyed me. It's no less than what the motherfucker deserves. In my haste and because of the knife I clutch like the savior it was, I fumble with the locks on the door. Finally, I throw the door open.

Naked, I run from the apartment to the stairwell. My nudity is the furthest thing from my mind. All I see is the possibility of escape, the possibility of rescue.

Later, after someone finds me and I find myself at the police station, I learn that he had me for three nights and two days. But he'll never fucking have me again.

1 The Attack

How did I get myself into this mess? All I wanted was to have a bit of fun. Well, fun for me. But I just had to get in that handsy asshole's face. All because I have a chip on my shoulder and had to knock him down a peg. My pride and temper are always getting me into trouble, which I need to learn to control. Maybe then, I wouldn't find myself in these situations.

In my defense, he did grab my breast and grope my ass, which I have a real problem with when it's unsolicited. The price I'm paying now isn't worth it though. Not that I made it easy for him to kick my ass. I put up a good fight, even with him outweighing me by a good fifty pounds, all in muscle. After all, having an ex-marine for a personal trainer doesn't allow for weakness.

Yet, still, here I lay, my face on the cold, filthy asphalt in the back alley. The scent of my blood mixes with the stench of alleyway trash and dirt. *Fuck*. Every breath is torture. Every breath makes my ribs burn.

That can't be good.

I assess my body and take mental note of my injuries. That dick must've broken some ribs or at least bruised them. My right arm is finally, finally, blessedly numb. The pain earlier was so excruciating, I must have blacked out. Now, I can't get my arm to listen to my brain. The left side of my face feels like I was in a Rocky movie. Those are the most immediate pains that grab my attention.

Clenching my eyes shut, I really wish I would've just ignored his unwanted touch and kept moving through the crowded bar.

I try and take deep breaths but the stabbing pain in my ribs paralyzes me. My vision fades to black again.

My blood runs cold at the sound of fast approaching footsteps. Shit! He's come back to kill me. Or worse, violate me. *Never again*. I try and get my voice to work, hoping someone is nearby, but my raw throat burns with the attempt. It brings on a coughing fit, making the pain in my ribs flare, as I struggle to stay awake. The adrenaline coursing through my body is useless. I'm defenseless as things are. My pain level surges.

"Shhhhhh ... It's alright. I'm not here to hurt you." A deep, soothing voice, like warm velvet, pierces through my panic. "I'm an EMT. I'm going to check you for injuries, then we'll go from there. Okay?" Relief floods my system and I nod the best I can. He must have seen the movement because I feel strong, yet gentle, hands moving systematically over the back of me. Warm, callused fingers brush against my skin and clothes. "Okay, I think it's safe to turn you over. I'm going to grip your shoulder and hip as gently as I can and roll you on the count of three. Good?" At my agreement, he positions himself to roll me onto my back.

I bite the inside of my mouth against the pain; as minor as it is compared to what I'm already feeling, it's inconsequential. That doesn't stop the guttural groan from escaping past my clenched teeth. Did that sound, unfamiliar and broken, as raw as my throat feels, come from me?

He rolls me onto my shoulder, dropping my body weight onto the injured joint. It feels like my shoulder is on fire, a million knives stabbing it, while someone tries to detach my arm from its socket. Tears stream down my face, mixing with the dirt, leaving filthy tracks in their wake.

I squint into a blurry face, my tears clouding my vision. At the sight of dark hair and light eyes, my fear rocks down another level. This isn't the prick who beat the shit out of me all because he couldn't take a hit to his ego. That asshole was bald and had eyes as dark as the night.

God, I hope my rescuer isn't attractive but it'd be my luck if he is. I mentally roll my eyes for even having a thought like that in this moment. How vain does that make me? My inner rant rolls right on until I realize the EMT is talking to me. I catch bits here and there, the repeated reassurances: "It's alright. It's okay. I've got you."

I want to ask him who he is, how he found me, but my voice refuses to cooperate. The pain is eclipsing every thought. The sound of his promise, *he's got me, he's got me,* this man, his presence—it takes the edge off the panic and when the peace of darkness welcomes me, I don't fight it. It wraps me up in its oblivion until there is no pain. There's nothing to be afraid of.

∞∞∞

Beep. Beep. Beep.

What in the fuck is that noise? Who the fuck is responsible? Don't they know I'm trying to sleep here? For fuck's sake. It's rather rude of them when I'm clearly trying to sink into nothingness.

For a few beeps, I float in between consciousness and sleeping like I'm dead. I'd love to sink back into the darkness and peace that the incessant beeping is keeping me from. It's not stopping so I admit defeat and slowly rise up to consciousness.

I regret that action immediately. Why am I in so much pain … everywhere? Everything fucking hurts. I stumble through an impenetrable fog and search for the answers. What caused this? This is so much more than the usual soreness from working out or even overdoing it and sustaining an injury. I roll my mind back to the last thing I remember and start from the beginning.

The morning started like every other of my mundane life. I got my shit ready for work so I could go straight there after my workout and showered, even if I was just going to get sweaty. Dressing in my usual workout gear—a black racerback tank, hot pink sports bra, black yoga pants with mesh on the side and my white tennis shoes—I threw my butt-length, brunette hair into a tight, French braid so it would last all day.

My little kitchenette was the first stop. I made some eggs, toast and prepped my first cup of coffee, of many, in a travel mug. The first sip hit just right. I closed my eyes in ecstasy. I might have an addiction to the stuff but if that's my worse vice, I'd take it.

I grabbed my already-prepped bag and dug for my keys at the bottom of the bag. The coffee warmed my hands as I locked up my studio apartment and headed towards my shitty car. While it's on its last leg, I can't afford a new one. The price of becoming a psychologist is a real bitch and a crappy waitressing job doesn't pay well.

The modest inheritance that my late mother left remains untouched, other than for school.

The drive to the gym was as uneventful as ever. I parked the car in the back, behind the gym. The restaurant where I work is close by.

I questioned the point of locking my car as I pressed the 'lock' function on the key fob. Who would steal it? It's not worth the cost it would take to fix. Another reason why I haven't shelled out the cash for repairs—if I had the money, that is.

I swung into the breakroom of the restaurant, putting away everything that needed to go in the fridge. I grabbed my uniform, shower gel, flip-flops and a towel from the locker to take to the gym, storing away my purse, before heading to the gym in search of a beautiful, welcome torture.

My trainer went hard, really putting me through the wringer with no room for slack. I welcomed the pain and discipline, that feeling of my life being in my control, in my tight grasp. The standard five miles of cardio before the real workout got my blood pumping and the subsequent hour of strength training pushed me to limits I didn't know I had, before he allowed me to head out. I retreated to the showers to freshen up before heading to work.

Nothing extraordinary happened there either. The few advances, from some female and one male client, were normal. Until a regular came in and sat in my section. My jaw clenched with irritation at the sight of the prick who's partial to my rack. But I've learned how to deal with perverts like him well enough and the rest of my afternoon blurred after my lunch break. A monotonous rush of clearing tables and serving food.

The day ended with a trip to the grocery store for fresh fruit and vegetables. Placing them in my trunk, I drove home and lugged my shit inside, storing everything in its rightful place before heading to the shower. I needed to get the workday sweat off me before heading out for a drink to relax.

Blow-drying my hair took a half an hour due to my hair's thickness and length. But once my hair was clean and dry, I changed into my favorite pair of bootcut jeans. They faded from a dark denim to a nice light blue and acquired an appreciated rip in the right knee. I completed the outfit with a plain white,

V-neck shirt over a lacy, hot pink underwire bra and a pair of charcoal gray tennis shoes. While the shirt showed more chest than I would have normally preferred, my double D's made cleavage unavoidable in anything other than a turtleneck.

Going solo allowed me to do what I do best: watch people. I prefer my own company to the awkwardness that comes with other people. I avoid drama in all its forms, whether that comes from the cattiness of women or from men who take every word as flirting or hit on me when I'm not interested—and I'm never interested.

I don't believe I have any real friends anymore. I stopped connecting with people after college, when people struggled to handle me after him. The go-to responses were either ignoring me or pretending like my life hadn't imploded.

I know I'm not normal. I know I struggle with 'normal' conversations. I can talk for hours about anything but the minute any personal topic is broached, a wall comes up. It's when the other person wants those supposedly innocent, pesky, little details that I close down.

So, I stick to the easy stuff. Like my trainer correcting or commenting on my form. Or going over a customer's orders to make sure I have everything right.

Past that, I'm not the most apt at being a friend. I can handle a meathead that can bench-press me but girl talk sends me into a panic. I adjusted to that though—now, I just have no friends. It's the only thing that makes sense. Take that universe! Cue awkward laugh and the sound of crickets chirping. I rolled my eyes internally. Even in my head, I'm an oddball.

I've come to the conclusion that people just suck. Why should I play Russian Roulette to find the good ones? It's not that I don't like people in general. Actually, that's not true. Most people do *suck. I know it's not all, but the overwhelming majority is dreadful. Or maybe it's me?*

I just can't connect with anyone anymore.

I shook myself out of my thoughts and smiled at the sight of the bar. Placing the car in park, I hopped out and pushed the entrance to the bar open. I slid up between two empty stools to place my order of a rum and coke. The bartender gave me a chin lift and started on my drink as I turned to find a spot to sit and relax.

My eyes brushed over the regulars in the crowd, scanning for the perfect spot to sit. Somewhere I could observe and not be observed. I was brought out of my perusal by the bartender.

He winked at me and slid my drink towards me on a napkin. "One rum and coke, for the lady." He was cute but not my type. Mostly because he was a Player with a capital P. Avoid, avoid, avoid ran like a mantra through my head. I put my cash on the counter, including my tip, and gave a salute with my drink before heading to take a seat.

That's where my memories become hazy. Was there a guy hitting on me? It's a struggle to recall the rest of the night. My head pounds with the effort but the memories leak through the fog.

The bald asshole materializes in my mind. The touch of his hand, unsolicited.

He definitely wasn't expecting the punch I threw at his cheek. Men never do. They never expect women to confront, rather than endure.

The silver tree of life knuckle ring that I was wearing, but did not account for, connected with his flesh. He dropped like a lead brick.

I should've just left it at that but ultimately, pride is my flaw.

I grabbed his ear and yanked his head back, dragging him onto all fours. He glared at me with blood running from the cut my ring made on his cheek, his nose bleeding. Did I do that? He must've smacked his head on the floor because I didn't touch his nose. Can't say I was disappointed, either way.

Just like I couldn't control my actions, I couldn't hold my tongue. I dropped my mouth near his ear, keeping my lips away from the pervert's flesh.

"Just in case my right hook didn't clue you in, I am not interested. Even if I was, limp, dickhead-looking pricks such as yourself are not my type. Did no one teach you to wait for permission before putting your hands on a woman?" I released my hold on his ear and pushed away from him. "No means no, motherfucker."

His friends laughing and pointing did not escape my attention.

Believing that to be the end, I sat and enjoyed my drink while watching a few rough-looking men play a game of pool.

I expected him to ignore me, pretend that I didn't exist after the embarrassing, for him, ordeal. That's the usual for men who take a hit to their ego. But not this cue ball-headed fucker.

I nursed my drink through the night before deciding to head home for some rest, moving through the bar, stupidly unaware of my surroundings. I didn't think to look around.

I headed out the door and turned in the direction of my car.

Cue ball grabbed me from behind, fisting my hair in his vicelike grip. Such a bitch move. How manly of the cowardly fucker.

He dragged me down the alleyway, using my hair as a leash.

Such a cliché. The guy grabs the girl and takes her down the dark, empty alley, oh my!

Except it didn't go down like that. I fought him with every step, raking my nails down his forearm, leaving scores of bleeding wounds.

This is where the knight in shining armor steps in. Except, once again, reality deviated from fantasy. Fairytales don't end with the villain beating the shit out of the princess.

There was no white steed. There was no prince.

And he didn't let me go.

"I'm going to teach you that you don't ever fucking do that to a man, ever again, you worthless cunt," he snarled in my ear, his breath hot and revolting against my skin. Smelling like stale beer.

He wrenched my right arm back and up until I felt a pop, until it felt like my shoulder was burning. The fire raged so hot that I screamed and screamed and screamed until my voice gave out, barely registering when he lost his balance and we toppled like dominoes.

Dickhead used my body as a prop, pushing himself up. His hand clenched against my arm, his grip sure, before latching onto my hair. He slammed my face against the concrete. His knees dug into mine with enough force to break my legs. Miraculously, I was spared that injury, at least.

I didn't expect him to stop there.

But he took off like a spineless mouse, retreating back into whatever sewer he emerged from. Something must have scared the dickhead off.

I blacked out before I could figure out what it was.

2 Dr. Baker

That explains the pain every-fucking-where.

I try to open my eyes but the light is blinding and the resulting nausea, from the assault on my visual senses, is instant and raging. I cautiously peel my lids open to slits so the light doesn't overwhelm me again. The nausea is better than earlier but as I try to open my eyes all the way, my left eye refuses to open any further.

Shit. That's not good.

With only my right eye open to full capacity, I notice the TV mounted on the wall—a TV that I don't have and that was not there earlier. And my bedroom wall isn't white.

I turn my head to the beeping sound. To the left of me sit all kinds of medical equipment. That confirms my suspicion—I'm in the hospital. I suppose it's better than still being in the alley but the debt this will throw on my shoulders isn't a great alternative.

I move to grab the water on the bedside table but the moment I move my right arm, my shoulder screams with pain, the nerves in my back and arm feel as if they're on fire. The beeping monitor goes into a frenzy.

Breathing through the residual pain, I move the fingers on my left hand, anticipating the same pain. When the pain doesn't come, I move my left wrist in small circles, slowly increasing the range of motion. So far, so good. My fingers, wrist and elbow are all good. But when I get to my left shoulder, I have to mentally psych myself up. Like ripping off a bandage, I move my shoulder before I can think about it.

My heart sighs at the absent pain but my head is starting to feel light and only then do I realize that I've been holding my breath. I let it out in one big huff. Big fucking mistake. The sensation of a thousand knives stabs me in the chest. I get my breathing back under control and the pain slowly subsides.

My ribs are likely broken and I'm guessing that escaped my notice because I wasn't taking deep breaths earlier.

I drop my left, uninjured arm hesitantly to the side of the bed, careful to avoid aggravating my ribs, and fumble for the call button that all hospital beds have. When I finally press the right button, a beep sounds in the room before a voice comes through the intercom.

"Just a moment, Nora," a female nurse voice says, "a nurse will be right there. Please don't try to get up."

What was probably minutes felt like hours before the door opens for the nurse. I'm still disoriented from the painkillers they pumped into me so my perception of time is off.

The nurse smiles at me from the threshold of the room. "Glad to see you're up, Nora. I'm going to page your doctor and grab your chart. Sit tight, I'll be right back." She disappears back into the corridor and the door shuts behind her. My bladder protests and demands release but I close my eyes and go over the rest of my body.

I focus on the areas that feel red-hot with pain. The left side of my face and my head are pulsing. My right shoulder is not in good shape. When I test them, my fingers seem fine and though my wrist twinges, it's bearable. But I have to be careful with every breath because, my ribs are, at the very least, bruised. In the lower half of my body, everything, except my right knee, is fine, which I learn when I try to lay my right leg down flat. That's a nice surprise because, with the way he was on both of my legs, at least they're not broken. My ass and hips hurt. The rest of me seems unscathed.

Resting my head against the headrest, I relax with the knowledge that I've had worse. Much worse. All I kept from that time in my life is the protective cement wall so I slam it up, halting my thoughts right there. That rabbit hole can wait for its Alice; I'm not going down it.

Just as I stop the spiraling, the door opens and admits an honest-to-God angel.

Holy mother of baby Jesus! If it wasn't for the pain attesting to my sentience, I'd think I was actually in heaven.

My doctor is stunningly handsome. That boy-next-door look, disguising a slight hint of bad boy potential, magnifies his appeal exponentially. His hair is a dirty blonde, clipped close to his head on the sides and longer on the top. The longer strands of his hair are styled in a swept-back look, leaving his jade-green eyes exposed. Almond-shaped eyes, framed by strong slashes for eyebrows, burn into mine with an intensity that has me feeling equal parts nervous and excited. His strong, squared jaw with a hint of stubble and full, luscious lips would make my heart race, if it wasn't already from the pain. His slightly-crooked nose only heightens his allure.

The white lab coat does nothing to hide his physique. He's easily over six feet and well-built, enough to indicate he either spends his hours at the gym or is otherwise physically active. A platinum wristwatch peeks out of his sea-green sleeve and dark, charcoal slacks envelop his thighs.

"Hello Nora, I'm Dr. Owen Baker. Do you feel up to going over a few things with me?" the deep timber of his voice, smooth like warm water, rumbles out, refreshing me. My heart stays high because of the pain but the lingering anxiety abates.

When I open my mouth to answer, my throat feels like someone sandpapered it before pouring vinegar down it.

Dr. Baker notices immediately and turns to the nurse who followed behind him. "Susan, can we get some lukewarm water for Nora, please?"

"You can't be my doctor." I rasp out before I can hold the words back. My eyes widen—at least, the right one does—at my uncharacteristic frankness. It's got to be the drugs!

His head tilts slightly to the left, puzzled, his lips tipped up, like he's trying to figure out if I'm being serious or funny.

"Why is that, Nora?"

"You're *way* too fucking hot to be a doctor." In my mind, I'm trying to dig a hole to hide in forever but the drugs lower my inhibition and obliterate my brain-to-mouth filter. "Plus, you don't look old enough to have graduated medical school." As I try to convince myself that I didn't just embarrass myself enough to hibernate for the rest of my life, Susan snorts and gives me a sympathetic look, like she understands my stupidity completely. She tries to rein in her amusement but, that just makes it worse because it's so much louder than it probably would've been.

"Of course, Dr. Baker, I'll be right back with that water." She escapes the train wreck and leaves me to deal with the situation alone— that, admittedly, I'm solely responsible for, but what ever happened to not leaving a girl behind? I snort and my ribs smart. Dr. Baker eyes me like he's concerned for my sanity.

If he only knew the half of it.

"Okay Nora, while we wait for your water, let me tell you what we know." He takes a quick glance at the clipboard in his hand before setting it aside. "You were brought in just over ten hours ago by an off-duty EMT. He found you in an alleyway behind a bar that he owns and stabilized you to the best of his ability before bringing you in. His statement has been verified and the relevant authorities are currently looking for the man who assaulted you. Surveillance footage from the bar and overlooking the alley is being reviewed and an officer will be coming in to take your official statement, when you're ready for that. You have the option to file official charges against your attacker. Do you have any questions so far?" Dr. Baker pauses as I shake my head in the negative before continuing, "I'm going to give you a brief exam as I go over the rest with you, okay, Nora?"

At my agreement, he pulls back the bed sheet. As he moves close to me, towering over me, a flashback jumps into my mind but I push it down before it can take root.

"Regarding your current condition, I'm sorry to say you've sustained a few serious injuries. Some will take time to heal. Your right shoulder was severely dislocated and has a hairline fracture." He relays the damage as he continues with the physical examination. His hands run over my head, careful to not put too much pressure on the injuries, before moving onto the next body part as he talks about it to me. "Your left orbital bone was badly bruised. You also have several bruised ribs. Thankfully, none were broken but they will still take some time to heal. During that time, they will cause quite a bit of discomfort when moving around but that can be controlled, if you're careful. The last major injury is to your right knee. Your patella has a fracture and the resulting swelling is going to be troublesome. The rest of your injuries are superficial scrapes and bruises."

"So, with all of that, there will be absolutely no heavy lifting or rigorous or unnecessary physical activity. I want you off of your feet, except to and from the restroom." He pauses to determine that I've absorbed all of that. It's a lot for sure but it could've been so much worse. Based on the level of pain, despite the drugs, I'm not surprised at the extent of the injuries.

Nurse Susan returns with my water and steadies my hand as I take a small sip. The water initially burns going down but the relief is enough to bring tears to my eyes. I squeeze my eyes closed, resting my head on the head of the bed and fight back my emotions. Once I start, there will be no stopping them and this is no place to cry.

Once I've locked down my emotional vault, I open my eyes. Dr. Baker and Nurse Susan meet my eyes without a hint of judgement or pity. For their kindness, I am grateful. I nod for them to proceed and take more sips from the paper cup.

"Now that we've got the easy part out of the way—" At my groan, Dr. Baker smiles before continuing, "I need to ask some questions about your emotional health and the events that led up to last night's attack. Do you think you're feeling up to that?"

I'm not sure if I am but I don't have much choice. Eventually, I'll have to answer these questions. It might as well be now. At least this way I can start working on moving past this.

"Yes." Though my voice sounds meek, at least it sounds even and more stable than I'm feeling. Dr. Baker's eyes flash before the hint of emotion is buried under his professional exterior, his lips set into a grim line. I'm not fooling him.

"Did you or do you know the man who attacked you?" he questions, carefully.

I clear my throat before I answer to give myself a moment. "No."

"Can you speculate as to why he did this to you?" His patience and kindness break the dam. I can no longer control the tears I kept at bay and they fall silently down my cheek. I hate crying, especially in front of company, and my ribs likely won't appreciate the show of emotion.

Of course, he has an empathetic, bedside manner! Of course, he has to be the perfect package! I think, trying to find the humor in a situation that has none. I gather my courage and start from when my assaulter touched me.

"Yeah, I can." I sit up a little straighter before recounting the events as I remember them. "I walked by him in the bar and he grabbed me. When people touch me without consent..." I let that sentence trail off but Dr. Baker gives me an understanding nod. "I hit him and gave him a piece of my mind in front of his friends. I suppose he didn't like the hit to his ego ... or to his face." Dr. Baker smirks at me but it falls off at my next words. "Looking back, I wish I would've kept walking and ignored him."

"Nora..." The scent of ginger and oranges permeates as he comes closer, overpowering the smell of hospital disinfectant that I dislike so much. When he speaks, he speaks with conviction. "This is not your fault. You didn't consent to his touch. Even if you had, and you changed your mind, that doesn't give him the right to assault you. This was a sick man with serious control issues." When he receives no response from me, he carries on, "Just to be clear, you've never met this man before and, besides hitting him when he touched you without consent and the incident in the alley, you didn't engage in any other way with him?"

"That's right. To the best of my recollection, I've never seen him to the best of my recollection and didn't have any further interaction."

Susan opens a drawer and removes something. Cleaning my IV with an alcohol wipe, she injects what she removed from the drawer into it.

"Thank you for answering my questions, Nora." His voice rolls over me as I relax back in my bed. Dr. Baker holds my hand and swipes his thumb back and forth over my knuckles, until I slip into the peace that only sleep can bring me now. The last thing on my mind is: *how the hell am I going to pay bills when I can't wait tables?*

∞∞∞∞

When I wake up, a soft glow is emanating from the light behind my bed and my mind is clearer and less muddled. They must have changed the drugs they were giving me.

I'm grateful to whoever dimmed the lights, rather than turned them off. I'm not sure how I'd react to darkness right now. My bladder cries for release so I reach for the call button and give it a firm press.

A different nurse, in black scrubs, walks in moments later. She smiles but, unlike Susan, it doesn't reach her eyes; it's, a smile that you'd give to strangers you accidentally made eye contact with. She seems less approachable than Susan. As long as she doesn't fuck up my care, I'm fine with her bedside manner.

Without providing her name, or even a simple 'hello,' she moves to look at the clipboard hanging from the end of my bed and checks my IV bag, not even bothering to ask why I pressed the call button.

"Is there any way I can use the bathroom? I need to go immediately please." My voice comes in a whisper that still feels too loud for the room. I look for my cup of water but decide to forego a sip until after I've been to the bathroom.

"Let me check with your doctor. I'll be right back." She turns on her heel and walks out the door.

Fucking fantastic.

I tell myself I can wait but after a few more moments in the empty room with my bladder close to bursting, I take matters into my own hands. I look at the machines next to me. Other than the IV, there's only an oximeter clamped on my pointer finger. I unclamp it and throw back the covers.

Shit, a knee splint.

While that complicates things, which the sling on my arm was already doing, I move ahead regardless. Conscious of my ribs, I slowly maneuver my legs over the side, careful that my right knee doesn't bend too much. My right arm is useless and contributes nothing to the cause so I grab the side rail with my left hand to hoist myself up.

In the middle of my struggle, the door opens, and Dr. Baker comes in. He stops short in the threshold before rushing to my side with disapproval on his lips.

"Nora, what are you doing? You shouldn't be up and about without assistance."

"I need the restroom. I paged the nurse but she said she had to ask first. I can't wait for someone to decide if I can use the loo. I have to go *now*."

With a scowl, Dr. Baker bends down and scoops me up into his arms, making my head spin. Even though he's gentle and careful, I still feel a twinge in my ribs as he carries me to my en-suite bathroom. The IV drip follows us, and my belly flips with the evidence of his strength and efficiency.

He sets me down in front of the toilet and makes sure I'm steady before he lifts my hospital gown and guides me down onto the seat. I'm mortified but he keeps his eye away from the lower half of my body and remains completely professional.

"I'll be just outside the door if you need help. Just call for me and I'll come back in. When you're done, don't try to stand on your own. I'll help you wash your hands and with anything else you need." He gives me a pointed, stern look before leaving and cracking the door an inch. I finish, cover myself and call out for him.

He opens the door immediately.

When he sees me staring longingly at the shower, he helps me to my feet and to the sink as he says, "You can't take a bath or a shower but if you'd like a sponge bath, I can get a female nurse to help you."

"Thank you, a sponge bath would be good. And thank you for helping me just now too. I know this isn't part of your job but I appreciate it."

Dr. Baker holds my gaze with a smile. "No, it's not normally a part of what I do for my patients but I don't mind helping you, Nora. Let's get your hands washed, then back to your bed where the nurse will give you your bath." Once again, he picks me up effortlessly and carries me back to my bed.

"I'll go and get a nurse and come check on you later. Get some rest and no more leaving that bed without help. Doctor's orders." he says with a wink and breezes out my door.

Good goodness, he actually winked at me!

While my heart still flutters in my chest, a different nurse to the nameless one enters with a friendly smile on her face. She sees the look on my face, *thanks, Dr. Baker,* and gives me a knowing, amused smile.

"Hello, Nora, I heard you wanted to feel like a human again. I think I can help with that," she jokes. She wheels her stand over to my bedside and helps with the bath. All throughout, she stays patient if I have to stop and talks like we're old friends catching up.

By the time we're done, I feel much better and fall asleep with a smile on my face.

∞∞∞∞

When I wake up, it's morning and I've been told I'll be discharged once I've given my statement.

A male and female officer enter the room. While they both seem cordial, the female officer is friendlier and is left to do most of the talking.

"Hello, I'm Detective Daron," the male officer says. "And this is my partner, Detective Brogdon. She's going to ask you some questions and I'm going to take notes. Is that okay?"

At my approval, Detective Brogdon begins with easier questions, easing me into the process. I'd already answered most of these with Dr. Baker but Detective Brogdon moves to the harder questions as we go through my night. I remember everything but, emotionally, I'm drained and can't talk about this much more.

As I recount how the attacker assaulted me, neither Detective Daron or Detective Brogdon interrupt me. Detective Brogdon gives me her undivided attention as her partner makes notes.

"By the end, I was in so much pain, my memory is fuzzy. I just heard someone coming to help after the bald guy left," I finish awkwardly. I don't feel comfortable calling him 'my' attacker. I want no part of his identity attached to mine.

Detective Brogdon hands me her card. "You have my condolences. My partner and I will do everything we can to catch this guy. Thank you for your time. If you remember anything else, no matter how small, please call me."

For a moment, I stay in the room in silence, recharging from the emotional drain that recounting the night was.

My friend, Kyle, comes to mind. Though he didn't start off as my friend, we've become fairly close and he's the only one I can think to ask. When I first met him, he was a client at the restaurant I work at. I thought he was interested in me but then I noticed that he treats everyone the same way. We became friends, connecting through our love for fitness.

With a mental sigh, I relent and dial Kyle's number. I'm just thankful that my phone somehow survived the attack and thankful to the nurse who returned it to me.

He picks up after the third ring. "Hey, this is Kyle."

"Hey, Kyle, it's Nora. Can you come and pick me from the hospital?" I pick at the mattress sheet beneath me as I say it, conscious that I may be overstepping, and the long pause does nothing to help my nerves. Maybe we're not close enough for this request.

"Nora." A sharp exhale carries through the phone to my end. "You have five seconds to explain to me why I'm picking you up from a hospital without any knowledge of you needing to be there. And I swear to God, Nor, if you're hurt, I'm gonna be pissed that you didn't call me sooner." Kyle's voice is hard and gravelly.

The anger in his voice shocks me into a stunned silence for a moment and my mind fills with flashbacks of another overprotective male friend.

But at his growl, my heart jumpstarts. I snap out of it, tumbling over the words without pausing to think.

"I need for you to not be mad at me right now. I'm on the edge of losing it and I need support right now. A rock, not your anger. Yes, I'm hurt, more than you'd like. It's not good. I'll explain more after you pick me up and take me home. But, please, Kyle, please, just come and get me. I just can't right now … I want to go home but they won't discharge me unless someone comes to get me." I blink past the unwelcome emotion.

I've been independent for so long and I don't want to have to depend on anyone, not even Kyle.

I focus on my breathing in the pause that follows, slow and steady for my nerves and my ribs.

Kyle sighs. "Of course, Nor, I'll be your rock. I'm on my way. We can talk when I get you home. What hospital and room number?" I relay the information and the line disconnects after a quick 'bye.'

Not even twenty minutes later, my room's door handle jiggles. My gut clenches before I remember I'm safe and the door opens to admit Kyle. He must have dropped everything to come here.

As his gaze rakes over me, I realize I haven't seen myself yet. I've avoided the mirror. The evidence of my reality is not something I can face right now but evidently, it must be *really* fucking bad because Kyle takes two steps into my room and pulls short.

His chest heaves with deep breaths that I wish I could take, if my body wasn't bruised and broken in more places than I'd like to acknowledge. He clenches his eyes shut for a second before opening them, his chocolate-brown eyes shiny and his voice tight and hoarse.

"I'll be right back, Nora. I just need a second. Just a few seconds and I'll come back and be your rock. Just—" With an apologetic look, he steps out back through the door.

Fuck. I've never seen him like that before, with that destroyed look in his eyes. I made the smile he always has on his full lips around me disappear. That almost hurts as much as my fucking ribs right now.

I distract myself from that thought because if I fall apart, it'll only hurt him further. So instead, I focus on him, rather than his emotional state, and how handsome he looked in his casual clothes. I've never seen him in street clothes before, only workout gear, that I can recall, and he looks equally handsome in both. His dark wash jeans and dark blue shirt pair well with the white sneakers on his feet.

When the door opens for him again, he's pulled himself together so I do the same. I sit straighter in my bed and right my hospital gown. *Might as well give the illusion of stability.*

He pulls the vacant chair closer to my bedside and sits down, raking his hands through his auburn hair. It's long enough to curl at the ends and product-free. For a moment, we only stare at each other and I drink him in. I feel fragile and breakable but the familiar planes of his face bring me closer to feeling okay. The roguish face that reminds me of bandits and pirates, the sharp nose and eyebrows with a killer arch. Everything is familiar and comforting.

He really is my rock right now.

I know I'm not beautiful—I pass as average in all aspects of life—but with the way my left eye refuses to open and the swelling on one side of my face, I'm sure I'm a sight to behold.

The urge to touch the swelling, like I can actually make it go down by pushing on it, is hard to resist but I know it'll explode with pain, especially since I haven't taken the painkillers they've given me. I avoid any medication, other than vitamins, because I'd rather grin and bear the pain than drug myself.

I smile to ease the tension but my split lip throbs with the act and it comes across as more of a grimace.

Kyle's eyes flash and he clenches his jaw before relaxing it.

"Nora … What happened? Why didn't you call me sooner?" Though his voice is soft and soothing, which I know is deliberate, I can sense the hurt. His compassion isn't helping. It's chipping away at the walls I've erected when all I want is to remain tough and get home. I can't fall apart *here*. I'll fall apart at home.

For what feels like the hundredth time, I close my eyes against overwhelming emotion. I can't trust myself to speak so I rest my head against the headboard until Kyle sighs.

Callused, warm fingers graze over my knuckles and at the unexpected touch, I resist the urge to flinch and fall into the soothing touch. "Okay," he relents, "Let's see what we have to do so I can take you home. I'm going to snag a nurse but I'll be right back." His chair scrapes back and I feel him standing. I focus on the touch on my hand, rather than the fact that he's standing over me. "Nora, whatever happened, we'll get through it. I'm here for you and here is where I'll stay, for as long as you'll have me. You hear me, honey?" I nod with my eyes still closed and with a squeeze of my hand, he lets go to leave and find a nurse.

I get my emotions back under control and have composed myself by the time he returns five minutes later, Dr. Baker in tow.

I let myself look and appreciate the hotness overload, let Dr. Baker's thousand-watt smile lift my heart and breathe in Kyle's stabilizing energy.

By the time I zone back in, I've missed the first part of what he was saying but I regret nothing. I needed a second, so I took it.

"So, as long as that's the case, you're clear to go." He hands Kyle an information packet and a card. "Take a look at that packet. If you experience any symptoms from there, or experience any trouble in general, call that number on the card." He gives me a look that doesn't leave room for argument and at my nod, he elaborates, "That's my personal number."

I smile in thanks, careful of my lip.

"I'll make sure of it. Thanks for taking such good care of Nora, Owen." Kyle shakes his hand and hugs Dr. Baker in the confusing way men do, slapping his back. Dr. Baker signs the release papers as I'm left to wonder how they became so familiar with each other so quickly. Maybe they know each other already, since Kyle is comfortable enough to use Dr.

Baker's first name. I'll ask later or maybe, it's none of my business.

"I'm going to go and get her a wheelchair. Why don't you bring your car to the entrance? We'll meet you out front." Dr. Baker steps into the hall and Kyle follows after making sure I'm okay.

Dr. Baker wheels the chair in and lifts the pedals to lock the brakes. He brings the clothes, that I hadn't noticed were sitting in the chair, to me. I certainly don't recognize those clothes and at my bemused look, he explains, "I'm afraid your clothes were beyond repair. They were already in a state before you were brought to us and we had to cut the pants away to treat your injuries. The shirt was basically non-existent when you came to us." Before I can dwell on the memory of the loss of another shirt, to another man, in another time, Dr. Baker continues, "These are some extras I had in my locker. They'll be big but that's not a bad thing with the state of your shoulder and knee. The less you jostle or restrict them, the less pain you'll experience and the less the risk of further injury."

He holds up the long, dark gray sweatpants. Next thing I know, he's kneeling down in front of me, waiting for me to put my feet in. I start with my left leg but he stops me with a gentle hand on my knee. "No, lift your bad leg first and I'll slide them over your foot. That way you don't have to bend it. May I?" He lifts my right ankle up without bending the knee.

"Yes," I croak, partly from the pain, partly from his proximity. Thrown off by my reaction to him, my face flushes and I avoid eye contact with the attractive doctor. Unfortunately, or fortunately, depending on how you look at it, that brings my gaze to his hands. There's no ring, no ring depression, no tan line on his left ring finger. *He's not married.*

I have no idea why my thoughts are digressing to the possibility of a relationship with him when I'm in no condition to date. I need to heal and recover—more than just physically.

Besides, he's my doctor and he can't get involved with me without risking his career. Granted, I won't be his patient much longer. But he's not even giving any indication that he's interested! Rolling my eyes at myself, I shut my thought process down right there.

"Lift your other leg and I'll pull them up." I slip my other leg in and he dresses me, while keeping my modesty intact. "I'm sorry but this is all I had. You'll have to go commando for the ride home." He stops to look at me. "In order to get the shirt on, I'll have to take off the gown first so I don't move your arm and shoulder any more than I have to. I, of course, don't have a bra but you shouldn't be wearing one right now anyway, with your shoulder the way it is. Is that okay, Nora?"

He's being so thoughtful and though my heart flutters with the thought that I'm getting special treatment, I remind myself that he's probably this considerate with all his patients.

I smile, reassuring him. "I trust you to remain as appropriate as you have throughout this whole ordeal, Dr. Baker. You've been perfectly professional throughout this entire experience and I know you're only looking out for me and my comfort."

A confused look crosses his face but it quickly disappears behind the professional smile. He removes the sling from my right arm before slipping the gown down my arm and picking up the black shirt he brought, which looks to be twice my size, at least. "I'm going to slip your arm in first and then pull it over your head. The rest should be easy from there, okay?"

At my agreement, he grabs my arm gently and moves it closer to the sleeve. The slight movement causes the pain to radiate down my arm and back, making me gasp and curl into myself, which only causes more pain to flare from my ribs. I moan as my head hits his hard abs, breathing as shallowly as I can without going lightheaded, and wait for the pain to subside. Once it's lowered to a dull ache, I apologize. "I'm sorry. I didn't think to brace myself."

Dr. Baker smooths his hand up and down my back, careful of the shoulder, as I continue to lean on him for support. "There's nothing to be sorry for, Nora. I'm sorry I couldn't prevent the pain. You can rest for a bit until you're ready to continue."

"That was..." I trail off, without ending the sentence. "I'm good now." I sit up and look into his eyes. There's heat and compassion there but when he blinks and reopens his eyes, only compassion remains. He quickly conceals the need so just the compassion remains. Did I only see the desire because I wanted to see it? The painkillers from last night must still be messing with my head.

Dr. Baker slips my head through the shirt and removes the hospital gown completely after the shirt falls to my chest, to protect my modesty, yet again. I put my other arm through the other sleeve. Throughout the whole process, his eyes didn't stray from my face, despite keeping me completely covered the entire time. "Color me impressed, Dr. Baker. Thank you." My face heats as I realize that I just unintentionally flirted with him.

His chest rumbles with his deep chuckle, the sound vibrating through my arm. I didn't realize my hand was still on his chest. "Would you believe that's the first time I've done this? Usually, the nurses do this part."

I quickly remove my hand from his body and mumble, "Sorry."

"Nora, stop apologizing. There's nothing for you to be sorry for. I chose to help you and I'm glad I did." He grabs the hand that's still warm from the heat of his chest and places it around his neck, leaning down to lift me into the wheelchair. Once he's deposited me there, he says, "There, all set. I'll grab your bag of personal items from the closet and we can go." He gets the plastic bag containing my wallet, keys and sneakers and hands it to me.

Dr. Baker releases the chair's brakes and wheels me to the entrance. Kyle is leaning against his car, waiting to jump into action, apparently, because as soon as he sees us, he rushes to the front passenger door of his black Tahoe with the dark-tinted window and slides the seat all the way back.

I smile at him in thanks, relieved to be getting out of the hospital. When I'm working here, it'll be different but I'm not a fan of being a patient. He smiles back and my heart sings at the sight of his dimples reappearing. He seems better, more refreshed.

"All set?" he asks Dr. Baker.

"Almost. If you'd take her bag, I'll take her signature and then she's good to go."

Kyle takes the bag and walks to the driver door as Dr. Baker squats slightly and hands me a clipboard with a paper and pen for me to sign.

I read every word carefully, absorbing the financial information, especially. It says that they will bill my insurance and anything my insurance doesn't cover is my responsibility, but since I'm a student and work part-time, I have to pay a high deductible fee. I only work part-time so I don't have health insurance or receive any benefits from my job. Everything I learn goes to school or my car and the money my mom left me is intended only for school.

I have no idea how I'll pay what is sure to be an astronomical bill but I still sign the damn paper as my mood plummets.

"Nora," Dr. Baker says, "I don't want you to worry about the financial stuff right now. Our hospital is very easy to work with and anything your insurance doesn't cover, we can take payments on. You tell us what you can pay and we will work with you as much as you need."

"I don't have insurance, except for what my school offers to students. I'm a part-time waitress and full-time psychology major," I confess.

Dr. Baker looks at Kyle and they share a look undecipherable to the opposite sex. Then he looks back at me and says, "Like I said, I don't want you to worry about this right now. Focus on healing. The bill will be there when you're ready to deal with it."

He takes the clipboard and rests it on the top of the Tahoe. He leans down and lifts me into the front passenger seat without aggravating my injuries, buckles me in and catches my eyes. "Nora, as I said, call me if you need me, not just if you develop complications."

After finding whatever he's looking for in my eyes, he closes the door, grabs the clipboard and wheels the now-vacant chair back inside.

3 Panic Attack

I wake to the sound of a car door opening and light pressure on my front, making my heart plummet and race simultaneously. My eyes snap open and I settle when I see Kyle undoing my seatbelt. I don't remember falling asleep. The last thing I remember is wondering what Dr. Baker meant by his last statement.

Was that his way of extending a hand of friendship?

If I wasn't confused before, I sure as hell am now.

Kyle lifts me up like Dr. Baker did, kicking the car door shut with his foot and carrying me to the front door of an unfamiliar house. We're at *his* house?

"What are we doing here? I thought you were taking me home," I question, wary of his motives.

"Nope." He grins like he won the damn lottery as he walks us into the house. The door is already unlocked, which he must have done before he came to get me from the car. "Didn't you hear Owen? You can't be by yourself until your next appointment. You staying here was the condition to you being discharged. You'll be staying here until you get an all-clear from a doctor to be on your own."

I'm not sure but the look on his face seems smug. Regardless, I've got to point a few things out.

"You do realize that could be until my fractures heal, right?" At his unwavering determined look, I say, "That's around six weeks."

"I understand more than you think I do, Nor. Speaking of, while you're here we're going to get a few things straight." The smug look stays before he shakes his head and continues on, "But that can wait until tomorrow, after you've settled in."

Setting me down on the huge, plush sofa he says cryptically, "Now I'm going to go and find some paper and a pen. I want you to start thinking of all the shit you'll need from your apartment so I can go get it, after we've had a late lunch and you've given me your address."

Before I can process what happened, he's gone and I'm still blinking at thin air.

I shake myself out of my stupor before taking in his house. I've never been here since our interactions, until now, were limited to the restaurant and occasionally the gym.

The double composite front doors are wooden with smoked, oval glass taking up the majority of the space. The glass is patterned with iron swirls designed through it. The doors open to a small entry way, where a small table sits for keys, and a mirror above the opens the space up.

The entryway leads to the living room, where I am. It's large enough to be spacious but not to be ostentatious. The U-shaped, soft-brown, leather couch seems right at home in the center of the space and against the soft tan walls. On the floor sits a large rug. The sturdy, iron-and-glass tables at the ends of the couch and a decent-sized, matching coffee table, complete the look. And, of course, a massive, flat-screen TV.

The kitchen, to the right, is separated by a bar with four, thick-cushioned, black barstools. The black marble countertops, with hints of tan, are home to state-of-the-art, stainless steel kitchen appliances. French patio doors open to a well-kept backyard with a gazebo and gorgeous patio furniture.

Funny, I never took Kyle as a guy to care much about interior design, nor did I realize he could afford all this extravagance, but he clearly put a lot of thought into this. Everything is simple, functional and flows well but of high quality.

The sound of a drawer closing to my left brings my attention to the hallway with several doors on each side and one at the end. I can't make out what the grayscale pictures hanging on the wall are, from where I'm sitting.

Kyle emerges from the second door down, of the left side of the hallway, holding a notepad and a pen. He sits down next to me and turns towards me.

"Okay, Nora honey, what's first?"

Shit! I was too busy gawking to think of the list he asked me to make.

My brain comes up blank so I say the first thing that comes to mind. "You have a really nice house. I'm surprised. You never struck me as a guy with such great interior decorating skills."

Hoooly shit! Did I just insult him?! That came out completely wrong.

Before I can stop myself, I start blabbering again, "I didn't mean it like that! I'm not saying I don't think you have good taste but it's all just so high quality. *Shit!* That didn't come out right either. Okay, I'm just going to stop talking now."

Kyle smiles a big, lopsided grin, making a dimple pop out. "Don't worry, Nora. I know what you're trying to say. I know I don't seem like I go for this kind of stuff and if I'm honest, I don't. This was a show house and turnkey. I bought it because of the location. So, yes, while this is nice and I obviously live here, I'm not necessarily into all this." He waves his hand around and chuckles. Putting the pen to paper, he says, "Now let's get back to your list."

Glad he's let me off the hook, I think out loud, "Okay, I'll need: clothes, preferably loose, toiletries, like my toothbrush, toothpaste, soap, facewash, face moisturizer, shampoo, conditioner, leave-in detangler, face moisturizer, body lotion, my comb and some hair tie. I'll also need my school stuff, so books, laptop. My cell phone charger. Oh! And comfy socks. That should be good." Kyle writes everything down quickly with typical man handwriting bold with slashes for the letters.

As soon as he's got "comfy socks" on the paper, my stomach grumbles so loud, it may as well echo in the room!

I give Kyle a sheepish look and he returns my look with a grin. He gets up and starts to make his way to the kitchen. "Guess that's my clue to feed you. Are you okay to sit there or do you want to try sitting on a stool? I'll prop your leg up on another stool with a pillow under it."

Hmm, staring at thin air or getting an eyeful of Kyle? As if that was a legitimate question! I'm not passing up a chance to gawk at him. Secretly, of course.

"Stool with a pillow, please!" I smiled, pretending like I didn't just yell that at him with way too much enthusiasm and my face hasn't turned red.

"The stool it is then." He comes back to carry me.

"You don't have to cart me around like this, you know. I'm pretty sure I can hobble on my own." I say, once he's placed me on my seat.

He looks at me and with a firm voice and says, "No. You might do more damage to your knee and hopping on one foot is just going to hurt your ribs. You can't use crutches either, because of your shoulder. This is the only option available to you so, suck it up, buttercup." He boops me on the nose and I already know he expects no argument.

Fat chance of that. His point is valid but I'm stubborn and not used to depending on anyone else. Being carried like a damsel everywhere, while nice, goes against every fiber of my being.

Just as I open my mouth to argue, he carries on. "What would you do if you fell? And what if you fell on your right side, Nora? It's not only just going to cause a shitload of pain, it will also set you back on your healing and could cause long-term issues. It'll only make things worse. And I'm not risking your safety."

52

Damn him and his logic.

But, as I said, I'm stubborn so I take a breath to launch into my argument—and find his lips covering mine.

I squeak out in surprise.

Kyle is kissing me. *Kissing* me. With *tongue*! Holy shit, can this man kiss!

This moment has featured in my dreams more than once but I always imagined he'd kiss rough and fast. But this—*this* is a slow and slick burn. I feel the heat building and building, energy sparks around us, until I lose all sense of anything except him.

His tongue plays with mine, coaxing me to take him into my mouth, to meet him where he is. I comply, chasing his tongue with mine. Our tongues swirl around each other, engaging in a dance that leaves me crying for more but at the sound of my whimper, he pulls back, our chests heaving. He's staring at me, while I stare back, wide-eyed. *What the hell just happened?* I untangle my hand from his thick, soft hair, still dazed. The nerves in my left hand are on fire, sighing at the remembered feel of his silky hair, so I place my palm on my thigh.

I'm still stuck on his swollen lips as his hooded eyes watch me. Eventually, once he's looked his fill, he turns away, grabs a cushion from the sofa and sets it on the stool next to me. He helps me prop my leg on it, with only a twinge of pain, and starts making his way through the kitchen.

My head is still shaken up from the kiss, or maybe the pain is making me delirious, but whatever it is, I can't control my tongue. "Wow, you sure can kiss." It comes out in an awed breathy whisper, but judging by the grin on his face, he definitely heard me. "I mean ... Kyle, what was that about?"

Finally, my brain is catching up.

Of course, I'm not blind. I know he's good-looking.

But...

I've known this man for a year and still don't know what he does for a living. I don't *care* what he does for a living but that just signifies how little I know about him. And then he goes and kisses me?

I don't know what to think but I know my lips are still tingling and I want to know more about the man I consider my only friend.

The sound of his voice pulls me out of my ruminations. "That's one of the things we need to make clear, Nora."

I watch in silence as he pulls out the ingredients for lunch. He places the bread on the countertop, before following that with lunchmeat, lettuce, tomatoes and mustard and ketchup. A bag of barbeque chips makes its way next to the rest of the items.

The kitchen fills with silence as he braces his hands on the countertop. His low sigh breaks it before he shakes his head and opens the drawer, reaching for a knife. As he works on the sandwiches, he says, "Nor ... I've been into you since we first met but you never showed any interest in me. When you called from the hospital, it was like a blow to the head and it hit me then that I didn't know what I was waiting for. What's holding me back? I was afraid of losing what we already have in pursuit of something maybe only I wanted." He pauses but I can sense he hasn't finished so I wait. "But I have to know or I'll always keep wondering and regretting."

He divides the sandwiches on either plate, adds the chips on the side and passes me one of the plates.

I buy time by taking a bite of the sandwich. As soon as the taste registers, I'm rendered momentarily speechless. He made it exactly the way I like it—heavy on the mustard, no ketchup. I'm baffled by this. We've only hung out maybe once and I hadn't realized he was paying attention.

As I carry on with my lunch, he lets me think in silence.

I realize that I *do* like him. I think we're compatible. He makes my heart race, makes me feel safe. But after the last few days, do I really want this? I'm not too sure I do. I think a relationship right now will be a complication I don't need.

I finish my sandwich, still unsure what to say. Sighing internally, I take the direct approach. "I like you, Kyle." His eyes light up, which makes this a thousand times harder, so I duck my head like a coward and finger the crumbs on the plate. As one crumb sticks to the tip of my fingertip, I stare at it and continue, refusing to make eye contact. "I do. But with what just happened, I don't think I'm in a place right now to start a romantic relationship, with anyone. I don't know what kind of impact this is going to have on me and my life. I still need to heal physically but I can't underestimate the emotional damage that I might have suffered. I don't know what's coming next and I can't take more uncertainty. I can't juggle a relationship with recovering."

I need him to understand that my love life should be the furthest thing from my mind while I'm healing physically.

Mentally, however—

I don't even want to consider that. I know those wounds don't heal.

It's not going to be an easy road.

Kyle gently takes my hand in his and gives a reassuring squeeze, urging me to look at him. When I give in, there's no hurt in his eyes and his voice is soft when he says, "I'm good with that, Nor. You *should* have the time to heal without the added pressure of a new relationship. I just needed you to know."

"Thank you."

I wait for him to finish his lunch. Once we're done, he takes our trash to throw in the trash bin, clearing all the ingredients away and putting them back.

"Alright, Nora honey, you wanna lounge on the couch for a bit or take a nap in bed?"

A dull throb started in my knee during lunch and the shooting pains in my shoulder are not letting up. The pain is exhausting me and I know I'll have to give in and take some painkillers, eventually. But as comfy as the couch is, I'm exhausted.

And I really don't want to be in his way.

"I'm getting tired so I should probably head to bed for some decent sleep. I should also get the prescriptions filled for my pain. Until then, do you have any ibuprofen or Tylenol I can take?"

"Yeah." He turns to a cabinet next to his fridge and hands me the pills from the bottle before getting a cold glass of water to wash them down with. "If you want to lay down, I'll get your meds filled and get your stuff from your house while you're resting."

"Sounds like a plan."

I should have taken the pills earlier. If they don't kick in soon, the pain will be unbearable.

Kyle rounds the counter and lifts me in his arms again. I'm not sure I'll ever be comfortable with being carried like a damsel but there's nothing to be done about that right now.

He carries me down the hall to the door at the very end.

He stops at the door. "Get the knob for me, honey?" I can't reach it from this height so he squats for me to turn the knob and push the door open.

As we cross the threshold, the first thing I notice is the *huge* ass bed, centered on the far wall, between two decent-sized windows that go from the floor to the ceiling. The bed is made up with a dark, comforter and piles of black pillows. And not just sleeping pillows.

Decorative pillows!

I imagine Kyle sleeping on a bed with decorative pillows and can't hold in the giggle that escapes. My ribs protest it so I control the humor and brace myself until the pain subsides. Kyle, ever patient, waits for me to gather myself in his arms again.

"Kyle, there's pillows on the bed. A *lot* of pillows," I tease, "Most that aren't for sleeping."

He realizes the source of my amusement and rolls his eyes. "Yeah, it was a turnkey house, honey."

My amusement doesn't fade entirely so the smile stays as he sets me on the edge of the bed and I get a look at the rest of the room. I mean even so, he still keeps them on the bed!

The bed is facing the door and a wall with another large TV. It's surrounded by an entertainment center, complete with a DVD player and a complex looking stereo system. To the right is a waist-high, black, wood dresser, with a mirror on top. To my left is a taller dresser in the same black.

There's a partially open door in the room, which opens to the master bathroom.

I narrow my eyes suspiciously—well, one eye. *Wait one second...*

This is *his* room! I wasn't expecting to go to *his* room. With how massive the house is, surely he has a vacant, useable guest room? If not, I'll take the couch. It's bigger than a twin bed!

"Kyle?" When he glances at me as he turns down the bed, I raise one eyebrow. "Is this your room?"

"Yeah," he answers, distracted, not even a little concerned by the tone of my voice.

I lose the sass and try to reason with him. "Umm ... I don't want to sound ungrateful but I can use a guest room or if you don't have one, I'll take a nap on the couch. I don't want to put you out."

He just looks at me for a beat before coming towards me and kneeling down.

This is the second, deliciously handsome man to kneel in front of me today. *That takes the number of men to kneel to me in my life to a staggering grand total of ... two!*

Kyle interrupts my internal rambling. "Nora, first, you're not sleeping on the damn couch." Immediately, I go on the defensive but he holds a hand up to stop the argument waiting to spew from my mouth. "Second, the other rooms in my house are an office room, an exercise room and a media room. My guest room doesn't have a bed. This is the only bed in the house. And in case it passed your notice, it's big enough for three people.

"Third, I want to be close, in case you need something. If sleeping in the same bed makes you uncomfortable, I can use the floor. But I'm not leaving the room." Before I can argue that I won't need him at night, he brings out the big guns and pulls on my heart strings. "Do not try to argue with me on this. I'm not just doing it for you, honey. I need to be close, for me, even if it's not in the same bed. For *my* peace of mind. Understand? "

Shit, he got me there. How could I deny him now? If he needs this, it won't hurt to share a room or, if I decide, a bed.

I submit without further protest. "Okay."

He gives me a soft, grateful look that has me sinking into his eyes. Eyes that promise the world. My attention falls to his lips, the memory of how firm and *soft* they were on mine earlier. How they guided me into the best kiss of my life so far.

Before I can act like a complete hypocrite and kiss him, Kyle moves back and stands over me. The silhouette of his shadow falls over me and suddenly, I'm not in his room, in his house.

I'm not warm and safe and sound. I'm back in the alley with that asshole looming over me, his hand pulled back to deliver the next soul-crushing blow.

I flinch away from him, raising my arms to protect and defend, out of pure instinct, and bolts of piercing pain radiate from my shoulder.

"Nora? Nora, honey?" Confusion bleeds to concern and understanding. "Nora, it's okay. You're safe. You're here, I'm here. That fucker isn't going to hurt you. He's not here, honey."

When I dare to open my eyes, Kyle's kneeling in front of me again, running his hand up and down my left shoulder, his other hand on my thigh. I focus on his eyes, pull the feeling of home from his chocolate-brown gaze to bring me back to the present. I'm crying hard and my ribs are aching something fierce but more than the pain, guilt and regret envelop me.

Because it's Kyle. I know it's Kyle. I can see it's Kyle. His gentle hands on my skin, the burnt metal smell that is uniquely him. It's all *him*.

I start to come back to him and his room but I can't stop crying. I cling to him with my good arm and the tears keep falling. I try to take some calming breaths and they hurt my ribs but I need the oxygen, so I can get control of myself again. All the while, Kyle keeps stroking me along my arms, hair, thighs, anywhere he can touch me, reassuring me that I'm safe and not back in that alley.

He says, hesitation in his voice, "Maybe I shouldn't leave you alone right now. I'm sorry, honey. I didn't mean to scare you. I'm so sorry, Nora." He whispers, "Shit!" before continuing to soothe me, "I'm here, Nor. You're safe in my house. He's not here. He can't get to you here, honey. Shhhh ... It's okay, Nor. I'm here." Kyle keeps repeating the same sentiments while I put myself back together.

Once it feels a little less like there's a bulldozer sitting on my chest and a dam breaking behind my eyes, I take a deep breath and rest my head against the headboard, even more exhausted than before. I reach for his hand and squeeze. "It's okay, Kyle. I don't know what happened. I'm s-sorry. I don't why I freaked out like that..."

That's not entirely true.

He's still smoothing his hands over my arms, legs, careful of my injuries and I wonder if he's soothing me or himself at this point.

"I'm going to call Owen," he says after a moment. "I think you just had a flashback. I want to see what he says. Do you think you're okay for a minute so I can go get my phone?"

I know that's what it was but I don't want to delve into that with him. I'm okay now. Maybe that's not entirely true but I can at least put on a brave face.

I nod in response to his question and release my death grip from his neck. I don't know when my hand got there.

Poor guy. I bet I scared him half to death.

Scooting up towards the head of the bed, with Kyle's help, I relax into the headboard with the support of the pillows shoved behind me. He tucks the pillow under my leg to prop up my bad knee and pulls the covers over me.

"I'll be okay, Kyle." After a second, I admit, "I think you may be right about the flashback."

Kyle looks at me but for what, I'm not sure. Reassurance that I'm okay or answers, maybe. He slowly backs out of the room with cautious steps, like I'm a crazed animal that he doesn't want to provoke.

I suppose, in a way, I am.

I freaked out when he stood above me. Him looming over me, it felt like I was in the alley all over again, that man's hits landing on my body without mercy.

I close my eyes against the memories.

I'll wait to see what Dr. Baker thinks before I say anything more to Kyle.

The panic drained me and I'm unable to resist the softness of the bed and covers, or the call of slumber before his return.

∞∞∞∞

Ding dong!

I start to come back to the surface from a light sleep.

Ding dong!

Good goodness! Why must there always be some ruckus waking me up?

My eyes drift open and closed but I can't seem to escape that liminal stage between sleep and consciousness. When I open my eyes, that I don't remember closing, it's to the sight of a dimly-lit room that I don't recognize.

It takes a moment to remember where I am and why. The 'why' part sucks but the 'where' part? Not so much. To know that Kyle cares enough to have me stay with him does something to my heart.

Hushed voices just outside the bedroom door carry through the barrier. I can't make out what's being said but the voices are deep, masculine, soothing. They lull me back to sleep and I drift off when I notice that the voices have stopped.

I open my eyes.

Or, at least, I thought I did.

I can't have though because, at the foot of the bed, there are two men who belong on the front pages of a catalogue standing there, looking at me. I blink a few times, waiting for the scene to change. *Nope.* They're still there.

Looking up at the ceiling, I mutter, "Lord, if I'm dreaming, please don't let me wake up," and shift to my left side to fall back to sleep.

To my mortification, two deep chuckles sound from the foot of the bed and my eyes fly open wide. I just said that *out loud!* I really need to stop doing that shit!

Dr. Baker greets me with a smile in his voice. "It's good to see you too, Nora."

I blow out a breath, bracing for the pain to hit and turn my attention to him.

He's still sporting that thousand-watt smile, though it's more of a grin right now. His clothes are the same but his tie has been loosened at some point and he's rolled his sleeves up to his elbows. Why does that automatically amp up a man's hotness? *Do I have a forearm fetish?*

I didn't think he could get any hotter but the absence of his white coat reveals planes of his body that were hidden before. His shoulders seem even broader and his hips leaner and if I didn't drool on Kyle's bed while sleeping, I sure as hell must be now.

Kyle standing next to Dr. Baker, trying to hide his amusement by covering his mouth with his hand and focusing on the foot of the bed, rather than on me.

I glare at them both but only Dr. Baker can see. But Kyle must *feel* the heat of my glare because his broad shoulders start shaking with silent laughter and Dr. Baker's smile gets bigger and bigger, more enthralling than I thought possible.

Jerks.

Kyle reins it in and clears his throat but the smile stays on Dr. Baker's face.

"Nora, I called Owen and told him what happened," Kyle says. "We both agreed that he should come and talk to you in person to see if we can prevent something like that from happening again. Or, if it does happen again, to understand the cause and figure out what we can do to make the episode easier on you."

That explains Dr. Baker's presence. When Kyle said he'd call him, I never imagined he'd come here. Frankly, I'm grateful he agreed to come at all. This is way above and beyond his obligations to me as his patient. Well, technically, I'm not even his patient anymore.

So why is he here?

Instead of questioning a good thing, I say, "Thank you, Dr. Baker. I want you to know I really appreciate this."

He smiles and accepts my gratitude graciously.

"Well, Nora, I'm here strictly as a favor to you and Kyle. And since you're no longer my patient, please call me Owen." Dr. Baker—no, *Owen*. Owen gestures to the edge of the bed and asks, "May I sit?"

"Of course."

I make a move to sit up but before I get far, Owen is supporting me Kyle is placing a few more pillows behind my back. Both men move slowly, like they're afraid I'll strike them or fall apart. I guess, considering the circumstances we met in and the situation now, that's justified.

Once I'm settled, both men sit on either side of me. Owen is to my right, facing me. Kyle, to the left, places a few pillows behind himself and rests against the headboard. They both grab either of my hands at the same time to which I lift an eyebrow in question, which they breeze right past.

"Alright, Nora," Owen says, "It sounds like earlier, you had either a panic attack or a flashback of the other night. Let's go over what happened, if that's okay with you?"

I like that Owen checks with me, rather than assumes, before jumping in. His attentiveness makes me feel heard.

I agree with a nod and he continues, "Are you okay with Kyle being here for this?"

Kyle stiffens next to me but, otherwise, doesn't react.

"Kyle is more than welcome to stay, Owen. In fact, I wouldn't want to do this without him," I say, not just for Owen, but for Kyle too, who relaxes and gives me a small, but genuine, smile.

Owen pats my hand in acknowledgement. "Perfect. Let's start just before your panic attack. Where were you and where was Kyle?"

With his help, Kyle and I cover everything leading up to and during the panic attack. He fills in the parts where I wasn't entirely coherent and recounts that I was crying and pleading for him to stop, to not hurt me anymore.

I don't remember saying anything.

Once we've finished, Owen appears deep in thought before coming to some sort of conclusion. "Okay, this is what I think. Kyle standing above you like that reminded you of your assaulter in the alley and it took you back to that night." He turns to Kyle. "So, for now, try not to stand over her while she's sitting down or in bed. When she's standing, it doesn't seem to elicit the same response. If that changes, we can revisit this plan. But as it is right now, try not to stand over her. If you do, move slowly and speak to her to keep her in the moment. That way she knows it's you and she has something else to focus on and keep her out of her head."

64

Owen waits a moment for us to agree. Then, he looks at me and continues, "Now, Nora, I think it would be a good idea for you take some self-defense classes, when you're able to, of course. I can connect you to a very good instructor, who I think will be a good match for you. If you decide he's not, I have no doubt he can refer you to someone he'll deem appropriate.

"Also, the off-duty EMT who found you, who I mentioned was also the owner of the bar, is a good friend of ours." Well, that answers the question of whether Kyle and Owen already know each other. "He has requested to see how you're doing. You have no obligation to see him and if you say no, we won't bring it up again. However, it is my opinion that you at least consider it, not just for him, but also for yourself. Meeting the man might help you.

"Lastly, your car was found a few blocks from the bar. I'm sorry to say that it's no longer in working condition. It's at a local mechanic's garage. He's agreed that the damage is extensive and is willing to make the repairs needed to get it safe for the road. Not that the car is worth fixing." Owen sounds mildly exasperated with a hint of amusement. "Honestly, Nora, how did you make it anywhere in that thing?"

I haven't even thought of my car yet. I haven't had the time or the energy. The repairs are going to put a serious dent in my finances. The meager savings I'd put aside to buy a second-hand car, someday, to replace this one, they're not enough to repair my current car *or* buy a new one.

I look to Owen and my distress must be clear on my face because his entire face softens. "I'm sorry, Nora. I was trying to lighten the blow with a joke. It was in poor taste. Please forgive my ignorance?" he implores with sincerity woven in each word.

I know he wasn't coming from a bad place so I just wave it away. I tell myself, *it's just a car, after all.*

"You're sure it's my car?" I press, hopefully.

"I'm afraid so, gorgeous." My mood plummets with my hope. "You don't have to worry. I trust the mechanic. He's the same one I use and an old friend from high school. I know he won't take advantage of you, like many would, just because of your gender. He's an honest man."

I mull that over. "I'd like to hear from the mechanic and see my car for myself, please. It's a big blow and seeing it, hearing from him, might help absorb the reality of it all. About the EMT, yes, I'd like to meet him, to thank him for helping me. As for self-defense training, I'm not sure just yet. But I'll at least meet with the coach you're recommending and we can go from there."

"All fair and easy things to accomplish, Nora honey," Kyle says, speaking for the first time since we finished discussing the panic attack. The two share one of their looks again, leaving me in the dark, before turning their focus back on me.

Kyle clears his throat and addresses Owen, "Do you mind staying here with Nora while I go to her apartment? She needs some of her things for her stay here and we'd also like to get her prescription filled."

I ignore the flutter of my heart at Kyle presenting us as a 'we' and focus instead on how much Kyle must trust this guy, since he's comfortable leaving him alone in his home.

But am I comfortable being alone with him? I don't think he'd do anything untoward.

But ... how much do I really know him?

Owen acknowledges Kyle with a glance. "As long as Nora is okay with it, I'd be more than glad to stay." He turns to me. "My shift finished this morning just after you were discharged and I have the next few days off so, any way I can help, I will, gorgeous."

With Owen smiling, no secrets in his eyes, and the strength Kyle emits, I know I inexplicably trust these men. They make me feel safe in a way I've never experienced before.

"I'd like that. Thank you, Owen."

"Okay," Kyle says, climbing off the bed with a squeeze of my hand, "I'll get my car keys and go get your stuff." He leans over, lands a soft kiss on my hair and gives me a tender look. "I'll be back as soon as I can, Nor."

"We'll be okay. Don't rush. But don't take forever either, please."

4 My Nightmare

Kyle leaves and, after a moment, in the distance, the front door slams shut and the sound of a rumbling engine follows. The bedroom door was left wide open.

I can feel Owen looking at me so I turn my attention from the gaping door to him.

"Nora, I'd like to ask you a personal question." Owen watches my expression but I keep it blank, I hope. He elaborates, "I have two reasons. I promise to tell you one and, depending on your answer, I'll decide whether or not to tell you the second."

Well, that was oddly cryptic. As far as I can tell, he's generally been very upfront with me, so this unexpected vagueness sparks my curiosity.

"Feel free to ask but I reserve the right to decline to answer." I respond with my own stipulation.

His lips twitch but he nods, sagely. "Understood. Are you romantically involved with Kyle?"

Wow. He just launches into that, reverting back to his blunt self again.

At first, I'm shocked by his frankness. When that's passed, I'm unsure if I should be mad or embarrassed at the probe into my private life. I decide to hold off on either, at least, until I know his first reason.

"No," I answer, wondering if I should expand. I decide to jump off the deep end. He's been open with me and I'd like to return the courtesy. "We discussed it when he brought me here but we both decided it wasn't a good idea until I've had time to heal, both mentally and physically."

"That's very smart. Which brings me to my first reason. I'm going to caution you against any physical intimacy for some time. Immediate romantic attachment after traumatic events, like you've faced, can have adverse effects, rather than benefits."

Does he know about my other attack? Surely not.

I nod my understanding and, after a moment of hesitation, he gives me his second reason. "My second reason is because I'm interested in courting you when you feel ready."

Uh … what?! If a slight breeze came right then, it would've blown me over like a feather.

While I'm processing *that,* he carries on. "I'll be required to wait at least six weeks per the MD board but I want you to know now that I'm interested in you and I would like to court you."

"You'd like to … to *court* me?" For some reason, that's that part I need clarification on. What an odd way to say he wants to date me.

Owen smiles.

"Yes. Dating, to me, seems so temporary. In the past, courting was the way to show a potential romantic partner that you seriously wanted them to be a part of your life. I think I will, eventually, want that with you. If you'd like you can also see Kyle, as long as he's aware of the arrangement."

The *screech* of a record scratch sounds in my brain. If this entire conversation hadn't thrown me off, this certainly did. "You what now?"

"I'm willing to wait for you to be ready, both mentally and physically, to court you. I'm also open to you seeing Kyle at the same time, if you so choose, on the condition that he's aware and agrees."

Wow! The good and proper Dr. Owen Baker is into open relationships. That's a development I did not expect. He seems so old-fashioned and gentlemanly. He just expressed an interest in *courting* me, for goodness sake!

Just goes to show that I don't know him at all.

That explains why he's so upfront and direct. Communication clearly matters to him. If open relationships are his thing, it needs to matter.

I mentally shake my surprise off and focus on the situation at hand. "Owen, I'll tell you the same thing I told Kyle. Yes, I *could* be interested in dating you but, right now, I need to focus on healing. For now, I'd be open to, and appreciate, your friendship. Whether or not I'd be willing to date both of you together, I'm not sure yet. I'm not ready to explore that just yet, not even in my head."

"I'd thoroughly enjoy being your friend, Nora." There's a knowing in his smile that I can't decipher and, frankly, have zero energy for right now. "Now, would you like to stay in here and watch TV until our brains rot ... *or*," he rubs his hands as he suggests what's sure to be a tantalizing option, by the way he's presenting it, "I can see what Kyle has in his kitchen and I can start dinner."

"You can cook?" *Could this man get any more perfect?*

His smile returns in a wicked grin at my surprise.

"Is it that surprising?" His eyes light up. "It relaxes me. I like making something from a bunch of different, seemingly random, unconnected things. It's kind of magical, if you think about it, to create something from nothing."

The excitement in his eyes conveys how much he loves cooking and I return his smile.

I see the glimpse he's giving me into his life and jump on it. "Tell me more about cooking."

That's all he needs.

He tells me about his favorite meals to make—tacos, because they are so simple, yet so satisfying—and his favorite food to eat is poached eggs with hollandaise sauce. Both poached eggs and hollandaise sauce are, apparently, a real bitch to make. We're both laughing at one of his botched attempts at making hollandaise sauce when the front door opens.

"I'm back!" Kyle calls out.

"We're still in your room!" Owen calls back, laughter still in his voice. "I'd better go and see if he needs any help." He runs his index finger from my temple down to the side of my face and around my jaw softly. It stops at my chin. Then, slowly, mindful to avoid quick movements, he leans in and kisses my forehead, his other hand cupping the back of my head.

It's so sweet and unexpected that I melt on the inside.

While my eyes remain closed, he moves away.

And then I'm all by myself, for the first time while conscious since I left the hospital.

I take a slow breath, as deep as I can manage, and hold for a count of ten. Then, I let it out even slower, reflecting on how I'm feeling physically. My shoulder and knee are starting to notch up on the pain scale.

Owen's voice drifts towards me from the hallway.

"I just want to give her a pain pill. I was starting to see pain in her eyes about five minutes ago and I don't want it to become unbearable. I'll come back and help after." Owen walks into the bedroom with a glass of water and a pill bottle in his hands and I'm already grateful. He's so observant. "You don't have any addictive tendencies, do you, Nora?"

"No." I answer with a smile so he knows I'm not offended by the question. "But I hate taking anything other than vitamins. I can't make sense of it but it's just how I feel. Can I just take half a pill, please?"

"Yes, you can have half. But if your pain comes back, I want to know. This will probably knock you out, which isn't bad because you should rest. I'm being a bad doctor, keeping you up."

Owen hands me the glass of water and retrieves a pill from the bottle. Setting the bottle and lid on the nightstand, he halves the one in his hand and gives one part to me. The other half goes back into the bottle, on which he secures the lid back on.

He waits until I've downed the pill, takes the glass and sets it on the nightstand and helps me lay back in bed before going out the door to help Kyle, leaving it slightly ajar.

As the pill kicks in and I drift to sleep, I think about how funny he is, how easy to talk to, to listen to. He's eloquent and a master storyteller with an ability to turn cooking into an engaging topic. Nothing of our time together felt forced. It all just seemed to come so naturally to him.

As I slip into dreamland, with the guys moving through the house, sometimes coming into the bedroom, moving things around, I conclude that I like Dr. Owen Baker and can see myself liking him more.

∞∞∞∞

My limbs scream at me to run, my body burning with pain.

The hits land again and again, concentrated on the same areas to maximize pain with minimal effort.

He grabs my arm and wrenches it behind my back, yanks. The sound of my shoulder dislocating comes before the pain, before the numbness. I can't feel my fingers. The tingly numbness travels and fuck! I can't tell if it hurts or if I'm numb or both but he's not done.

The roots of my hair pull, my scalp lights up with fire as he jerks my head back with his handful of my hair. I'm practically bent over his arm. He's still got a hold of my wrist and he squeezes to the point of pain as he roars, "You think you can do that to me? You think you're such hot shit that you don't have to face consequences?! That you can fuck anyone!" His voice drops to a cold whisper that's worse than the yelling. "Well, sweet ass. I'll show you just how hot you are."

With a shove, I fall on the floor. I try to catch myself but with my now useless arm, I can't and he slams my face into the tile. My knees hit hard and I already dread the swelling tomorrow.

He kneels between my legs and grabs my hips and, with a ruthless yank, gets me on my knees with my head still on the ground.

No. Not this.

No, no, no, no. Please, no!

I try to fight him but he's stronger and in a better position and I'm not at full form with all the injuries I've sustained.

He unfastens my pants and takes them off.

I wake to an agonized scream, both familiar and not.

I bolt upright and instantly regret it. The scream cuts off into a groan of pain. It feels like my torso is on fire. Fuck! I try to take careful breaths through the pain.

The door slams open, making me jump high enough to almost fall off the bed in terror.

Two hulking figures burst in, rushing towards me.

I curl into myself, into the headboard, away from the dark figures advancing towards me.

He's back. He's *back* and he's not alone. I can't go through that again.

I frantically look for something, anything, any-fucking-thing that can pass as a weapon. I won't go down without a fight.

The two men stop advancing and they both hold their hands up, palms out, as if they are trying to placate me. In my frantic search, I just barely register one of the figure's lips moving but I can't make out what he's saying over the roar of blood rushing in my ears.

I look to the other man and his face looks so devastated that it gives me pause.

Why does he look like that?

I look back to the other man. Jade-green eyes, blonde hair. *I know him. Wait, I* know *him?* I look to the other one. Auburn hair, chocolate-brown eyes. *Home.* A soft light turns on in the room.

"It's okay, Nora," a deep, rumbling voice says. Soothing voice, soft words. "You're safe. You're not in the alley anymore." He continues repeating that but I'm stuck on what he just said.

The alley. What alley?

Then, it all comes back. The attack in the alley, the EMT, the good and proper doctor, the useless car.

I look to the other man.

Kyle, my rock.

He looks so distressed that I just want to hold him until those dimples reappear but I can't bring myself to move or say anything. I'm still trying to get my nightmare to leave. I try to slow my breathing down and focus on the other man.

"I'm Owen," he soothes, his hands still in the surrender position, "I was your doctor in the hospital. I'm here now because Kyle called me to help him with you. Kyle's right here and we won't let anyone hurt you, gorgeous."

That's the third time he's called me that. I don't know how he can think that when my face is still swollen and the bruising is horrible. My left eye opens more fully now but that doesn't help with my appearance. The blood vessels burst when the man from the bar hit me so the white of my eye is all red. I'm the furthest thing from *gorgeous* right now.

"Nora, honey," Kyle coaxes, "We're here to help you, not hurt you. You're safe in my house. You're safe with us." Kyle tries to break through the last remnants of my hazy nightmare. It's working; their words, their voices, are bringing me back.

"I'm here. I'm safe. I'm with you both. I'm here, not in the ... alley." I stumble over the last word. I wasn't in the alley but I can't tell them that.

Tears still run down my face unchecked and I'm sure my nose is running too. What a sight I must be.

I just can't muster the will to care right now.

"Can we come to you now, Nora?" Owen asks. They both look like they need the proximity, just as much as I need to have them close.

"Yes," I sob, "Please."

I can tell they're restraining themselves as they slowly move to either side of the bed, climbing in with me. Being closed in on either side almost makes my heart race but I remember who I am, who I'm with.

Kyle moves behind me, one leg on either side and I lean into him. He puts his strong arms around me, holding me tight, holding me together. He keeps saying the sweetest things and kissing the top of my hair. Owen takes my left hand. The warm skin of his soft fingers runs over the back of my hand, tracing random patterns that trail all the way from my hand to my wrist. He reaches the sleeve of his shirt, that I'm still wearing, then glides back down, ever so slowly, staying quiet as Kyle whispers to me.

When I relax enough that I start to drift off again, Owen asks Kyle if I've slept since I've been here.

"Not since I left her and you came in with me," Kyle responds, the tension seeping back into his voice, now that he thinks I'm asleep. "But she was only out for maybe five minutes, max. Should we be worried?" I want the stress from his deep, baritone voice gone. But I'm so exhausted and I can't make my lips or my fingers move.

"It's not uncommon for people who've been through trauma to experience nightmares or night terrors. It's part of the mind trying to come to terms with what happened. It also could just be the trauma itself messing with her. If this persists, or even if it doesn't, she should probably get some counseling to heal."

"She's a psych major, Owen." The voices sound further away but I'm still coherent enough to understand what's being said. "She's graduating after this semester. I think she knows most of what a therapist will say."

"That may be. But even if she knows these things and has the insight to recognize the issues she's facing, applying treatment methods is much more difficult without support. It's always easier to see the answers from the outside looking in. Even therapists sometimes need therapy and her finishing her undergrad means she hasn't even started her psych courses yet, so I doubt she even has the tools she needs to deal with this. With her emotions involved, it's going to be difficult to separate herself enough to see things clearly, if she can even manage that. We can talk to her about it tomorrow after we take her to look at her car and talk to Silas."

That's when I lose my battle to stay awake and sleep claims me once again.

∞∞∞

When I wake, it's to Kyle on one side and Owen on the other. This time, I didn't have any nightmares and I wonder if I can credit that to them. I have no idea how they managed to get comfortable without waking me.

When I awoke in the middle of the night in pain, they were both lying next to me, one on each side, with me snug in the center of the bed. A pillow had found its way under my right leg and I don't know who to thank for that. I drifted back to sleep, comfortable and warm.

Now, Kyle is still on my left, with one of his thighs draped over my left leg, weighing it down in the most soothing way. He's wrapped around me as much as he possibly can be without squishing me. Out of the two men, if I'd been asked to guess who'd be a snuggler, I would not have guessed Kyle.

Owen is on his back, his fingers intertwined with my right hand but other than that point of contact, there are a few inches between us. I try to slip my hand carefully from Owen's but at my slightest movement, he opens his beguiling jade-green eyes and looks at me.

"What do you need, gorgeous?" Though his voice is rough with sleep and deeper than normal, he seems wide awake. I guess, being a doctor, being up at the drop of a hat is a skill he's mastered.

"I just need half a pill again. The pain is back," I whisper so I won't wake Kyle.

Owen sits up in bed and that's when I notice that he's only in his plain, white undershirt and slacks. The dress shirt has been discarded on a chair in the room, where his shoes and belt also are. His hair is sticking up in all directions on one side and flat as a pancake on the other. It is *adorably* sexy.

Rubbing his eyes, he swings his legs over the edge of the bed. He sits there for a second, running his hands through his hair and it is miraculously back to looking perfect once again.

He moves toward the door that leads to Kyle's master bath, taking my glass with him. The faucet runs and stops and Owen reappears with water in the glass. He snags the pill bottle and gives me the remaining half from earlier and the water. "Here you go, Nora." His voice is still only a sexy rasp.

I pop the pill into my mouth and chug the entire glass of water down, wetting my parched throat. I thank him but he waves me off, takes the glass and sets it down on the nightstand.

He climbs back into bed where his hand finds mine again. I smile at the mutual desire for a physical connection as I try and find sleep once again. Once the pill kicks in, sleep comes easily and, thankfully, dreamlessly.

∞∞∞

The sound of a shower rouses me from sleep. This time, it takes less time than before to remember where I am and why.

I take a beat to take a physical inventory of my injuries and how they are today. My right shoulder and knee still feel stiff and my face is tight again from swelling. A dull throb is starting to pick up in various places. My ribs have yet to contribute their share to the pain but it's still early. I expect them to confirm their protest at my existence at any moment.

My eyes are gritty, my mouth feels like sandpaper and my teeth feel fuzzy and gross. I'd rather pretend my hair looks more like attractive bedhead than the rat's nest it feels like.

Owen's not in bed anymore, Kyle's trying his best to pull a starfish to the left of me, but evidently, I'm interrupting his emulation of the sea creature. The covers are draped on his waist and the waistband of his boxer briefs are peeking out under the material. He's on his stomach, snoring lightly, with his face turned away from me. Since he filled his quota for cuddles during the night, I appreciate having this to wake up to instead.

The shower turns off and, a moment later, Owen emerges with nothing but a towel around his waist.

Yum-*my*! This morning just keeps getting better!

Drops of water run down his chest to two glinting barbells in his nipples that I would not have expected. But he clearly keeps surprising me and I keep underestimating him. The V-cut of his eight-pack abs call to me like a siren and my tongue runs dry. I'd love to quench my thirst with the water going to waste on that towel.

He's slimmer and leaner than Kyle's bulk but still muscular. They both hold merit and this morning, I have both right in view.

Owen looks up and catches me ogling him, stopping short. A grin paints over his lips and I want to roll my eyes, even as I flush pink.

"I didn't mean to wake you. I was going to borrow some of Kyle's clothes and start breakfast. Any special requests? Or things you don't like?" That grin, a mirror image of yesterday's, doesn't let up. *Yes*, I was looking *hard* but can't he at least pretend to let me get away with it?

Of course not. I'd expect nothing less from Dr. Doesn't Beat Around The Bush. I grin in my head at my own lame joke and answer him.

"Whatever you make, I'll eat."

He grins wider at that because apparently, my inner vixen unleashed at the sight of his Adonis belt and even innocent things sound flirtatious. "Yes, but what do you like?"

"I usually prefer something light but packed with protein," I clarify and then, the ramble comes because he still hasn't moved or covered himself and one of the water droplets is drawing seductively close to one of the barbells. "Gotta start my day off right or it's all gone to hell and I won't even try to eat right for the rest of it."

Be still my beating heart! *He's just your friend, he's just your friend.* I shouldn't be thinking about him like that when I just asked for platonic friendship yesterday!

I watch the muscles on his back ripple as he goes over to the dresser, moving with agile grace and an innate, masculine strength. He grabs some clothes from the top and turns back towards me.

"Nora, if you keep looking at me like that, it's going to make my promise to stay friends very difficult to keep," he states in a rumble as he walks back into the bathroom with the borrowed clothes in hand and closes the door.

"Then you need to keep your clothes on around me," I whisper under my breath to the closed door.

"Who does?" Kyle says in a rough voice, making me jump and my tummy do a flip.

"For Pete's sake! I didn't know you were awake." I place my hand on my chest against my rapidly beating heart.

"Sorry, honey. Didn't mean to scare ya," he murmurs with his face still in the pillow. He lifts his head and peers at me through narrowed eyes, with his hair a sleepy mess. Unlike Owen, he doesn't need a moment to return to the land of the living, so there's no display of adorable lethargy.

Kyle props himself right up on his elbows with a spring in his step. Even after just waking up, he's lithe and alert. He runs his eyes over my face; though looking for what, I'm not sure. Maybe he's just assessing my swelling and bruises.

It's a moment before he speaks again and when he does, he clears his throat first so it's smoother this time around.

"How are you feeling this morning, Nora, honey?" Kyle asks as Owen comes out from the bathroom, dressed in black sweats and a gray, cotton t-shirt.

"My knee and shoulder feel stiff and my face is tight. But no pain, as of now. That doesn't mean anything though; the day's still young," I joke.

The expressions, filled with compassion and concern, make my eyes water but I'm just done with crying. If they keep looking at me like that, I won't be responsible for the resulting tears so I just look away.

"I was going to make breakfast, Kyle. Anything you prefer? Nora has already requested light with protein," Owen quips, saving me with a subject change.

"Protein sounds good. I'm going to take a quick shower. Nora, you think you'll be okay to take one by yourself or will you need help?" Kyle asks me.

I don't know but, as much as I'd like running water right now, it probably isn't a good idea to enlist Kyle or Owen's help. I inwardly sigh and resign myself to my reality with a mumble, "I'll just take a sponge bath."

"If you want, you can take a bath, Nora," Owen informs me. "It might even help with your stiffness."

"Maybe. Let's see how I feel after I get moving around a bit."

Kyle springs out of bed and I can't stop my jaw from dropping as he moves to the bathroom and stretches on the way.

His boxer briefs leave nothing to my very active imagination. His muscles flex and pull and I'm deep in my head with all those muscles when Owen appears in front of me.

"Nora," he calls my name in a teasing voice, "You're doing a *very* good impression of a Venus flytrap."

I shut my mouth with a click of my teeth and glare at him. A toddler throwing a tantrum is likely more intimidating because Owen just chuckles and heads out of the bedroom with a shake of his head.

Jerk!

Five minutes of me lounging later, Kyle returns with a towel around his waist, much like Owen, with no regard for the state of my heart. He disappears into the closet after pulling some articles of clothing out from the dresser drawers and reappears fully dressed, almost as sexy as he was a minute ago. A white, cotton t-shirt stretches tight across his chest and arms, while faded blue jeans hug him in all the right places and a pair of clean, white tennis shoes hang in his hand. Pulling out a pair of socks from the same dresser, he sits on the bed and works the socks and shoes over.

I wonder if there will come a day where I'm not mesmerized by the way his biceps contract and release with his movements. Regardless, today is not that day.

Ever-thoughtful, he says, "Do you think you can make it to the bathroom or do you need help?"

I want to try on my own but I'm not sure how I'll fare.

"I want to try and see how I do but could you maybe go with me?"

He agrees with a chin lift and helps me to my feet. I put most of my weight on my left foot and test my right by slowly adding weight until I feel a twinge in my knee. Not even half of my weight has gone onto my bad leg but the pain's already intense enough that I know I'm not going to be able to walk on my own.

Damn it.

But I don't want to keep inconveniencing these guys so I try again. My knee buckles and the pain is immediate and sharp. I almost go down but Kyle catches me before it's too late. He tries to be gentle but, in his rush, he grabs my elbow and it jerks on my injured shoulder, making the pain in my body increase tenfold as it radiates down my knee, arm *and* back. I wince and moan and rest my head on Kyle's shoulder as I hiss through clenched teeth. *"Fuck!"*

"I'm sorry, Nora. I'm so sorry." Kyle steadies me and then removes his hands, like he can't bear to touch me and cause more pain, but his hands stay outstretched in case he needs to catch me again.

"It's not your fault. I was stupid and put more weight than I should've. I can do it if I take my time. I just don't want to keep burdening you guys."

Kyle's eyes flash and his voice hardens, harder than it's ever been directed towards me. "Cut that shit right there. Stop. Right now."

I'm so surprised that I just stand there on my good leg at a loss for words. "You are not a burden or an inconvenience. If we didn't want to be here with you or for you, we wouldn't be. It's okay that you need help, Nora. An asshole beat the shit out you." His jaw ticks. "It's going to take more than a few days to heal and get back to doing things on your own. Let us help you and make it as easy as possible." He blows out a breath and the tension from his shoulders falls, as he jokes to soften the scolding he just dished out. "Besides, you won't be able to keep us away. In case you haven't noticed, we kinda like you."

"Okay, Kyle," I relent. "It's just not easy for me to ask for help. But I'll work on it."

"If it's too hard for you to ask, then I'll just do it without you asking and I'll make sure Owen knows to do the same."

I feel a bit like an errant child, caught with my hand in the cookie jar. I huff at him but give him my good arm and let him help me to the bathroom. I try to hobble but he practically lifts me by my good side and we make it to the bathroom with far more finesse than I would have managed.

"Okay, do you want to try a bath? I can help you get in and when you're ready, I'll come back in and help you out. Or I can help with a sponge bath," Kyle offers.

"I'd really like to try a bath. I haven't bathed properly since that night. I feel gross."

He nods and moves to turn on the faucet. He plugs the drain and comes back to help me undress as the tub fills. Once I'm out of Owen's sweats, he helps remove my sling and splint. The shirt stays on so only my lower half is uncovered. When the tub is full, he pulls the shirt over my head while keeping his eyes on the wall behind me. Without looking, he lifts me into the tub. It's a very impressive display of his strength and self-restraint.

I sink into the warm water and sigh slightly as my muscles release tension I hadn't realized I was holding. Kyle turns and leaves, only returning back to put a towel behind my neck and move the body wash and shampoo closer to me, on the ledge of the tub. He goes to leave again but stills before he leaves. "Just give me a shout when you're ready and I'll bring your towel and clothes and help you out." Then, he levels me with a warning glare. "Don't try to get out on your own, Nora. I'll be pissed if you do."

"I won't, I promise." I assure him.

He leaves and I enjoy the warmth that eases my sore, stiff muscles. When enough time has passed, I wash awkwardly. My

84

right shoulder makes that a battle but I manage, even if it does take me longer than usual. I have to get creative when it comes to my long, tangled hair though. I'm just wishing for some conditioner when Kyle knocks on the open door.

"You doing okay? Need anything?" He checks in. I can't see him so I'm hoping he can't see me either.

"Did you get my conditioner from my apartment?" I ask timidly.

"Yeah, sorry, I'm not used to needing that. Guys don't generally use a separate one. At least, I don't. Two-in-one works the same." I hear the shrug in his voice before he gets my conditioner for me. I submerge myself in the bubbly water so it covers me before he comes.

He's about to leave when he sees my hesitation and gives me a warning look.

"Actually ... can you help me work out the knots in my hair? I washed but my arms are tired and it'll make brushing easier if I can get this done now." I'll have to be careful with the way I'm sitting to not expose myself.

"Give it to me and tell me what to do," Kyle agrees rather quickly.

I hand him the conditioner and explain that he needs to start at the bottom or the knots will only get worse. He squeezes some conditioner in his hand and rubs them together, then starts finger combing my hair from the bottom up. By the time he's done, I'm so relaxed that I'm laying back in the tub with my eyes closed, trying not to fall asleep with my hair over the side.

Kyle has just finished when Owen taps on the door frame.

"Sorry to interrupt, but breakfast is ready. If you're almost done, I'll set the table."

"All done, just need to get sleeping beauty out, dried and dressed, then we'll be right there." Kyle answers for us since I'm incapacitated with drowsiness. Owen leaves and Kyle rinses my hair as I sit up, making sure I am covered in the places that matter.

I wait until he has my towel and helps me stand, before I screw up and forget that I need help and almost fall trying to step out. Kyle curses and wraps the towel tightly around me before he lifts me up bridal style and sets me on the bathroom counter.

"Sorry, I forgot," I apologize, sheepish. He sighs and kisses the top of my head then hands me my toothbrush and toothpaste.

"You really need these. I didn't want to say anything but your breath could knock over a goat," he teases lightheartedly.

"Jerk," I tease back with a smile on my face. It probably *could* knock over a goat.

I get to brushing while Kyle dries my hair with a second towel and then begins the daunting task of combing my hair. He starts at the bottom, slowly untangling the remaining knots out. It feels so natural, my movements become automatic and I don't think when I unwrap myself to dry with the towel around me.

"Nora." He stops the hand that's undoing the towel. "Let me get another and I'll help but let's keep you covered," he says with a warning in his voice.

"I didn't think. I'm sorry, Kyle." I just keep making this harder on him. "I'm not trying to make things difficult for you."

His eyes soften and he cups my head in his hands.

"You don't have to apologize for being you, Nora. I just know me and I'm not sure I could keep my hands to myself if you took off the towel just now. Just give me a second to get the towel and I'll help." His voice is so soft and his eyes tell me he wants me but he knows I'm not ready. If that's not the *sweetest*, most *selfless* thing...

He helps me dry off with the extra towel he returned with and gets my feet into my underwear. I pull them all the way on before encountering the next dilemma.

"Ummm ... could you help me fasten the bra? I can't get both my arms behind my back to do it." I ask, hesitant to not cross any boundaries. He just moves his hands to my back and fastens it on the first try. "Wow, impressive," I say, shocked.

He laughs.

"It was luck. I'm usually taking clothes *off*, not putting them on."

I roll my eyes and smile at the predictable, male response.

He holds up a pair of loose, burgundy sweats. I stick my feet in the legs and he helps pull them up. Next, he gets one of my shirts, bigger than most of the rest of my shirts and a light gray color. He pulls it over my head and I try to get my bad arm into the sleeve but after a certain point, I can't lift it without the pain getting unbearable.

"I don't think I can get my arm high enough to get it into the sleeve."

He pulls the shirt back off, removes his and puts that one on me. Of course, it's ginormous on me and much better to maneuver around. He stands back and studies his handy work, nodding in approval.

"My shirt looks better on you anyways." He winks and picks me up, depositing me on the bed to search his dresser for another shirt.

Interesting that the one he picks is the same light gray color that I was going to wear.

He helps me stand and carefully, slowly, we make our way to the kitchen, getting there just as Owen puts the last glass of orange juice on the bar countertop. Kyle sets me on the stool and props my foot up on the one next to me with a pillow under it.

I swear, these guys think of *everything*.

The food looks as good as it smells. Plates of omelets with spinach, mozzarella cheese and tomatoes sit in front of us all and *that's* the moment my stomach decides to imitate a whale's call and my face flames along with my ears.

"Anyone else hungry?" We all chuckle at my bad attempt at a joke.

The smiles stay as Owen sits next to me while Kyle stands on the opposite side of the counter, facing us.

All three of us dig in and, in no time, we're done.

"That was the best omelet I've ever had. Thank you, Owen." I say as Kyle clears the plates and cutlery while Owen and I sip our morning drinks.

"Hey, wait, why didn't I get offered coffee? Can I not have any right now?"

Owen glances at me and lowers his cup.

"No, you can, but the juice has vitamin C, which is good for your immune system. Often, when someone is injured and under immense stress, they can get sick because their body is too busy repairing the damage to fight off any foreign, harmful pathogens. This will help to prevent you from getting sick. You can have some coffee, if you'd like, but only after you've finished that glass."

I nod and gulp the rest of my glass but before I can beg for coffee, Kyle finishes loading the dishwasher and turns to us and says, "I was thinking we could take my Tahoe so Nora can ride in the back with her leg up on the seat to keep it elevated."

"That's perfect. Nora, you should take some ibuprofen to help with your swelling and the pain. I'll take your pain meds with us, in case you end up needing something stronger but the ibuprofen should be enough, so long as you don't let the pain get too bad." Owen slips into professional doctor mode right in front of my eyes and I just can't resist the urge to disrupt it.

"Is my face that bad?" I ask in fake horror. Owen's eyes snap to mine and he looks like he wants to kick his own ass but I can't keep a straight face for long. When a smile breaks free, so does a chuckle and he rolls his eyes with a smirk on his handsome face.

"Ha, ha, you're a hoot."

"I certainly think so," I say, immensely proud of myself. "Let's go meet your mechanic friend."

Kyle grabs his keys and wallet as Owen carefully lifts me and carries me to the garage. Maybe it's Kyle's speech in the bedroom or how much I'm being carried around but it doesn't feel as uncomfortable anymore.

When we're all buckled in, Kyle backs out and closes the garage door with a button on the overhead Tahoe console before we're making our way to the garage where my supposedly-irreparable car is.

I hope it's all just a really bad joke.

Right now, I need a little more humor and a little less life-disrupting stress.

5 Job Offer

"Can we swing by a drive-through for some coffee?" I mask the pleading in my voice by issuing a warning, "If I'm not caffeinated, I'm going to be cranky."

Kyle's smiling eyes catch mine in the rearview mirror.

"Yes, you little gremlin. I'll get you your caffeine fix." He looks at Owen and explains, "She can be grouchy as hell if she doesn't have at least one cup of coffee in her. You've now been warned. Be prepared for permanent coffee detail and be very glad you gave her permission to drink coffee, because otherwise..." He stops short with a full-body shudder as I gape.

"I'm not *that* bad!" I interject, completely affronted. "Kyle doesn't like doing cardio!" I tattle to Owen, whose grin sits wide on his face.

"I'm sure Nora is peace-personified at all times." Owen, my champion, says, not missing a beat. His forehead is bunched in a frown, his voice holds a scold, but the glint in his eyes is unhidden, "And, Kyle, as a doctor, I have to say I'm disappointed. You know better than most that cardio is good for your heart."

I can't hold in the snicker that escapes at the sight of Kyle's unimpressed face and the sound of Owen's Dr. Professional voice. Trying to hold in the laughter just makes it come harder and the tears come quicker. "Okay, I give! Please don't make me laugh anymore," I say between bouts of laughter, holding my front. "My ribs can't take anymore."

Owen sends a smirk my way before changing the subject. "So, Kyle, you know what we both do for a living. I'm sure Nora wants to know more about your work too." My ears perk up at the topic. I mentioned to him yesterday that Kyle's work is still a mystery to me.

"I design and make high-end custom fire-arms," Kyle provides, giving Owen an odd look.

Finally! I have no idea what that entails but at least I now know he makes guns. Apparently, expensive ones.

"I didn't know that was something you could do independently. I've always assumed that firearms are part of a mass production."

"Yeah, it's a real thing and a very lucrative industry, after you've established a client base. Luckily, I didn't have a problem doing that." He pauses like he's not sure about revealing the next part. "I did four years in the Navy. My buddies from my unit are always looking for their next toy. They're regular clients and they send new potential clients my way as well."

Kyle continues, answering questions I hadn't even formed yet. "Occasionally, I have contracts with the government. Mostly, that means testing weapons they're looking to purchase on a large scale to make sure they're good quality and worth the price. I have an office space, which doubles as a warehouse, not far from my house. It's where I do most of my builds and tests—there's a small, indoor gun range for that—and also where I hold client meetings. Other than that, it's mainly for storage and I work mostly from home. It's more convenient for me to handle business and the creative side from my workshop at home."

Well. My curiosity is piqued. That just goes to show there's always something to learn, even about friends. I make a mental note to ask to see his workshop sometime. Maybe I could convince him to take me shooting? Not that I'm going to be able to shoot anytime soon.

"So," I tease, "You know your way around guns pretty well, huh?"

Kyle pauses for a second and shifts in his seat. "I guess you could say that."

That look in his eyes says I'm not getting the full story so I call him out on it. "Spill the rest, Kyle."

He huffs at my bossy tone and glances at me in the rearview mirror.

"How do you know I'm holding something back?" When I only look innocently in response, waiting, he rolls his eyes. "Fine. I'm a leading expert on firearms building, quality control, all of it." When he stops again, I motion with my hand to carry on and he rolls his eyes again, his cheeks flushing a light pink. "Fine!" he says, more forcefully, "I kinda more than know my way around guns. I'm an expert sharpshooter and hold the record for long-range shooting with a handgun and rifle."

"No fucking way! How have I known you for a year and didn't know this about you?!" This is a *massive* deal. Well, I don't actually know how big of a deal it really is but it *sounds* like a massive deal!

"It isn't something I like to advertise. Some people get weird once they find out this shit. I didn't want you to see me any differently than you do." What I glean from that is, most people think he's either bragging when he reveals his success or jealous of him or, maybe, they're just afraid of pissing him off and getting a sniper bullet to the head while they're walking down the street because holy hell, he's awesome.

While I'm busy fangirling, he continues, "It's not a part of my life in any active sense. I do still go shooting but that's mostly to test new builds before they go to clients or recommend firearms with specific specs to them. I don't compete in any competitions anymore."

The unease in his voice is bleeding through so I let him off the hook. Besides, I got my question and *more* answered. I can tackle convincing him to take me shooting later.

I smile at him and turn to my next victim just as Kyle turns into a local coffee shop's drive-through. "So, Owen, other than being a doctor and an aspiring cook. What else do you do for fun?"

The conversation pauses while Kyle places the orders. Black coffee for him—predictable but how does anyone drink that! And a mocha Frappuccino with caramel drizzle for me. Owen shoots me a look at my order. I shrug. I like getting my caffeine buzz and sugar high all in one, so shoot me. It's my only guilty pleasure.

"Did you want another cup, Owen, or something else?" Kyle offers.

"I'll take a green tea, thanks." When the orders have been placed, Owen addresses my earlier question. "I don't get much time for it but I enjoy equestrian activities, particularly, polo. I played in college but being a doctor keeps me busy now."

"Horses! I *love* horses!" I squeal. "I used to have one when I was younger but when we moved to the city, we couldn't afford to board him, so my mom said I had to sell him." I cried so much when I had to give him away.

"Well then, you just so happen to be in luck. I've got stables at my house so anytime you want to visit some horses, come over. You're welcome to come and ride with me any time after you've healed properly."

When my drink finally makes it into my hands and we're out of the drive-through, I take my first sip of coffee since the morning of the attack. The moan that escapes me is unbidden. It's oh so good!

A throat clears from the front and I open my eyes to Owen, turned slightly in his seat, looking at me. We lock eyes for a beat and the heat in his gaze is scorching. I look away, my cheeks flushed—whether from embarrassment or desire, I couldn't say—and focus my attention on the window, refusing to acknowledge Kyle's eyes on me. The silence stretches for the next few miles but shifts from awkward to comfortable.

When the building comes into sight, I'm in awe. The sign on the front of the building reads: King's Custom Cars. The garage is more like a high-class showroom for custom cars, nothing like a mom-and-pop's garage.

I wonder how I, a part-time waitress and psychology major, am just surrounded by successful people lately before another thought takes over: *how the hell am I going to afford this place?*

We pull into a well-maintained, well-occupied parking lot and park a few spaces down from the door. As Kyle comes around to help me get out, I leave my empty cup on the seat next to me to dispose of later and Owen goes inside to let his friend know we're here.

I look up and the light reflecting from the numerous windows covering the two-story building almost blinds me. The main headquarters take up a quarter of the block and the other quarter is occupied by what looks to be the garage.

As Kyle helps me inside, the stares from strangers walking to and from their cars unsettles me but I try to shake it off. Of course, they'll look. We're walking at a snail's pace and I likely look exactly how I feel—like I got the shit beat out of me.

Kyle, however, in his determination to get me inside in one piece, doesn't even seem to notice the attention. His patience is unending. He matches my pace and I'm pleasantly surprised that he's letting me walk. How awkward would this be if he was carrying me like a helpless princess right now! I'd much rather use him as a walker.

As we make it to the door, Owen holds it open while we make our way through.

The inside is clean and spacious. The reception desk to the left-center of the wall is taller than usual and accommodates a pretty, redheaded woman. Long waves of copper-red hair graze against her shoulders as she works on the computer in front of her. Light sky-blue eyes, set in a round-shaped face, are focused entirely on the screen. She appears tiny but I suppose anyone would, in front of a desk that massive—it only just reaches above her mid-torso.

There's a glass elevator to the left and, to the right, there's a white marble staircase with a silver, metal railing that sweeps up to the second story.

It all seems very clean and professional and nothing like I'd have imagined a mechanics shop.

Owen leads us to a waiting area. It's in a nook under the stairwell, well-furnished with several plush, black leather chairs and a matching couch. Kyle helps me to the couch and props my leg up before sitting in one chair, while Owen is on the other end of the couch with my leg reaching across the expanse to graze my toes against his side.

The connection soothes my nerves a little because I know I don't belong here. I look like a bum in my sweats. Kyle's in nice clothes and though Owen is in Kyle's t-shirt and sweats, he still looks presentable.

Both men talk about some of the newer car models that the showroom boasts while I distract myself by taking note of the magazines on the glass and stainless-steel coffee table. On the wall, there are framed photos of all sorts of luxury vehicles: sleek trucks, SUVs, gleaming motorcycles. All carry the King's Custom Cars logo on them.

As I'm looking at the body of one particularly glossy, powerful-looking, black motorcycle on the cover of a magazine, a huge man descends the stairs and heads toward us.

"Nor—" Kyle begins but my attention is riveted towards the approaching man.

He's about as tall as Owen, but stockier. The bulk of muscle he's carrying is closer to Kyle's size and the planes of his body suggest that his figure is a byproduct of hard work, rather than hours spent in a gym. Though he's not as chiseled as the other two, he still looks like he could crush me with one of his massive hands.

His dark-brown, almost black, hair, sets off the color of his striking blue eyes. It looks like ice frosted over in those eyes; so light, they're almost glowing. Thick eyebrows, a cut, strong jaw and a straight, proud nose. How can one person be so good-looking? Lush and full lips, with an enviable cupid's bow, only add to his masculine appeal. His black t-shirt is tight across his chest and biceps, as big as my head. A flat stomach leads to slim hips, encased in black boot-cut jeans and black work boots that look like they've seen better days.

Owen stands to meet the hulking stranger in another confusing man hug. They grab each other's wrists and pull each other in for a hug that ends in loud and hard slaps to the back. It looks like that should leave a bruise and I'm still bemused by the display, as always, when they back away and smile at each other.

"It's good to see you, man," Owen's friend says in a gravely, deep voice that makes shivers run up my spine.

"You too, Silas."

Silas. It suits him.

Owen takes a few steps towards me and stops, saying, "Let me introduce you to the lady I was telling you about."

As Owen helps me stand, Kyle comes to my left but I'm too focused on the cold heat of Silas's glare as his jaw ticks to be much help. The anger in those icy eyes would unnerve me but I have Kyle on one side, Owen on the other, and a strange feeling that this man isn't angry at me.

He's angry *for* me.

Not even my friends after him were as enraged at the injustice as these men have been. Two strangers, one friend. And they don't even know that I've faced worse.

Silas's shoulders are still bunched with tension as he balls and releases his fist. His growly voice is tight with rage as he says, "Tell me whoever did this to her is eating his meals through a straw."

Owen shakes his head in disgust. "I can't, but the police are looking for him." When Owen notices Silas's questioning eyes on me, he says, "Oh yes, I'm sorry, this is Nora Molano. Nora, this is the friend I mentioned, Silas King."

King! His name is on the damn *building*. This guy is more than a mechanic; he's the owner of this luxurious garage.

Kyle and Silas jerk their chins in greeting before the frosty-eyed giant turns his full attention to me.

Under the weight of his full attention, the world stops. He looks at me, really *looks* at me, taking in every detail, from the very crown of my head, to my untied hair, falling free around me, to my feet in tennis shoes. I know he doesn't miss a single bruise, scrape, or detail.

The intensity of his gaze ratchets up when the men at my side stiffen as Silas moves towards me.

"Slowly, brother." Silas stops at Owen's caution. "She's been through quite a bit and has some triggers we need to be mindful of."

I'm thankful for their thoughtfulness. Though I don't feel threatened by Silas from this distance, it's impossible to deny that he's massive. I don't have to be sitting down for him to tower over me. He might be the same height as Owen but he's bigger and I know he might send me into a panicked flashback.

Silas acknowledges the advice with a chin lift before sharing a look with Kyle that I can't decipher. Finally, he advances again, slower this time, as he keeps me with him with that gravelly voice.

"Hello, Nora. As Owen said, I'm Silas. Anything you need, transportation-wise, I've got you." He reaches me by the end of his introduction and takes my hand in his. His bear paw is twice the size of my hand swallowing mine right up. Calloused skin caresses mine, bringing me to a vague memory of my EMT rescuer running his rough hands over my skin, checking for injuries. It's the only pleasant memory from that night. Rough hands have always calmed me.

His hands were pampered and soft as could be.

"Uh," I flounder, unsure how to respond, "Thank you?"

He still has my hand in his. Then, he does the last thing I would've expected from this, or any, man: he brings my hand to his lush lips and kisses my knuckles, brushing them back and forth with his thumb. Kyle stiffens more than he already has while Owen's light chuckle sounds next to me.

"Silas, give her a moment to get to know you before you invade her space." Owen warns him with an indulgent tone in his voice. "I'm sorry Nora. Silas is a very touchy guy. If it makes you uncomfortable, just tell him. He'll back off."

I look into Silas's frosted eyes. This isn't a man who wants to harm me. In fact, he looks like a man who'd give his life to protect mine. I smile shyly at him to reassure him that I'm okay with him before replying to Owen.

"Clearly, as you can tell from my current state, I don't have a problem letting anyone know if I don't want them to touch me."

The coiled tension in Silas's frame tips me off that this was the wrong thing to say. He's so tense, it looks like he might snap. In a voice that's so low and lethal, that I feel a very real, menacing chill up my spine, he says, "Some asshole touched you, you said no and then he beat you for it?"

I bite my tongue to hold it. I'm not scared of this man, but I don't know what to say right now. From his reaction, I can tell that he's projecting his own anger, maybe anger at the general mistreatment of women, onto my situation, so nothing that comes from my mouth will make this any better. And I don't know him, but I do know that lies, however white, will not be appreciated so I don't downplay the severity of my situation. I do the only thing I can think of. I clasp his hand, still in mine, tighter and pull him into me. His balance doesn't falter and he doesn't fall into me but I fall into him, hugging him as best as I can with how much taller he is than me and my injured arm. The man's frozen at first. But when he thaws, I know I'm in for a crushing bear hug.

I don't want to upset him further but I also don't want my bruised ribs to become broken.

"Careful. I have a few bruised ribs and a few other injuries."

He takes a deep breath and, on his slow exhale, he wraps his arms around me carefully for one of the best hugs of my life. I feel warm and engulfed in the pressure of his embrace, in his strength, and my nerves sigh wherever his body connects with mine.

"I'm so sorry this happened to you, doll," Silas whispers in my ear. "I swear that motherfucker will pay for this. He'll never touch another woman without consent again. He'll never put his hands on a woman *ever* again."

I just hold on.

A warm hand lands on the middle of my back as Owen comes to stand at my back. "Okay, Silas. Let her go so she can take a look at her car and discuss her options."

Silas releases me and steps back carefully.

"Come on, doll. Let's go talk shop before Dr. Baker blows a gasket and explodes into a lecture on time management." He winks as Owen rolls his eyes and Kyle takes my good arm, wrapping it around his waist.

Silas takes the lead and guides us through the building, with Owen at the rear. We stop in front of the elevator, waiting for it to arrive, when Silas directs a question at Owen. "You going to send her to Heath?"

"I mentioned it to her, yes. She said she'd check it out and see from there." I give Owen a probing look so he explains, "The self-defense coach I told you about. His name is Heath. He's a friend."

"Why am I not surprised by that?" I ask absently as we get into the elevator. Silas has his phone out and he's typing away on it until we reach the second story. The doors open to let us out just as Silas's phone disappears into his pocket and he leads us to a spacious conference room, holding the door open as I lean on Kyle for support.

A long conference table takes up most of the space in the room. It's empty, save for an office phone in the middle, and furnished with ten chairs, four along each side and one at each end. Kyle helps me into one of them. "You good, Nora honey? The pain's not too bad?"

I smile at Kyle, checking in with my body before replying, "Nope. Manageable."

He lands a kiss on my hair.

As Owen props my leg up on the chair next to me under Silas's watchful eyes, Kyle takes a seat to my left, with Owen taking the seat to *his* left.

Silas shuts the door for privacy and waits until we're all seated before sitting at the head of the table.

"Okay, Nora. This is where we're at with your car," he starts. "When it was brought in, I personally looked it over, as a favor to Owen. It's not good. Even before the damage that I'm assuming was done by the fucker who hurt you, it wasn't good." I lift my hand, palm out, stopping Silas.

"Wait, what?" I frown, confused. "What damage?" I know my car's in bad shape, it has been since I got it, so when they mentioned it not being worth the money it would take to fix, I just assumed they meant the existing issues with it. This is the first I'm hearing of any damage.

All three men share a look that says a thousand words, clearly none meant for me. I'm getting irritated by all the silent conversations but before I can muster up the courage to call them out on it—*if* I can muster up the courage—Silas starts talking.

"When it was brought to the garage, all the windows were smashed."

Those words stop me short but Silas doesn't give me a second to process before throwing bomb after bomb on me. "All four tires were slashed and the front driver's seat's upholstery and padding were destroyed. Anything that could've been sold for parts was gone. In short, it's going to cost more to repair not only the damages but, also, to update the maintenance to make it safe."

Fuck. *Fuck!*

All my hopes of having a working vehicle are dashed into a muddy puddle and stomped on. Forget having it fixed, I might not even *have* a car. I only have the sorry remnants that the fucker left behind.

Fuck!

Now, on top of having what's likely to be a twenty-thousand-dollar hospital bill, likely more, I need a new car. And I can't work to compensate for the cost of one expense, never mind two, since I can't work for at least six weeks. Hell, I couldn't even walk from the elevator to the conference room without using Kyle as a crutch!

I quickly calculate what I have left in savings and my heart plummets further. I don't even have enough to cover two months' rent. My lease on my apartment has six months left so it'll cost me more to break it than I can afford.

I prop my forehead on my left hand and just stare at the table, racking my brain on how I'm going to pull any of this off. I can't see a solution. I close my eyes and fight back tears of hopelessness.

What am I going to do? I don't even have enough money to *live*.

Kyle puts his hand on my lower back and starts gently rubbing. I resist the urge to shrug away the comfort because even though I don't want to be touched right now, he's only trying to help.

I look up when Silas starts speaking again.

"It just so happens that I can loan you a vehicle until you can find a permanent replacement."

The offer makes my heart lift but I know I can't accept it. My pride won't allow it. The cars he has on offer I couldn't afford to lease them for a day, even if I *was* working. There's no way in hell I can accept it for free. Not only would that put him out of pocket—granted, not by a lot—I'm not a charity case.

I'll find a way.

"Thank you for the offer but no. It wouldn't feel right to me." It's a generous offer but ultimately, my self-respect must take priority. It's all I have left. It's all I've *had* left for a while. "But I would like to see my car, please."

The memory of the events leading up to the recent attack surface and my heart starts beating fast. My pride is what got me in this situation. I shake my head and refuse to resent myself for my self-respect.

I'd be nothing without it.

"Of course," is his simple response, with only acceptance. "We can take a look at your car now, if you'd like. I have it in my bay in the garage."

The guys all stand and Kyle hovers, waiting to help me up. The open wound of compounded loss feels heavy on my chest and the uncertainty of the coming future makes the ground feel like it'll yield under my feet at any second. His hand wraps around my left bicep and it doesn't feel like a crutch anymore; it feels like a handcuff.

I shake his hand off and snap at him, "I can do it."

His hand stays suspended in the air, frozen, as his eyes widen slightly, before a shutter slams down on his emotions and he backs off, face blank. But he keeps close enough to catch me if I fall and a twinge of guilt twists my gut. I grit my teeth against it. I need this.

I *need* this.

I bend as far as I can with my ribs and, with my left hand, I pull my leg from the second seat and set it down on the floor. The chair slides back on its wheels easily, with only a slight push. That's the easy part. For the rest, the wheels are going to be more of a nuisance than a help.

I place my left hand on the table for stability and, cautiously, follow it with my right hand. I push up with my left leg, blowing out a breath to center myself. When I'm on both feet, my weight falls on my right leg more than I intended and I hiss and wince at the pain. In my peripheral, Kyle's hand rises and falls, like he was going to reach for me but didn't know if he should, but I've already caught myself before he had to.

And that makes me smile wider than I have in a week. The split lip pulls with the movement but I couldn't hold myself back even if I tried. I did it! It's such a small thing, so seemingly insignificant, but I can't stop the pride at my accomplishment.

I look at the guys, hoping they'll share my excitement, and though Owen is smiling, they all have an undecipherable look in their eyes, a kind of awe that I can see but don't understand. Silas's eyes are still on my lips, where a smile still rests, though it's turned more quizzical now, and I touch my lip with my fingers to see if it's bleeding.

Nope, *all clear*. I mentally shrug the weirdness off.

The elation dwindles with a pang of self-hate. I snapped at *Kyle*.

Kyle, who's opened his home to me, who's been my support since he heard about the attack, who's been my rock since the moment I asked and since the moment he promised. Who was, just now, as proud of me as I was, even after I pushed him away.

I motion for Owen and Silas to carry on and, as they leave the room, I hobble to my rock and close the distance between us. I offer him my hand in question, and when he takes it without hesitation, I smile sheepishly. I use the hand to hobble even closer and into him and wrap my arm around his waist, lay my chin on his chest and look him in the eyes. "I'm sorry for snapping. I shouldn't have taken my frustration out on you. Forgive me?"

He smiles back.

"There's nothing to forgive. I understand your frustration. I'm a bit on edge myself with everything that's happened." He wraps his arm around me and gives a light squeeze, kissing my forehead. "We just need to stick together and we'll get through it."

As we move to the door, I wonder how I found someone as great as him. I'll forever be thankful that he framed the situation as a 'we.' Because I'm still leaning on him but now, it feels like maybe he's leaning on me too.

We file back into the elevator. I keep hold of Kyle's hand and rest against the glass wall of the elevator, exhausted and dreading the walk to the garage. *Oh, how the mighty have fallen.* Only a week ago, I was as active as Kyle but with all this healing, my energy reserves are at zero. Kyle must have noticed because when the doors open, he waits for the other two to file out. Then, without asking, he picks me up in his strong arms and I smile inside, knowing for sure that we're okay. There was no hesitation or doubt in his movements.

Owen and Silas are waiting outside, discussing a replacement for someone called Sara. They don't even turn to look at Kyle and I, as Owen says, "Nora could handle it, I'm sure."

"Nora could handle what?" I question.

Owen turns to me. "Silas needs a replacement for his receptionist. She'll be leaving for maternity leave in a couple of weeks. They haven't found anyone they like to fill the position while she's gone and I was just thinking, if you need to work while you're healing, this would be a good fit since it's not too physically tasking. You could go back to your job at the restaurant when she's ready to come back."

Silas looks to me. "That's not a bad idea, if Nora wanted to help me out."

I roll my eyes internally. I know exactly what he's doing by making it seem like I'm helping *him*, when, in reality, we all know he's doing *me* a solid. But this isn't a handout so if it works for both of us, I'm taking this opportunity with both hands. After all, I've got a lot more bills to pay now.

"When would you need me and for how long? I have school and need to check with the restaurant to make sure they'll take me back."

"I'm willing to work with your school schedule and I'd need you next week so that Sara can hand the role over. It's not complicated but I need someone to take over because it's a pain to run back and forth every time the damn phone rings.

And don't even get me started on the paperwork." He makes a disgusted face that brings a smile from me.

He offers to introduce me to Sara and, at my assent, we head over to the reception desk, where the tiny redhead's sitting. He smiles sweetly at her, which she returns, and my heart jumps at the sight. That smile could bring down nations.

"Sara, I've found your temporary replacement," he says, sweeping his hand to me. "This is Nora. Nora, Sara."

Sara rounds the corner and her belly emerges from behind there a few seconds before the rest of her. Maybe it's because she's petite but it looks like she's ready to deliver at any point. I'm still gaping at the bump and how cute she looks with it when she comes up to me and holds out her hand. I watch my grip as we shake hands because her hand is so small and I've never met someone who seems as breakable as her.

"Hi, Nora! I'm so glad you can do this. You're really getting me out of a bind here. Now I don't have to worry about coming back to a warzone!" She laughs and it hits me then that she didn't even blink an eye at my battered appearance.

In my heart, I say my 'thanks' for that and answer with both a warning and a joke. "Don't thank me just yet. You haven't come back to my organized chaos. I can't even make sense of it sometimes!"

We grin at each other and I'm still reeling from the fact that I just had a moment with someone other than the guys when the front doors open.

An incredibly tall man, taller than all the guys surrounding me, enters. He's well-built, with the kind of muscle, and walks with the kind of grace, that says that he can fight. His red hair, the same shade as Sara's, is shaved on the sides, while the strands on top are long enough to be pulled back into a man bun. A good week of facial hair covers his face.

Good goodness! Where are all these hot-as-hell men coming from and why haven't I seen them before?

A t-shirt, branded with a gym logo that I recognize, covers his upper half. I've never been to that gym but the reviews and word-of-mouth rave have made it a dream of mine. On his lower half, he's wearing jeans that showcase his muscular thighs and black tennis shoes.

He's a fucking giant but he carries himself with cat-like agility, light on his feet with loose-limbed movements.

Sara waddles over to the new guy, quicker than I'd have thought she could move with her big belly, and throws her arms out for a hug with a squeal. "My favorite little brother!"

He smiles and hugs her, lifting her off the ground and teases in a deep-timbred voice, "Your only brother, little hellion." I'm just watching to make sure he doesn't squeeze the baby right out of her but she doesn't seem to care. In fact, she's laughing when he sets her down and ruffles her hair before turning to us.

His eyes land on me and my every muscle tightens to the point of pain as he swells to twice his size with tension. A worrying shade of red takes over his face and I'm so worried he'll explode, I brace for impact and it's a good thing I do.

"Tell me you were in a car accident and that's why you're hurt. If someone did this to you, I'm going to kill that motherfucker!" He bellows at us but I know he's talking to me … or at me? I back up a step into the nearest wall, which turns out to be Owen.

The giant's gaze shifts to Silas and this time, I'm sure he's pissed at him. The giant of a man clips out in a low, gravely growl, "You should've fucking said something to me, prepared me for this shit."

Sara lays a palm on his chest, which is as far up as she can reach on him and yells right back, "Maybe, don't scare the daylights out of her before you've even been introduced, Heath!" In any other situation, to see this teeny, tiny woman holding back a mountain of a man with only one hand would have been funny, but, in this instance, it most certainly is not.

Owen and Silas don't seem at all fazed by the yelling but Kyle and I are both on edge. I suspect Kyle is only reacting to my anxiety, ready to jump into action at the drop of a hat.

Heath takes several, heaving breaths through his nose and lets them out slowly with his eyes closed. When he opens them again, I'm surprised that he doesn't have blue eyes like his sister. His are a beautiful gray, though the fire and rage still burn in them. Once he has control of himself, he approaches us slowly, as if he's trying to not frighten me.

I'm not sure if I am scared of this man. Surprisingly, after his initial reaction, I don't think I am.

"I'm sorry if I freaked you out," he says, in a much gentler voice that has me relaxing against Owen. At the tension easing in me, Kyle relaxes too, proving my earlier theory. "I have issues with people hurting others unless it's in the ring or consensual." When he sees that I'm not scared, he continues, "I would never hit a woman. I might get angry and show it but I swear, I'd never take my hand to you or another woman in my life."

Assaulting memories cry out for attention and *shit!* I'm going to cry in front of everyone. The tears come unbidden, unwelcome, and I can't stop them. Heath's eyes fall to my wetting cheeks and reddening eyes and he looks like he wants to rip me from Owen's arms to comfort me. But he won't because he doesn't want to scare me again and for some reason, that makes me cry even more.

I turn into Owen and shove my face into his neck, loosening the rein on the emotions a little. He guides me to a chair and holds me as I fall apart, his hand smoothing up and down my spine.

I hear whispering not far away and catch some of Kyle's retelling of the events that recently transpired.

"Flynn was the one who found her?" Silas asks.

"Yeah, he brought her in." He continues after a pause, "He wants to meet her."

Just as I've controlled my breathing and lifted my head, the tears still running, I see Heath lowering into a squat to kneel next to us, staring into my eyes.

"I'm so sorry you had to go through that, sweetheart." Heath's voice comes out as a low rumble. "I'm the self-defense coach Owen told you about. I'm here because I got a text from Silas that I should come meet someone who might need my services. He's a pushy asshole like that. I'd like to coach you so you can prevent this from ever happening again and so that you can heal, mentally, physically, in every way."

His voice is so soothing, his words so gentle, and his acknowledgement of my precarious mental state makes me forget that this man is a stranger and makes me grab onto him. He pulls me into his lap with my insistence and then I'm in his lap, crying even harder into his shoulder. He *thumps* onto the floor on his butt and just lets me cry and cry until I'm all cried out, at least for now.

I sniffle and look up into his beautiful gray eyes that look wetter than they did a moment ago, and breathe in the scent of wood polish that clings to him. My voice is barely a rasp when I say, "I might not be able to do much until my fractures heal. But when they do, I'd very much like to learn."

He nods, free of judgement.

"I'll be here when you're ready. Until then, I'd like to help you and your new entourage"—he winks—"with anything you might need. In the meantime, we can work on the psychological aspects of getting past your trauma. It's all a part of my program."

I didn't know his program is so involved but I'm thankful that I'll have the help I know I'll need.

He stands, with me in his arms, and Silas leads us toward the garage. Sara shouts a greeting and reminder to see her next week on our way out. As I wave to her over Heath's shoulder, I see Kyle and Owen behind us, their heads joined together, deep in discussion.

6 A Full House

Sounds from every direction and of every kind assault my senses before we've even stepped into the garage. Passing the threshold increases the decibel level to the point where I'm almost tempted to cover my ears. The scent of gasoline, with a hint of disinfectant, reaches my nose.

Five bays, on each side of a long, wide aisle, hold one vehicle each. Some are on vehicle lifts; others, on the floor with their hoods up. Everything from luxury vehicles to more standard models fill the garage as men and women work hard in the massive room.

I don't have to search for my car for long before Silas leads us to the middle bay. I stiffen in Heath's arms at the sight of a vehicle I would deny to the last breath is mine, if it wasn't for the license plate.

I can't fathom why someone would do this to an already-crappy car and I allow myself to wallow in self-pity for a moment, before shaking it away. There's no point crying any more about something that can't be undone but I can't hide the shock that's clear in the whisper of my voice.

"How could someone do this?" I whisper and shake my head in disbelief. *Fuck this. I'm done being miserable.* I throw my head back dramatically, careful of my shoulder, and sigh dramatically. "I might scream."

Heath rumbles with laughter against the left side of my body, while the rest of the guys grin. At least Owen is trying to be secretive about it, as he covers his face, but I can see the way he's watching me, looking out for signs of a breakdown.

This should be the straw that breaks the camel's back, but I refuse to fall apart.

Reassured that I'm emotionally okay, Silas says, "I'm not going to insult you by trying to sugarcoat anything, doll. I can't even use this as scrap. It's too damaged and wouldn't hold structurally. I could sell you a car but they're all custom."

"Silas, I can't afford one of your cars." I protest.

He nods in understanding and gives me a sympathetic look.

"I could still loan you a car."

"And not have me pay for it? No. I'm not looking for a handout!"

"Well, I don't need the money. And I don't *want* your money either. What I *want* is peace of mind that you'll have safe and reliable transportation when you need it. That can be your payment."

It's clear he thinks he's either found a loophole or a solution that works for both of us, but it doesn't work for me. I can't take advantage of him like that.

"I'm sorry but I can't. It's too much."

"Okay, how do you plan on getting here for work? Or to school? Or to your appointments without a car?"

All valid points, of course, but all that I have no response to. I can't maneuver around a bus in this state and I certainly can't afford taxis. And if I'm not accepting his car, then I'm also not okay with them paying for my taxi, which I know will be their suggestion.

"What if," Silas barters, in a consolatory tone, "you give me fifty dollars a week until you find a replacement car. You'll be responsible for gas and any upkeep but you have to bring it here for any maintenance. Deal?"

I know he's trying to be nice but it grates on my pride. He's pressing so hard and I know it won't put him out of pocket. I should take it but I can't. Any car that he lends me will be worth

112

much more than two hundred dollars a month and I can't take advantage of him like that, even if he doesn't need my money.

"No and that's final," I say firmly, making it clear that this discussion is over.

All the men share a look and must come to the same conclusion because suddenly, I'm seeing matching grins on four faces and I just know I won't like their suggestion.

"That's fine, Nora," Kyle says, too smug for his own good. "We'll just rotate your transportation detail."

Underneath the smugness is a determination and I know I won the first round but I've lost this one. Even if I protest, they'll just deposit me in their cars and carry me wherever I need to go. Hell, I might even have to put up with a child lock. And, of course, since one's my doctor, one's my new roommate and one's now my employee, they'll know my schedule. I huff and glare at each one of them in turn.

That's when they all burst with laughter.

I could fight them on this, since this 'solution' eats a lot of their time, but I know it'll be a losing battle and I also damn well know that I'm looking forward to spending time with each of them. I cross my arms, pouting, and change the subject over the sound of their fading chuckles. "I'm hungry."

Heath gathers himself first. Still smiling, he heads back the way we came. "Then let's feed you, sweetheart." Over his shoulder, he yells, "Onwards, fuckers! We must feed the beast, lest we feel her wrath!" I roll my eyes at his theatrics.

As we file back into the building and pass the reception area, Sara looks up from her computer.

"Hey, guys, Flynn called. He wanted to know if you wanted lunch. I told him you were all here so he said he'd come over so you could go out for lunch. He suggested Mexican food. And of course, bring me back my usual, please." Oh, she's *good*. She said the last part like it's a no-brainer and like it was a request, but it wasn't. They also can't say no to feeding a pregnant woman, especially not without facing my wrath that they apparently fear.

"Like we'd come back without food for you. You think we don't value our balls?" Heath shoots back.

I'm leaning against Heath when the front door opens in sync with my warning. "Good because if you didn't bring her food, I'd beat *all* of your asses."

A rich laugh comes from behind us and I turn to see a strangely familiar man over Heath's shoulder, laughing with his head bent and his hands on his hips.

"I knew you were a little spitfire!" he says, chuckling.

I recognize his voice from the night of my attack. A deep, soothing voice. *It's alright. It's okay. I've got you.* And I'm filled with gratitude. This is the man who saved me. If it hadn't been for him, that asshole never would have run away.

When he looks up, the gratitude turns to wide-eyed awe. Just like the rest of the men, he's hot beyond belief. His brunette hair, the same shade as mine but healthier-looking, is shorter on the sides, but not shaved like Heath's. At the top, his hair is wavier, curling at the ends, and a few inches longer on top. His smile is infectious but I'm too busy gaping to smile back. Metal glints from inside his mouth. When he stands to his full height, he's about as tall as Owen and Silas.

Blue jeans and red converse cover his lower half and a lime-green shirt, tight over the cut surface of his chest, abs and arms, makes his skin glow. Unlike Owen's swimmer body, my rescuer has the build of a football player. Both his arms are covered in sleeve tattoos and various bracelets; one is in just black ink, while the other has every color of the rainbow and more. There's a black ring on his left thumb and a silver one on his right hand's index finger, with a blue one on his middle finger.

But more than *anything*, more than even the relaxed, hipster, Rockstar energy he exudes, I'm drawn in by his eyes. One is freshwater blue, the other as green as the sea. I've never seen anything like it. It's like he's the walking personification of two bodies of water that meet but do not mix.

Heath sets me down as my rescuer approaches.

"Hey, little spitfire," he says, in a voice that I will always associate with the feeling of coming out of a bad storm and into a warm embrace. "I'm Flynn. I'm the one who found you the other night."

Before I can respond, he's pulling me into a firm hug that makes me want to climb him and wrap my legs around his hips and never come unattached.

He takes a big breath and whispers in my ear, "I'm sorry we met under the circumstances we did but I can't say how glad I am to see you on your feet. I can't wait to get to know you."

I shiver against him and I know he feels it but he doesn't say a word.

Oh man, I'm in trouble. He's *smooth*, I can already tell. I just met him but he's already in my head, as much as the others. I pull back and look into his stunning eyes with a grin. "I also can't wait to get to know you."

He smiles back before wrapping an arm around me and making his way to the front door, taking me with him.

"Let's eat. I'm starved!" Flynn announces loudly, to no one in particular.

"You're always hungry," Owen says from behind us.

"I'm hungry too," I stage whisper to Flynn as we step into the open air.

Kyle unlocks the Tahoe with the key fob and everyone, except Silas and Heath, heads that way. I watch which car Silas

115

and Heath are going to and whistle low at the sight of a *huge,* lifter, black, Toyota Tundra. Several of the guys chuckle at my appreciative reaction.

With Kyle in the driver's seat and Owen in the front passenger, Flynn helps me into the back, slides in after me and props my feet on his lap. Once everyone's loaded up, we follow Silas and Heath to the restaurant.

At the restaurant, I end up between Owen and Flynn, with Silas directly across from me, Heath to his left and Kyle on the right, closest to the walkway.

The food comes quickly after we place the order and I spend most of my time talking to the guys and observing them, trying to get an insight into these men who should be strangers to me, but feel like friends.

Owen is the most logical out of the group. He, like Kyle, likes to sit back and observe and only contributes to the conversation when he has all the facets of the discussion. Silas, too, also has a personality made for leading. He's dark and mysterious, with a playful side that only peeks out when he's talking to me, not the other guys. He's got a protective streak that makes him well-respected in the group dynamic. More than once, I notice how much they value his opinion.

Heath, as funny and as involved as he is, is equally as focused on his surroundings as his company. He's hyperalert to everyone and everything, whereas Kyle is happier to observe my interactions with the guys than engage actively in the conversation.

Flynn's the fun loving, happy-go-lucky flirt of the group. He flirts shamelessly with me without any hesitation. He also blows right through the bubble of my personal space. Through lunch, my legs were on his lap, his hand was under the sweats and he was absently stroking my calf but I don't mind. He's respectful and never makes me feel uncomfortable.

I don't know how I fit into this group of dominant, testosterone-filled men yet. Every time the attention was focused on me, my nerves were shot but maybe that's because I'm still figuring out my place in the group.

The portion size was massive and I hate that I can't finish it. It's the best food I've ever had! I don't want to waste it. The guys are talking amongst themselves as I gape at their empty plates.

"Man, you guys sure can eat. Where do you put it all?"

"In case you didn't notice, we're big strong men," Flynn teases. "It takes a lot to fuel these bodies." He removes his hand from my leg and flexes his bicep.

Owen, who looks amused by his friend, catches my eye. "Did you want any dessert, Nora?"

I do but if I eat another bite, they'll have to roll me out and get a crane to lift me into the Tahoe. I smile at him. "Maybe next time."

When the check comes, with Sara's food, the guys start arguing about whose turn it is to pay. Funnily enough, they're all fighting in favor of paying. While they're distracted, Kyle nabs it, winks at me and slips from his seat, ninja-style. He returns to the other four finally reaching a consensus that it's Heath's turn.

They all look for the bill, then at me, like I got up, hobbled to the front desk and paid the damn thing when I can hardly move. *Men.*

"Nora, do you have the bill?" Silas asks in a serious voice.

Kyle comes to my rescue with a rib at them.

"I paid it while you guys were clucking like old hens about whose turn it was." They all chuckle and get up to leave, with Heath carrying Sara's food.

This time, Silas helps me to the Tahoe. Once I'm settled in, he looks me dead in the eye and I narrow my eyes suspiciously. "*Whaaat*?" I stretch the word out.

"When you're with us, you never pay for anything." His tone is very serious. "I find out you do and I'll tan your ass, doll. You got it?"

My eyes widen and my voice comes out in an amazed whisper, "You'd *spank* me?!"

"You do, after this warning, abso-fucking-lutely." He kisses my cheek then shuts my door and gets in his truck. I'm a bit alarmed, and unexpectedly turned on, by his comment and the kiss certainly doesn't help my current state of arousal any.

Flynn opens the door a beat later and climbs in after I scoot over. I tattle to him, leaving out the kissing part. "Silas just told me he'd spank me if I paid for anything if I'm with you guys."

Owen and Flynn look at each other but Owen speaks for both of them.

"He's serious, gorgeous. You don't pay, not with us. It's a guy thing. If you do, he'll find out because we'll tell him."

"That goes for me too." Kyle interjects as he starts the truck and backs out.

What in the actual fuck?

"You guys *do* know this is the twenty-first century. Right?" They all just look at me, unimpressed by the argument. "I'm perfectly capable of paying my own way!"

"We know you are," Flynn says. "This isn't about that. It's about us and the type of men we are. We pay for our women. That's just the way it is. I wouldn't recommend fighting on this one. You'll lose and just piss us off."

I cross my arms and huff out a reluctant, "Fine." I don't like it but this is not the hill I want to die on.

And when did I become their woman?

And what does that even mean?!

∞∞∞

I don't remember falling asleep but I'm roused from sleep with a slight jostle, to the sensation of being carried. The scent of orange and ginger invades my senses and I curl into Owen.

Before I can breathe in his presence for long, I'm being lowered onto Kyle's familiar bed and I'm out as soon as my head hits the pillow, before Owen's fully extracted his hands from my person.

∞∞∞

I wake to a darkened room and darkness in my head. The sun's gone down and the cobwebs of a lingering nightmare cling to me. Sweat runs down my body, through my tangled hair, and I force myself up to try to get my bearings.

It's too dark to make out anything. The door leading to the hallway is closed and the only light is coming from the bathroom, where the door is cracked an inch but it's not enough.

I scoot over to the edge of the bed, inching closer to the bathroom door because I really need to pee, and stand with only a slight wobble. I can do this. If I can stand without support, I can do this too. I don't want to need the guys every time I need the restroom.

Shuffling seems like the most painless way of getting anywhere so I do a little penguin dance and stop in front of the toilet, avoiding the mirror as I pass by. After I've relieved myself, I move to the sink to wash my hands. With my hands braced on the counter, I drop my head and breathe deep and slow, minding my ribs. It's time. I have to face the reality at some point. And it's *finally* time.

Slowly, I lift my head.

My lips fall open, my eyes widen and, without my bidding, my hands travel to my face, touching at the wounds and bruises before falling to my sides, heavy as lead. If this is how I look now, how much worse did I look the morning after the attack?

The left side of my face is black and blue from my hairline all the way to my neck. The swelling around my eye has gone down, but not by much, and the white of my eye is still streaked with red. There's a small cut on my cheek and my lip's split, swollen to twice the size it should be. There's bruising all along my jaw and left temple.

I'm a mess.

My hands on the counter support my weight as I finally succumb to the reality that I've been beaten, again, and this time, the guy's still out there. That night plays on repeat in my head and I break.

I fall apart.

The tears keep coming and I don't even try to control them anymore.

I mourn and grieve and sob for my job, the loss of my car, my empty bank account and no way to support myself. I sob because some dickhead thought he was entitled enough to touch me and I'm left with the consequences of standing up for myself while he runs free, unchecked. My chest caves in and my ribs hurt because he's free out there and I'm healing and will be for a long time.

How is that fair? How is it fair that I have to bear the consequences of his shitty actions and he might never be caught?

The knock of a door penetrates through the fog of despair that's settling around me. Warm, chocolate-brown eyes meet mine and I'm so thankful I'm not alone this time. *I have Kyle.*

He comes to me.

I have Owen.

He picks me up.

I have Silas and Heath and Flynn too. I don't know how or why but they're trying to become permanent fixtures in my life and at least I'm not alone this time.

He holds me and I cry for the broken girl who put her broken pieces back together, alone, after *him* and the broken pieces this newest asshole left that I don't have to pick up by myself anymore.

Because I'm not alone anymore

Kyle holds me tighter and tighter and though my limbs protest, I finally cry myself out in his arms. He strokes my hair as I sniffle against him. We sit there for long, silent moments before he lifts me in his arms and helps me back into bed, kneeling next to me, careful not to stand over me.

" Nor..." he says, sadness in his eyes. He closes his eyes and shakes his head as I hiccup from the last of the tears. "Let me go get you some water. Are you in any pain? I can get you a pill from Owen. He has to leave soon but he wanted to come and say bye. I can ask him to call later if you're not up to meeting anyone right now."

"He can come in. I'd love some water and just some ibuprofen, please." There's not much physical pain but I know it'll come so I might as well get on top of it.

While Kyle's gone to get the pills and water, Owen comes in and sits next to me on the bed.

He holds my hand in his, such profound grief in his eyes that I have to swallow over a tight throat. "It'll get better, gorgeous. Time heals all wounds. If you need us to, we can find you a therapist."

We sit in silence for a moment. He knows I heard him but I don't want to talk about that right now. "How long before you have to leave?"

It's irrational but I feel connected to him, to all of them, and I don't want him to go. How this connection came to be in such a short amount of time, I can't fathom.

"I have about thirty minutes before I absolutely have to leave."

"That's not much time. Lay with me?" I'm being selfish but I need him close.

Wordlessly, he just crawls over me, next to me, careful not to jostle me. He fits my body into his so we're pressed as tightly as possible, touching from shoulders to feet. I relax into his warmth and just breathe him in.

Kyle comes in, gives me an ibuprofen and some water and once I've taken the medication, he takes the glass and leaves, closing the door on his way out.

I look down at Owen's arm around my waist and trail my fingernails against his skin. The memory of how at ease they all were with each other at lunch comes to me. "It's so odd that you've all been friends for years. I'm not sure where that puts me."

"Where do you want to be?" Owen asks.

I think on that for more than a few moments but come up blank.

Before I can formulate an answer, Owen continues, "We all want you in our lives, Nora. You're fun to be around and fit easily with us, even if you don't see it yet. You bring something we've been missing. Gorgeous," he says in a tone that asks me to look at him so I do and our eyes meet over my shoulder. "I'm glad you had Kyle in the last year. We all are. But now, you also have the rest of us. You have me. You have Silas, Heath, Flynn. Even Sara. We're there if you need us, Nora. You're ours just as much as we're yours now."

I turn my face away from my good and proper doctor. He has such a way of making me feel wanted and valued, like I bring something that no one else can. They all do really. I've never felt so *not* alone. I like belonging to these people and I like that they say they belong to me.

In his arms, I slide into a restful sleep, only rousing slightly when Owen leaves with a kiss on my cheek and a promise to check on me soon.

Sometime later, Kyle comes in and slips under the covers with me. He pulls me to him and I snuggle into him as best I can.

We don't move all night.

∞∞∞∞

In the morning, I wake to an empty bed. I rub the sleep from my eyes and shuffle to the bathroom like yesterday.

This time, I don't have to brace myself to look in the mirror. I take a good look at the reflection that looks back and when my heart starts beating in time with pulsing despair, I shut that shit down because *this* is the girl, *this* is the face, that my new friends feel connected to. I *am* worthy.

That thought brings me some strength, despite the bruises that are yellowing at the edges. Instead of dwelling on that, I focus on the good. The swelling has *finally* gone down considerably and only my lip and my eye are slightly raised now. Nothing too horrible.

I formulate a game plan for the day and make a mental checklist. I need to call the restaurant and explain that I'll need to be on leave until my fractures are healed. Hopefully, I'll still have a job by then. I also need to check in with my professor about an assignment that I'd turned in just before my attack. I need to start looking for a car; the cheaper, the better. And my landlord will want a call too.

With a list of things to accomplish today, I turn on the shower and undress myself. I take off the sling, that I'm wearing twenty-four seven at Owen's insistence, and pull my bad arm through the hole before whipping the shirt over my head. I unclasp the bra and let it fall away. The knee splint is a challenge.

Once that comes off, I test the water temperature and step in, letting the water cascade over me and ease the stiffness in my muscles. I let go of my worries for a few minutes and just *exist* and relax.

"Nora," Kyle calls with a knock. "Are you alright? Do you need help?"

Now, *this* is a dilemma. I do need his help but I'm not in a bath this time. He'd have to come to me while I'm in the shower and I don't want him to think I'm coming on to him. But I can't wash my hair properly with one hand.

I decide he's a big boy and can say 'no' if he wants to so I brace for the consequences and call out to him.

"Yes, please, just with my hair."

Kyle opens the door to the bathroom and hooks a towel next to the shower. The shower's big enough for five people so, unless I move to the door, there's no way he'd be able to help without coming in.

"Ummm ... Kyle," I start, unsure of myself. "I don't want to give you the wrong impression but I really do need help with my hair. If you'll be uncomfortable, I can manage."

Before I've even finished, he's started undressing down to his boxers, opened the door and stepped in like it's nothing.

"Give me your shampoo," he says and I hand it to him. He squeezes some into his hand and massages my scalp. "I know this is awkward for you but I'm not going to take advantage of the situation. I'm just here to help with whatever you need."

The pressure of his fingers feels so good that my eyes drift closed and a quiet moan slips from my lips. I instantly stiffen. How *shitty* of me!

"I'm so sorry, Kyle. I didn't mean to do that." I start to turn around, so he can see how truly sorry I am on my face, but he grabs me by the upper arms firmly and holds me in place, only touching me with his hands.

"Don't. I know you didn't, Nor." He continues massaging the shampoo into my hair as he talks. "And I want you to know that, even though I do still want you, I have no expectations for anything sexual or romantic right now. We're both adults and can keep our hands to appropriate areas. Let's get through this so we can get past the difficult part."

I hum in agreement as he finishes with my hair. Then, his hands travel down, further, further, stroking my arms and my neck, stroking my shoulders with a silky touch that glides over my skin. A shiver sets down my spine, from the base of my skull to the bottom of my tail bone. I brace my left hand on the wall in front of me and hold still while he finishes soaping me up.

His voice jolts me out of the fog that his touch created.

"Okay, you're good for a rinse and then I'll condition for you."

As much as I'm enjoying myself, I don't want to make this longer for us, so I rinse and hand him my conditioner. This time, he pays close attention to the ends, remembering from last time.

"You're very good at this, you know." My face flames. Was that inappropriate? I try again and blurt without thinking, "I mean, you're good with your hands. *Shit!* I meant to say, you give good head." I pause as that sinks in. "Oh, fuck, I'm going to stop talking now. Thank you very much, Kyle."

And thank you very much, stupid brain! What in the actual hell, Molano?

My face flames further as Kyle chuckles behind me and I'm about a second from bursting when Kyle's chin grazes my shoulder, his lip against my ear, and he whispers the most tantalizing words, "Oh, I know I give good head, Nora, but you haven't seen anything yet."

My bloods ignites. *What the hell was that? And how do I request a repeat?*

"Now rinse and get out so I can shower."

I yelp at the smack that lands on my left cheek and leap into action, rinsing as quickly as I can and hightailing it to dry off. When I step out, Kyle's boxers fly past me to land with a wet plop on the floor. Good goodness! What the shit is happening? And, once again, how do I request a repeat!

I scurry faster and hear him laugh out right.

By the time, I'm dried and wrapped in a towel and working on combing my hair, Kyle steps out and grabs his towel, wrapping it around his waist. My hands still mid-brush because *ho-ly* hell, he's packing! I think I might faint. And my imagination is vindicated to know it was *very* accurate.

Before I can continue with untangling the knots, he comes up behind me and takes the comb from my hand gently.

126

Without a word, he starts on my hair, reaching the parts I can't. I watch him in the mirror, awed by this amazing man that's done so much for me in such little time.

And I'm not sure if it's a topic I want to discuss right now.

"I like you, Nora," he shocks me by saying. "Even more so as I learn more about you. I'm not going to act on it but I can't promise that I won't flirt with you."

I appreciate the honesty so I return the favor, starting what's sure to be an uncomfortable conversation. "Kyle, you're not the only one who's expressed an interest in me." At my confession, his jaw ticks and he doesn't look happy with that development but it looks like I only confirmed what he already suspected. I think back. That must mean he saw when Silas kissed me! I shake my head internally before carrying on. "But I can't focus on that right now. I need to try to get my head right. Just give me some time and space without pressure, please."

This is exactly what I was afraid of. They're all alpha males. There's no way I could casually date one of them, never mind more than one simultaneously, which was Owen's proposal, and expect them all to be okay with it. All it will do is jeopardize our budding friendships.

But so far, no one stands out from the others. Maybe, if I give it time, I can get to know them better and everything will be clearer. For now, though, I'm a slave to the passage of time because I'm not ready to go down that path yet.

He finishes with my hair and kisses the back of my head. "Just know I'm here no matter what happens, Nora honey."

With that, he heads into his bedroom, closing the door as he goes. I close my eyes and take a careful breath. I have to be careful or this is going to get messy.

On the sink, Kyle left some clothes for me earlier.

God, he's so sweet. If I bite into him, I'll get a tooth ache. That makes me feel worse than day-old shit for the current situation. Why can't I just choose him and be done with it? I've known him the longest and I know him the most. But my heart's hesitant to take the leap and I know I'll regret it if I choose.

I aggressively brush my teeth while beating myself up in my head. I rinse my mouth and spit the water out, wiping my mouth on the towel with such pressure that my split lip almost reopens. Frustrated, I slam the towel down on the counter, my hand going with it, getting angrier at myself.

Stop it! There's only one way to deal with this situation and that's to treat them all like friends.

Decision made, for the time being, I focus on getting dressed and grab my underwear. I have to do a weird wiggle to get them over my hips one-handed before moving onto my bra but I can't fasten it behind my back.

Damn it! Mother-dicks!

I resign myself to my fate and call out, "Kyle! Can you help me, please?"

It only takes him a second before he's there, dressed in worn jeans and a black t-shirt, his feet bare.

I'm holding the bra to my chest for modesty. "Can you help fasten my bra, please? I can't reach."

I feel like shit asking but it would be far worse to go braless. It would be uncomfortable for both of us or *all* of us, if the rest of the guys show up today. *Short-term discomfort, long-term benefit*, I remind myself.

He twirls his finger for me to turn around and fastens the hooks when my back is to him. He grabs my shirt, another loose one, and helps me get into it. It's easier than yesterday, maybe because of the practice.

"Thank you, Kyle. I know this isn't easy but I really do appreciate it."

His grunt of acknowledgement sounds from near the threshold of the bathroom door and I realize he's already on his way out, his back to me. He leaves the door halfway open and I sigh in the direction of the room.

Nothing to be done about it now.

I step into the faded, bootcut jeans that he left but my mind's wandering and I bang my knee on the sink pedestal. The pain is sharp and immediate, and so is my scream.

I almost go down but just manage to catch myself with my left hand on the bathroom counter.

Kyle rushes back in to help but the pain and the stress from the residual nightmare and this whole situation—it all collides and makes my heart race and suddenly, I'm in a ball on the floor, as small as I can be. My knee's throbbing and how the fuck did the man in the alley get in my apartment? He's standing over me, kicking me in the stomach and chest.

He grabs my hair and drags me up, my legs scraping against the ground. I whimper as he pins my arms down to my sides but it's not him anymore. It's an older monster, a worse one.

His hand slides down into my pants and cups me.

"This is mine!" he spits, rubbing my pussy, "You don't keep it from me. You hear me, you bitch?! And you don't fucking share it with another man!" He yanks my head to the side, his other hand closing around my throat and his hot, wet, revolting kiss is on my neck.

I'm whimpering like the bitch he calls me, trying to get out of his hold but he was always stronger than me and time and the gym hasn't changed that. My mind interjects, *how did he come back, how did he find me, how did he fucking find me*, but then his hand tightens on my pussy and I'm screaming, pleading, "Please, don't! I won't try to run again. I'll stay and we can be happy! I swear, I'll stay! Please just let me go so I can catch my breath?!"

I'm so desperate for him to stop, I'd promise to marry him just to get him to let me go.

His grip loosens and I don't hesitate. I jerk from his grasp and take a few steps away, breathing heavy, and lunge for the butcher's block on the counter in our shared kitchenette. I grab the biggest fucking one I can get my hands on and turn and strike out, catching him in the chest and then I run but I'm not going anywhere! It's like I'm on a fucking treadmill and safety is getting further and further away.

I'm still screaming. I'm still in a ball on the floor.

Someone's holding me, rocking me, talking to me.

Talking to me?

No, talking into the phone.

A male voice, steeped in panic.

"I don't know but this wasn't just from her attack! I think someone else hurt her." Pause. "No, I don't mean that night. No, this seemed different. *More*! I don't fucking know! Just get the fuck over here and help!" Something clatters to the ground, a phone? And then, he's talking to me, "Ssshhhhh ... it's okay, Nora. You're safe. It's alright, it's okay. I've got you."

I've heard those words before, in a different voice, and they penetrate. I grab onto the lifeline that's dangling in front of me and pull.

The floor beneath me is cold. My hair's still wet. "No one's here," he says.

No one's here.

"*No* one is here," he soothes again, with more emphasis. "I'm Kyle and you're at my house, remember? What's today, honey?"

Kyle.

It's alright. It's okay. I've got you.

His voice pulls me back to reality.

"K-Kyle. You're Kyle and I'm safe," I breathe out, more for myself, stumbling over the words but settling into them because *of course,* I'm safe. Kyle is here. He's got me. "Today is Monday. I'm at your house." The words keep coming and I keep talking but don't hear what I'm saying, "I'm not with him anymore, I escaped, I got out. He can't hurt me anymore. I got away. He's in jail. I'm safe. He doesn't have me anymore. He doesn't have me. You've got me. He doesn't have me. You've got me."

I don't notice Kyle stiffening against me as I repeat my mantra.

"That's right, honey, you're here. He can't hurt you. *It's okay. I've got you.* I've got you, Nor. It's okay. You're safe with me."

He keeps rocking me, telling me I'm safe and he won't let anyone get to me.

I don't know how long we sit there on the bathroom floor. I don't know if or when I stop crying.

But I know he's got me and I want to believe I'm safe.

7 My Secret

I'm still shaking when a loud bang comes from somewhere in the house.

Kyle shifts when his phone rings.

"We're in my bathroom," he clips out. "I don't give a fuck how you do it. I can't leave her here like this. Bust it down if you fucking have to!" He yells, making me shrink away from him, and whimper. He freezes and tries again, much softer, with less anger, "Get in here now. She's barely hanging on and I'm losing her again." The phone clangs to the floor again and he's holding me and rocking me and a distant, vacant, hysterical part of me wonders if the phone will dent.

The bathroom doorway fills with two silhouettes that my mind takes a minute to register as Flynn and Owen. Owen kneels down and shuffles on his knees over to us, while Flynn, my rescuer, stays back.

"Watch your voice," Kyle warns them. "Anytime I start to raise mine or get angry, she goes back to whatever the fuck flashback she was in. And it wasn't anything like last time, Owen. Someone else fucked with her, a lot ... and I don't think it was just beatings."

I barely hear what's being said. Only tones of voices and facial expressions register and, right now, Owen's looking at me like he wants to beat the shit out of someone. I cower into Kyle more, turning my face into him, afraid to incite Owen's anger.

"Owen, I get you want to hurt whoever did this to her but now is not the time for that. Change your facial expression, man." Kyle warns, picking up on the trigger. When I dare a peek at Owen again, his face is neutral.

An angelic voice, singing a version of Dermot Kennedy's *Glory*, reaches me and that, with Kyle's embrace and Owen's presence, allows me to come further out of an all too familiar nightmare. I close my eyes and just breathe in time with the tempo Flynn's setting and my body starts to relax without any prompting from me.

"Keep singing, Flynn, she's relaxing. I'm going to call Silas and Heath. They'll want to be here for her." Owen backs away, still shuffling on his knees, and only stands once he's at the door. He immediately pulls his phone out and disappears into the bedroom.

Flynn crouches down and crawls to me, still singing. When he's done with *Glory,* he starts singing *Sleep Baby Sleep* by Broods. The slow, mellow songs make the lifeline thicken and solidify and I pull myself out further.

I lift my head and reach out to him. He sits back and opens his arms in an invitation for me to sit on his lap. I crawl awkwardly on my good knee and drag my other leg, moving from Kyle's lap to Flynn's. My head ends up on his shoulder, my back to his chest, his legs on either side of my extended ones. He wraps me up in him and holds me as tight as he dares. Kyle sits with his back to the wall and his head resting on it, watching us, watching *me*, like a hawk, with his knees up and his forearms resting on them.

"They'll be here in ten minutes," Owen says, when he returns, "You can tell us what happened when they're here. That'll also give her some more time to calm down and maybe she can help clear a few things up."

The song ends and Flynn shifts to humming a tune that sounds similar to my favorite song, Louis Mattrs's *Fear in Me*. It's a beautiful song that breaks my heart and before I know it, I'm singing. All the guys sit on the bathroom floor, still wet, still cold, and just listen.

It's getting easier to breathe, even as the tears run, so I end *Fear in Me* and move on to *Trying Not to Love You* by Nickelback. I'm in the middle of *Ending* by Isak Danielson when

Silas and Heath show up. They don't interrupt. They just sit on either side of the bathroom door, their backs toward us and listen.

As the final lines of *Ending* leave me, my eyes are closed and my cheeks are wetter than ever, not just from the breakdown but also from the songs. They all touch me so deeply.

I open my eyes, though I don't want to. I just want to sit here with the guys but I know what I said. I know what they heard. I know they'll want details. And I *should* give them the truth.

But I don't know how.

I open my eyes to Owen and am filled with relief at his presence. He knows how to get difficult things out of people. He's here. They're all here. Is it too much to hope it'll be okay?

"Heath, get Nora, please, and bring her into the living room when she's ready," Owen takes charge and still watches me. He turns to the other men. "The rest of us, let's go. Give her a moment." They all move out, careful not to trigger me again.

It's just me and Heath when he slides in the bathroom and sits next to me on the cold, tile floor, waiting. He doesn't say anything, just sits with me, until I look into his handsome face.

I confess, "I don't know how to do this."

He smiles a sad smile and turns toward me, crossing his legs.

"Well, that's what you've got us for, sweetheart. Ready to start healing?" he asks.

The words make the tears prick behind my eyes but I nod and he picks me up, standing in a wickedly smooth motion. He carries me down the hall into the living room.

Everyone's seated when we enter. Kyle's on the far side of the U-shaped couch, with Owen beside him and Silas, next. Flynn is on the other end to Kyle. Heath puts me next to Silas, before sitting on my other side, sandwiching me between them. My thighs are touching both guys.

Silas puts his arm around me, pulling me into his side so I'm pressed up against him with zero space between us. My other thigh's pressed against Heath's and his hand's in mine. I wonder if I reached for him or if he reached for me.

I've never felt safer than I do in this moment. I suspect that's why they've positioned themselves like they have.

Owen takes the lead, completely focused on me, after we're all settled.

"Nora, are you comfortable with Kyle telling us what he saw and heard in the bathroom? Then, if you're okay with that, you can fill in any blanks when he's done?"

I swallow audibly.

Once they know, they'll leave because they'll know I'm nothing but trash. Nothing but tainted goods. *Well, this is where the fairytale ends.* Best to rip the band aid off quickly and get it over with.

At least it's happening now, before I *really* get attached to them.

"Yes, I'll answer any questions you guys have when he's done, if you're still here."

Owen gives Heath a knowing look but doesn't say anything. He looks to Kyle and prompts him impatiently. "When you're ready, Kyle."

"I was in my room, getting dressed, when I saw Nora go down and try to catch herself. I wasn't quick enough to get to her in time and I panicked and forgot. I didn't realize that I fucked up and was standing over her." Kyle stops to take a breath and addresses me for the first time since I came down from my panic. "I'm so fucking sorry, Nora honey. I didn't think. I just reacted."

"I'm not mad at you, Kyle. I get it. I'd have done the same thing." It really wasn't his fault but I know he saw me in the throes of the attack and I don't think my attempt to ease him helped.

"She curled into a ball and started saying things like 'please don't hurt me again' and 'I'll do what you want, if you just let me go.'" He pauses and I chance a glance at the others.

Blank expressions all around.

Is this it? Is that all it took? But Silas is still holding me close, touching me as much as he can without pulling me into his lap.

"At first, I thought it was from the alley attack," Kyle continues. "But then I noticed that she wasn't just afraid like last time. She seemed defeated, like she knew she couldn't stop someone from hurting her. Then she said, 'not again, please, not again, I can't do it.' That's when I knew she was in a different flashback and I called you, Owen. I just waited and sat there with her until she started to come back."

He takes a deep breath and turns to me with an apology in his eyes. "I'm sorry, Nora, but I can't keep what you said from them. They're a part of this. They need to know if we're all going to help you." I can see the pain in his eyes and, instead of feeling comforted, I just feel sad that he has to carry it with me. He turns back to the guys. "She started saying 'I'm at your house. I'm not with him anymore, I escaped, I got out. He can't hurt me anymore. I got away. He's in jail.'"

He turns back to me, while I'm still in shock. I don't remember saying any of that.

This time, it's Flynn who talks. "The guy from the alley hasn't been caught yet, Nora, and you didn't escape. He was a coward and ran off. Who else hurt you?"

The heavy weight of their stares shifts to me. Silas isn't looking at me but I know he's waiting for an explanation, just like the others.

My hands are both touching Silas and Heath so I clench my toes and brace for the fallout.

"Before I moved here to Arizona two years ago, I lived with my roommate. We were friends in high school and moved into an apartment together. For the first six months, things were good. I was living life and having fun. Then, when I started dating, my roommate became possessive, even though we'd never been together and I never expressed an interest in him.

"After the first few dates with a guy I'd just started seeing, my roommate waited for me to get back late one night and he attacked me in our living room. He beat me and kept saying that I was his and how could I do that to us? I didn't know he was obsessed with me. He hid it very well. I did notice that he didn't like me talking to any guys but I thought it was because he was looking out for me." I laugh without humor at the memory of how stupid I've felt for the last two years. Every time I remembered the times he'd make a comment about some random guy that came up to talk to me, I got pissed at myself for not noticing the warning signs.

"He held me in our apartment for three days until I could escape. He beat me several times and—" My breath hitches and I have to stop.

"It's okay, Nora," Silas rumbles, stroking my back. "Take your time. We aren't going anywhere."

I blow out my breath and try again.

"He raped me, more than once. I was a virgin before that." Several of the guys curse.

Flynn gets up and bolts into the kitchen. One down, four to go. I knew they'd leave once they realized I was tainted.

"How did you get free, Nora?" Owen asks me gently.

I pull my attention from watching the direction that Flynn disappeared to. I don't know why Owen's asking for more details, when he's just going to leave like Flynn but what do I know?

They can leave if they'd like but maybe it's good for me to tell my story so I answer, "It was on the third day, after we'd just finished having lunch. I was cleaning the kitchen and he was going to r-rape me again. He came up behind me while I was putting things away and put his hands on me." I decide to leave out the part where he raped me one last time before I escaped. "By then, I'd had enough. I just … snapped. I fought back and when he was distracted, I grabbed a knife from the butcher block we had on the counter. I swung out behind me and got him in the chest. It was just a superficial slash but it shocked him enough to give me a chance to run. So I did and I ran into another tenant in our building who was going to the grocery store. She ended up taking me straight to the police station. I pressed charges and they went to the apartment and arrested him. He didn't even try to run. He's in prison for now."

I wait a breath for them to be disgusted and leave but they all just sit there in tense silence.

Finally, Heath speaks up.

"Nora, sweetheart, did you get help for the trauma?"

Why is he asking? They don't have to pretend to care. I look into his eyes and wonder what put the sadness there.

"Not enough, apparently, I thought I'd dealt with everything but I guess I didn't."

"That's not necessarily true," Owen says. "This new attack could've triggered things you've already dealt with and reignited them. It's been known to happen."

Just leave. Just leave. Why won't you go?

"This is fucked up. How do we help her, Owen?" Silas.

Just leave. I'm a fucking mess. Why won't you go?

"We have to be aware of our actions around her and when she has an attack, be there for her until she can come out of it." Owen starts listing things to do to help me, like they'll be around for that. "Once we identify her triggers, we can help her avoid them. Get her into counseling, if she wants that."

Flynn comes back into the room.

"She shouldn't be alone." *Leave. Why did you come back?* "Not just because of her injuries but if she has another attack, she needs to know she'll be safe during and after." *Why won't you go?* "She's welcome to stay with me anytime she wants to."

They nod in unison and I snap.

"Stop! Just stop it! Stop pretending you care! Don't act like you'll be here to help me and then just leave. Just fucking go already!" I yell desperately, breathing as heavy as I dare by the end, but my ribs still burn with the movement. They're all looking at me like *I'm* the crazy one. Well, if I'm so fucking crazy, why are they still here!

I take some calming breaths and try again, this time, calmer. "Don't look at me like that. I know my shit is a lot to deal with and nobody wants to take it on. It's okay. It's fine. I understand. Just don't drag it out." The calm seeps into pleading but they're still sitting motionless, just exchanging glances in that fucking annoying way of theirs.

Why are they still here!

"Right," he says, smacking his hands on his knees. That's the universal sign, isn't it? That's the sign that he's getting up to go. But instead of standing, he falls to the floor on his knees.

What? I think, confused.

He's still tall enough, even kneeling, to cradle my face in his hands. "Let's get a few things straight right now. We"—he removes one hand to gesture around the room—"aren't going anywhere. You're stuck with us. It's okay if you don't believe that yet; we'll convince you. We'll *prove* it."

He waits a beat for me to absorb that before continuing, "My sister was raped when she was younger." My breath catches. *Sara?* "Nora, we know all about the fucked-up shit that goes through your head after a traumatic event like that. We can deal. We *have* dealt. And in case you haven't noticed, we've already adopted you into our family so like it or not, you're stuck with us unless you tell us to go. And I'm saying *you* tell us to go, *not* your trauma. That fucked-up shit in your head that tells you to push us away for our own good. That's your trauma talking, not you, and we don't abide by that shit. So," he says, his tone lighter now, "Now that we've cleared that up, we aren't leaving you. In fact, in a week's time, you're probably going to be sick of us. Shall we move on to who you're staying with this week and when?" Without waiting for my answer, Heath turns his attention to the others and they all start going over schedules.

I just sit there, with Silas's arm wrapped around me, warm and safe, in shocked silence. They work everything out without my input.

Kyle has to finish up a rifle he's working on and doesn't know how long he'll be or when he'll be home. Owen and Flynn have prior commitments and Heath's got two self-defense classes to teach in the day. So, I'm going home with Silas tonight, after he takes me for breakfast and to my apartment for anything I need.

Once they've finalized the details, Kyle disappears into the hallway and returns with my laptop bag and a change of clothes. He helps me put my arm sling, as well as the leg splint, and though I'm not much help, he gets it done quickly and efficiently.

When he's done, he gives me a kiss on my forehead where his lips linger.

"I'm in this, Nora honey. You've got my number and Flynn is going to program everyone else's into your phone so you'll be able to reach any of us, anytime you need."

He steps back and Owen quickly takes his place. He opens his arms and I can't stop him from wrapping me up in his warmth. I'm starting to forget why I wanted to.

"It's going to be tough but we'll be with you every step of the way, gorgeous."

He eases me back and then, Flynn is curled around me like a cat. He holds me the longest and I forget that he walked out, I forget to wonder why, because nothing else matters and Heath was right. That *was* my trauma talking.

"My little spitfire. We've got you in this."

Owen and Flynn leave the house and after I watch them go, I turn to Heath. As the biggest, he should be the roughest but it's the exact opposite. He's the gentlest and he holds me with such care, that it almost makes me cry again.

"I'm so sorry this happened, sweetheart. I'm sorry you've been alone for so long," he whispers. "But you don't have to be alone anymore and you won't be. We're all here for you. My sister will be there for you too, if you need to talk to someone with shared experience. I made sure her number got programmed into your phone, with the rest of ours. She knows you might call but I haven't said about what. Whether or not you tell her, or how much, is up to you. I'll text you soon so we can set up a training schedule for your self-defense classes." He turns to Silas and they share a look but it doesn't set me on edge anymore. With a final hug, Heath leaves out the front door.

Silas stands and carries my stuff in one hand and supports me to his big-ass truck with the other. He lifts me into the front passenger seat before rounding the truck and getting into the driver's side.

Kyle, who followed us out, hands me my phone and buckles me in and, with a kiss on my cheek, he's gone too.

When we're alone, Silas starts the truck and says, "Where to, doll?"

"Ummm ... surprise me?" I say. He glances at me and smiles before pulling out onto Kyle's street and heading out of the subdivision.

After ten minutes, Silas pulls into a parking lot with a bunch of stores and some restaurants in a strip off the road. He helps me across the street to a restaurant I've never been to. It's busy inside but we're seated quickly. The menu is extensive and everything sounds delicious.

A friendly, extremely pretty waitress comes over. "Hi! I'm Maggie, what can I get you?" she asks in a perky, cheerleader pep kind of way.

Silas doesn't even glance at her, he's so engrossed in the menu, and only lifts his head to order.

I decide on the cheat day wrap and Silas orders an open-faced sandwich. We both get a coffee and water for drinks. She heads off with our order and I peer up at Silas.

Placing my hands on my lap, I wring my fingers. I want to make sure he isn't freaking out about my past. "Are you okay?" That was a big load for him to take on.

He stares in my eyes for a moment, making my belly do a hard flip.

"*You're* asking *me* if I'm okay? Doll, with everything you're going through right now, *I* should be asking you that, not the other way around." He runs his thumb along my knuckles. "Doll..." Silas sighs. "I'm fucking furious that you've had to endure all that, let alone from someone who didn't deserve your trust. I will do whatever it takes to show you that you don't have to fear me. Yeah, I'll get mad and, at times, I'll show it but

142

I'll never use my anger against you to hurt you, Nora. I want to know how to help you. What do you need from me?"

Our waitress comes back and sets our drinks down.

"Need any creamer or condiments? Your food should be out in a jiffy."

She directed the question at Silas but he lets me answer, keeping his attention on me. It makes me feel like I am the only woman in the world so I smile at Maggie, more confident now.

"No, we're good, thank you."

She walks away, looking a bit disappointed, but what could I do?

"Just more of what you're already doing," I reply to his earlier question. "I need patience and understanding. Other than that, I think it'll just take time."

He gives me a soft look that hits me right in my heart but changes the subject at the slightest hint of my unease.

"What do you need to stay at my house for at least a week? I don't want you to have to worry about carting shit around with you, every time you come to stay with me."

Well, this topic isn't any less uncomfortable for me. I don't want them to buy me anything. I don't want to owe them anything and I definitely don't want to mooch off of them.

Silas reaches for my leg under the table with his free hand and props my foot on his knee before pressing harder on the subject.

"Nora, don't make me ask again. If I didn't want you with me, I wouldn't have offered. And if I didn't want you comfortable, I wouldn't have asked. I want you focused on healing, not on your missing fucking shampoo or your lost hair tie. Now, tell me your list of where we need to go so we can get it done after breakfast." I huff at his bossiness, then remember his comment about *tanning* my *hide* and realize bossiness likely comes naturally to him.

Before I can tell him my 'list,' Maggie appears with our food, setting it down in front of us.

"Need anything else?" she asks.

Again, she doesn't even spare me a glance. I'm not jealous but I am pissed at the shitty service. Yes, he's hot, but he's not her only customer.

"Mustard," I blurt out to wave away the awkwardness of her staring at Silas with no response from him. Also, I love the stuff. I eat it like most people eat ketchup, on *everything*.

"Mustard coming right up," she says, without looking my way and sways her hips as she's walking off.

I resist the urge to roll my eyes. Could she lay it on any thicker?

Putting Maggie out of my mind, I get back to the requested list. "Just the usual stuff, a few essentials and some bigger shirts for my arm." I wave at him with my right hand with a silly smile. "Everything we can get from Target."

"We'll go to Nordstrom," Silas says, tucking into his food like it's no big deal.

Meanwhile, I'm over here with my mouth falling open and my jaw on the tabletop.

"No!" I yell before bringing it down a notch. "I don't need anything that extravagant, Silas."

He doesn't say anything, just stares at me with those icy eyes as he chews. I know he's trying to unnerve me into relenting again but I arch a brow right back and dig into my food. Clearly, we're at a standoff.

Maggie brings the mustard. She slides it across the table and into my water glass, knocking it all over the table and me in the process. I jump at the shock of cold water on my skin, my knee forgotten for a second, and try to get out of the way. Silas jumps as well and my knee hits on the underside of the table. "Fuck! Ow! Fuck, fuck, fuckity, fuck, fuck. Damn, mother-*dicks!*"

I'm cursing like a sailor by the time Silas rounds the table and pulls me out. He swoops me into his arms and glares at Maggie, who, *surprise, surprise,* loses the smug look just as he turns to her. Suddenly, she's all repentant.

"Oh my gosh! I'm so sorry! Let me get you a napkin," she says, rummaging for the napkins, an expression of fake horror on her face.

"Don't fucking bother," Silas growls. "Get me the check and get me your manager. I'm taking her to the bathroom to dry off and when we get back, you'd better be here with both."

He sneers at her one last time and strides off to the *men's* room!

"Silas, I'm okay. It's just a little water. It'll dry on its own." He doesn't miss a step. "Silas, I can't go into the *men's* room!"

"Quiet!" his voice is clipped. "I want to look at your knee more than anything."

He gets the handle with his elbow and shoves the door open with his back, swinging me onto the counter. He leaves me there to check the stalls. Once he's satisfied we're alone, he locks the door and comes back to me. "Brace yourself up on your hands so I can get your pants down."

I can't help it. It's so ridiculous, I burst out laughing. "Well, at least you bought me breakfast first!" I manage to get out between my laughter.

His lips twitch with a repressed smile and he shakes his head, amused, so at least he's lost some of the anger.

Setting my palms on the counter, I lift myself up until my shoulder protests. I don't get far before I drop back down with a wince. "Fuck, my shoulder doesn't really like that."

An arm bands around my waist, and then I'm up and my pants are down. Just like that. He didn't even exert himself!

He kneels down and holds my right knee in both hands, examining it closely.

"I don't think you did more damage but just to be sure, I'll call Owen and see if he wants to look at it when we leave."

I'm still stuck on him taking my pants down so effortlessly as he lowers my leg.

"I don't think anyone's ever taken my pants off that quickly before. You sure do move fast."

He chuckles. "Nowhere near fast enough for me, doll." And, he winks! *My heart.* Hell, my stomach gets butterflies.

Big, bad, tough Silas, fucking winks at me!

He pulls my pants back up to my ass cheeks and sets me on my feet. I catch him glance at the mirror behind me as I bend to pull them up the rest of the way. "Don't think I didn't see you looking, slick."

He gives me a devilish grin and out pop two panty-dropping dimples. "I don't remember saying I wouldn't." I roll my eyes. "Come on, I've got a waitress to chew out and we've got shit to do. Let's go before I decide to kiss the shit out of you."

I shut right up at that and he swings me back up and into his arms.

When we get to the table, Maggie's there, wringing her hands and nervously looking at Silas. Seems she's lost the infatuation in the face of his anger. Next to her stands a man with a huge belly that hangs over his belt. When he catches us coming, his anger turns to worry and he stands a bit straighter.

"I'm so sorry for the accident, sir."

That's all he gets out before Silas fulfills his promise from the bathroom. "If that was an accident, I'm fucking Mother Teresa. She did that on purpose because she was jealous that I wasn't giving her my time or attention, which, for the record, I do not owe her. I suggest you have a talk with your staff about professional behavior toward customers." Silas sets me down and pulls out his wallet and tosses two twenties on the table.

I'm amazed he knew exactly what the waitress was up to. Even when he looked like he wasn't paying attention, he could see everything.

"My girl here has a broken kneecap and, as I'm sure you can tell because you've got eyes in your head and so does Maggie, she's had a rough week. Your waitress was petty and childish." He pauses and pointedly looks at Maggie. "Now, apologize so we can be on our way."

Maggie immediately complies. "I'm so sorry. He's right I was jealous and shouldn't have done that."

He picks me up without acknowledging her apology and heads out the door without a backward glance.

"I-You-Wait-*What* just happened?" I stutter, trying to find the right thing to say.

"No one treats you badly anymore, doll. If they do, they answer to me," Silas growls. He balances me on one knee, digs his keys out of his front pocket and disengages the locks. I reach out and open the door for him to set me on my seat. With one hand on the door and the other on my seat, he looks me right in the eye and says, "The days of you taking people's shit are over, doll. None of us will let that shit fly and you shouldn't either." The door slams shut at my shocked face as he stalks around to climb into the driver's side.

I swivel to face him once he's seated. "Who said I take shit?"

"Doll." He gives me a pointed look. "You don't have any fight in you right now and anyone who sees you, sees that. Maybe you're not usually like that but with what that asshole did to you, I'm willing to bet he beat the fight right out of you." His jaw muscle is ticking away as he waits for me to say something but I'm too shocked to speak. He just called me out on it. I didn't even realize I'd lost my spark. "That shit isn't going to happen anymore. The. Fucking. End. Find your fight, Nora, because until you do, we're fighting for you."

He starts the truck and drives to Nordstrom. I wonder if this is one of the things I should fight about? I'm not sure if I like this development or not but I think I'll go with it and see how it plays out. It shouldn't be that bad, right?

Silas parks as close as anyone can to the entrance without parking in the handicapped spot and I'm amazed at his luck. How the hell did he get such a good spot? The couple of times I've come here, I've had to walk a mile from my car.

We go straight to the personal care section and I decide to not be difficult about it. I grab everything I need. It's not like he'll let me leave unless I do. Likelihood is, he'll throw one of everything into the shopping cart. I'm surprised he doesn't rush me. He just helps me reach for anything that's too high or too low for me and remains patient when I have him pick something up and put it back ten times.

Then, he moves us onto the clothes section and I forewarn him, already anticipating a fight.

"Silas, I have my own clothes. I just need a couple of loose shirts." He gives me a look that says I was defeated before I even tried and I sigh and give into my fate. When I try to push back, he threatens to take over the decision making and that works to quiet me down. Lord knows he won't even check the price tag.

At the end, I've got new jeans, that I definitely can't wear right now, shirts that are loose enough for my arm, socks and, much to my embarrassment, underwear and bras.

By the end, I'm exhausted and I know I'm not hiding it well. My protests are getting less and less frequent and I'm favoring my good leg.

"I'll go find someone to bring this shit to the register. Be right back." He backs me up against an empty wall, points at me and orders, "Don't move."

Very soon, he returns with an employee, Janice, and I wonder what got her—the glare or the good looks. We smile at each other and when she rolls her eyes and points at him with a 'this guy' expression, I know it was the glare and my smile widens.

He picks me up and leads the way to the register with Janice wheeling the cart behind us. At the checkout, he sets me on my feet gently and fishes his card out of his wallet. His *black* card. *Woah*. But I don't care how rich he is, I still balk at the total and I still feel guilty.

"Nora, don't even think about it. If it helps, just remember, I didn't get this for you. I got it for me so I can rest easy knowing you're only focusing on healing." He kisses my head and asks for the bags to be brought to the car.

I'm in his arms again and it hits me that I feel right at home here. Being surrounded by him, it feels nice and secure. It only took three days for me to start enjoying being carried around everywhere. I rest my head on his shoulder, breathing the scent of engine grease and something spicy, and allow myself to bask in the feeling of being cared for.

No one's cared for me like this since mom died, just after I turned eighteen.

"You tired, doll?" Silas pulls me out of my thoughts.

"Yeah," I say, because I am, but that's not why I'm leaning on him. "Shopping always takes a lot out of me. Add my injuries to the equation and I'm about as ready for a nap as a baby."

"I'll get you home and you can lay down." He unlocks the truck and helps me in. I buckle myself in and he drives up to the entrance to retrieve the items he bought. It's all loaded up in minutes and he hops back in and drives to his house.

I'm excited to see where he lives but I don't make it for the full drive. Hell, I'm asleep before we're even out of the parking lot.

8 Bright Silas

I wake from my nap slowly, in a really soft, warm bed, cuddled up against a very firm, warm body. My hands are on a well-defined, naked chest, my face against a corded neck and my head resting against a firm jaw.

If I could wake up like this every day, I'd be in heaven.

I flex my fingers against some delicious chest hair when a rumble sounds in my ear.

"You awake, doll?" The vibrations of his words are under my hand and against my cheek and my body's shuddering with desire.

I smile at the gravel in Silas's voice and prop myself up with my left elbow, stroking my thumb along his stubbled jaw.

"Yeah. Did you carry me in?" I'm trailing the scruff on his face with my fingertips when my gaze meets his frosty, ice-blue eyes and I get lost in them.

He returns my look with a heating one of his own.

"Yeah, I carried you in, doll. Now unless you want to get to know me on a seriously biblical level, we need to get up."

He does a slow sit-up, taking me with him, turning me as we go, so that I'm sitting next to him, instead of straddling his leg like I was. Every inch of his body meets mine and, *let's just say*, he's massive *everywhere*. In the back of my mind, as my hand cradles his shoulder, I wonder how many hours he spends in the gym maintaining his physique.

But once I come out from my admiration and feel Silas's skin again mine, I realize that I'm not entirely dressed, though I was when I went to sleep. I quickly pat myself and, whew, I *still* have *undergarments*. Otherwise, I'm in an oversized, black t-shirt and no pants. Unlike the one from earlier, this one dwarfs me and has that spicy scent that eludes and intoxicates me, shooting straight to my core.

"Uhhh ... Silas?" My concern must be all over my face because I don't have to word it for an answer.

"I tried to let you sleep in your clothes but you kept tossing and turning, getting the pants tangled up. I didn't want you to hurt your knee so I took them off. When I came back from the bathroom, you already had your shirt off. I tried to let you sleep alone but you wouldn't settle unless I was right next to you. You kept tossing and turning and couldn't rest. Hence why you're wearing my shirt because I'm a fucking hot-blooded man, not a saint, and I was trying to behave. Then we fell asleep together. You like to cuddle, by the way, and I don't mean normal cuddling. I mean clinging-like-a-baby-monkey cuddling." By the end, he has a shit-eating grin on his face and he looks mighty proud of himself. I find myself grinning back, even though it hurts my split lip, and when he sees I'm amused, not offended, he gets up.

Sweet firm baby ass cheeks! The man has on a pair of black boxers that leave nothing to the imagination. And since Kyle's, *um*, package exactly matched my imagination, I know I can trust it.

Oblivious to my ogling, he goes into what must be the bathroom. I'm too busy staring at his backside to confirm. And not just his ass, but his back and shoulders too. Holy hell, they're ripped. The dimples in his lower back wink at me and if this was a century ago, I would've swooned and fainted and needed smelling salts. Just how many dimples does one person need? For Pete's sake, he's already got a pair on his face!

The door closes and I shake myself out of a rapidly-forming fantasy that involves things I can't do, due to my injuries.

Instead of lamenting over a reality that can't exist, I focus on the room's décor. Surprisingly, everything is bright and uplifting, which is *not* what I was expecting. Beneath me are blindingly white sheets that feel like Egyptian cotton that I want to float on. The comforter is a light denim color and extra fluffy. Oversized, overstuffed pillows line the top of the bed but there's no headboard or footboard. There's no entertainment system and only two nightstands on either side of the bed. The waist-high dresser holds the only picture in the room.

The walls are a soft, sea blue that go nicely with the bedding and the rest of the furniture is a light, cream gray. On the far wall from me is a painting of a beach, with the ocean looking calm and inviting. The floor is a slate-colored tile in a chevron pattern. It's all very picturesque and looks like it's designed for relaxation.

The toilet flushes and, after the faucet turns on and off in quick succession, the door opens and my jaw hits the damn floor.

Earlier, I only got a back view and the front does not disappoint. I can't pick a favorite. He has that yummy V-line and washboard abs with pecs that Zeus himself couldn't rival. I'm too busy ogling all the man candy to notice that I've been busted. He comes right up to the bed and puts a fist on either side of my hips, lowering his eyes so they're level with mine. He gets so close to my face that I have to resist the urge to chase his lips for a kiss.

"Nora," he warns, with a hint of bossiness and a lot of male satisfaction. "As much as I appreciate the appreciation, stop looking at me like that before you get more than you bargained for."

I blink and close my mouth and mentally shake myself out like I didn't almost drool all over his lovely, blue sheets. I hold my head up higher, ignoring when my face burns, because for once, I'm not lying when I say I didn't mean to brush my lips against his! A light comes into his eyes that I don't acknowledge and breeze right past, pretending that my voice isn't strained, *when it really fucking is*. "Can I use your bathroom?"

"Nora, when you're here, treat my home like yours. You don't have to ask to use anything. You're a part of our family now and we don't keep things from family, be it material things or emotional issues. We share everything, with no exceptions. I have nothing to hide so feel free to explore. Got me?"

I feel a warmth in a place in my chest that's been cold for years but I ignore it and try to push the surge of emotions into my black box of things to avoid. I'll come back to it later.

I nod my understanding, feeling a little more at home and a lot better.

Silas backs off and gives me some space. "Do you need help with the bathroom?"

Unlike when Kyle asked this morning, I know I'll need help and I'm trying to get better at admitting it. *Progress!*

"Yes, please. Getting there and then, with my hair." I gesture to the tangled mess on my head. It's been down since my time in the hospital because I can't tie it back by myself but I want to at least try. It's much more convenient to have it out of the way.

Silas gathers me in his arms and picks me up like I weigh nothing, easily striding into the bathroom. It's not huge but it's decent-sized and has a nautical theme. Vibrant blue tiles wrap all around the wall and ceiling and colored tiles in different hues and a hodge-podge pattern cover the floor.

We pass his-and-her sinks with white countertops and he sets me down in front of the toilet, that has its own little section, cut off from the rest of the bathroom. Already anticipating my needs, he helps me take off my sling and knee brace so I can get my panties down easier.

"Just shout when you're ready for help with your hair." He backs out into the main bathroom and closes the door.

With a soft sigh, I awkwardly lower myself down, relieve myself, flush and try to get up but fail. There's nothing to grab for support.

I almost feel like groaning in frustration but yell for him instead, "Okay, Silas, I'm ready!"

He comes in not even a beat later, still in just his boxer briefs. not even a beat later. Would it kill the man to put on some clothes? And did he *have* to stand just outside the door? How awkward.

He helps me to one half of the his-and-her sink and stands behind me with the comb and brush he bought earlier this morning, waiting as I wash my hands. I look up to catch his eye but catch sight of myself in the mirror instead. The swelling has almost gone down but the bruising is still horrible. I try not to dwell on how off-putting it all looks but it's hard with a perfect specimen of man behind me.

He starts to work on the tangles with the wide-toothed comb, starting from the bottom and moving upwards, without needing direction. That's interesting. I had to tell Kyle what to do.

"Do you help a lot of women with their hair?" I inquire, only half-teasing. When he sends a probing look over my shoulder, I elaborate. "Most guys don't do it right and start from the top with an aggressive hand. You started from the bottom and have a gentle hand. How'd you know to do that?"

He throws a smirk my way at the unintended compliment before sobering up for the answer.

"When Heath's sister was attacked, she stopped taking care of herself for a little while. We all took turns helping him with her. She's like our sister too. According to her, I was the best at doing her hair." He shrugs it off like it's no big deal but I know better. It was a big deal, not just to Sara but to him, too.

He has this fire that's normally absent in his eyes. This one isn't borne from arousal or lust. It's the satisfaction that comes from the memory of helping a loved one in need. Based on what I know and what I've guessed about him, I bet it killed him that he couldn't do more for her or protect her in the first place.

The rest of the time, he works silently and methodically through my hair, and untangles all the knots without so much as a pull on my roots. He follows that up by shocking the shit out of me even further by saying, "Do you want me to braid it?"

"Can you do that?" I ask skeptically.

He just gives me a smirk and a shake of his head that says he's disappointed I underestimated him and starts *French-braiding* the thick mass. Of all things! It looks good, way better than mine, which always come out sloppy and loose.

"Hold this, doll? I forgot a hair tie." He hands me the end of my braid and goes back to his bedroom.

I inspect the braid closer and when no faults show up, I smile a wicked and giddy smile. He *really* fucked up. Now I'm going to have him braid it all the time.

Silas comes back and wraps the tie around the ends of my hair as I plan my future abuse of this newly-discovered talent.

"Thanks, Si," I say, playing with the plait. "I need to call the restaurant and email school so I can get things situated with them until I heal up." When I turn in his direction to ask for my sling and knee brace which are on the floor, I don't realize that he's frozen. "Si? Can you help me with the sling and brace?"

I don't understand what's happening or what brought it on but, without a moment's notice, I'm wrapped in his thick, corded arms. He lifts me so the tips of my toes just graze the floor and nuzzles my neck, holding me there for a moment. I decide to just go with it and hold him back as tightly as I can while he works through whatever he needs to work through.

It feels so good to be held, with no fear of violence and no expectations of sexual favors.

He sits me on the counter without giving an explanation and I don't ask for one. After securing the sling and brace, he helps me slide off the counter and back into the bedroom. I wait on the bed, kicking my good leg out back and forth, as Silas gets me some of my new sweatpants, courtesy of his generosity. He helps me step my feet into them and pull them up.

I'm glad he chose these ones for today. They're dark blue with orange stars in a polka dot pattern and a big, fat 'SUPER' on the butt. I thought they were quirky and when Silas laughed his head off at the sight, that just solidified my decision to get them.

"Come on, Little Miss Super, you can sit on the couch to make your calls and use your laptop." Suddenly, he's grabbed me by my good hand and pulled me into him with such force, that I go down like a domino and squeal like a pig. But before I can fall too far, Silas bends down and picks me up in a princess carry, stomping through the house like a big bad wolf.

I'm giggling and slapping my hand on his chest.

"Silas, put me down! I can walk now! This isn't necessary!"

"Of course, it's not necessary, but it's fun." With a tweak of my nose, Silas deposits me on the couch with a very theatric, "M'Lady."

I like the company and alone time with him. It brings out a playful side of him that I haven't seen yet.

As he wanders off, I look around. *Geez, how loaded are these guys?*

Larger versions of his bathroom tiles are present in the living room with a sky-blue couch to match and a wooden coffee table and matching end tables. Here, the walls are a sandy beige and seascape photography are hanging on them in various places, surrounding the television on the back wall and over a fireplace. His house definitely has a theme; with only slight variations, the central focus is the ocean.

The dining room, furnished with a white wood table for six, sitting on a plush, gray rug, separates the kitchen from the living room. In the open kitchen, the cabinets are all white with seashells for handles and the countertops are a soft gray. The aqua sea green backsplash in a honeycomb pattern is the only color and the tiles are the same as his bedroom.

I would not have matched such a pristine and chic, but cozy, home to such a rough-looking man.

By the time I've settled into the couch and pillows, Silas enters, dressed in old jeans, with mysterious stains and random rips in them. The old, black shirt has definitely seen better days.

With my phone and laptop in hand, he approaches me slowly. At first, I'm confused at his careful movements but at the question on my face, he explains, "I don't want to trigger you and send you into a panic attack doll."

As the heat of his body settles next to the curve of my hip, a bit more of the wall I've built around my heart crumbles down and that warm feeling spreads inside. It's been happening more and more, anytime the guys do something with my wellbeing in mind, with no expectation or goal, other than my healing.

Making the effort to heal was inevitable, with or without them, but they do everything possible to make it easier. They don't hover, they give me space when I need it and they don't overcrowd me as they check up on me. It's a relief to know they'll let me walk on my own but be there to catch me if I fall.

I give him a big smile, which is half-teasing and half-appreciation, and sing his name, "*Si-las*, you have a girly house."

His lips twitch and he shakes his head. At the amused exasperation on his face, I let out a little laugh and move on.

I look at him in silence for a second.

"You guys are really good at this." At his head tilt and puzzled look, I elaborate, "All this trauma stuff, and how to deal with it." Then I remember Sara and how they helped her after the attack and take back my words. "I'm so sorry. That was insensitive. I didn't mean to bring up bad memories. It's just … I just meant that it's nice to have help this time around." His silence is his way of prompting me to disclose more and, I have to admit, it's a damn good tactic because I'm talking without intending to. "Before … all my friends acted like I was damaged or just ignored my situation. Eventually, when I couldn't get my shit together quick enough for them, they quit calling and coming around." It's hard to talk about how that made me feel but I suppose he deserves to know why I am the way I am? I sigh. "It made me feel dirty, like I was unwanted, defective, because I couldn't heal in a second after—Well, anyway, I was already in a bad place and that didn't help."

"Nora," he says, lightly, in a tone that says *listen to me and hear me*. "You don't owe us anything, not even full disclosure. All we want is honesty. I know I'm practically a stranger to you but I'm not a stranger to what you're going through. Thank you for trusting me. I'm glad that I'm here to help and I know it's not going to be easy for you, even with us here, but I do know that, as long as you want us here, you won't be alone." He pulls away and comes to standing a few feet away to give me some space. "I have some stuff to do in the garage outside. If you need me, just call or text."

Then I'm alone with my thoughts.

After a breath for courage, I call the restaurant, already anticipating my boss's reaction. I close my eyes and lean my head against the couch when he says, "We're very sorry to hear about what you've been through, Nora, but—"

I knew that 'but' was coming but it still makes my heart drop. They say that while I have their condolences, they can't guarantee that my position will be there when I'm able to come back. They need to fill the space and it wouldn't be fair to the new hire to be fired when I'm ready to come back. I understand.

It sucks but I understand.

At least I'll have the job at Silas's while I'm recuperating. After that, I'll deal with the rest when the time comes, once I've healed.

Putting another setback out of my mind, I grab my laptop and log into my school portal.

Thankfully, before the events of the weekend, I had turned all my assignments early to prepare for a relaxing weekend that didn't happen so that's one less worry. I email all my professors to let them know, in as little details as possible, that I had an accident and that, though I would still be continuing classes, the next couple of weeks would be rough while I healed from the worst of the injuries.

I'm not concerned about most of my professors. I know they'll understand and work with me. But the professor of my math class, he's a real jerk and an unrelenting hard-ass. He doesn't tolerate excuses or late submissions for any reason, which I understand because he has pre-set due dates, but how was I to know I'd get attacked? Not that he knows that that's what happened to me. I just have to hope he'll understand without asking for more detail.

I submit the last of the work I had completed early but couldn't turn in until today.

Next, I call my landlord because I know he worries. He's a great guy. Just passed fifty years of marriage to his wife. They have the kind of marriage I used to dream about. Maybe my loft isn't anything to write home about but he does his best to help if I need it.

It takes around an hour to get everything done to my satisfaction, mostly because my landlord wants every detail and

160

multiple reassurances that I'm alright, that I'm not alone. I finally end the call forty minutes later and my stomach growls as my phone chimes with an incoming text.

It's Flynn. *Owen and I got done early. Wanna do lunch with us?*

I smile, my spirits lifting. *Do you read minds like Owen or did he tell you to ask? Or did the sound of my stomach growling travel through space and time all the way to you?*

I'll text Silas and see what he wants. We can bring it to his house. I'll get you something light but filling. Cool?

If you screw this up, I reply, deciding to mess with him a little, *I'll never let you pick my food again so don't fuck it up.*

Noted. I wonder how I can feel his smile through a one-word text. *See ya soon, my little spitfire.*

These guys are too much—and just enough.

I work on an essay that's due at the end of the week for one of my classes until Silas reappears thirty minutes later. I give him a cursory glance over my laptop, still engrossed in my essay, but do a double-take. How did he get so covered in grease and grime in just a couple of hours? It's like he dipped his arms up to his elbows in motor oil! He even has a few streaks on his face. I completely understand the old clothes now.

"The guys texted," he says, not stopping on the way to his room as he wipes his face with a washcloth. "They'll be here in a few. Owen wants to look at your knee. I'm going to wash up and be right out but don't freak when they just come in. They have a key."

That catches my attention. "You must be close if they have a key to your house."

He stops at the mouth of the hallway and turns toward me.

"We all have keys to each other's houses, cars, jobs. Owen's place of work is the only exception. We're as close as can be and we're brothers in every sense of the word, except for blood. Now you're a part of that too, Nora. Just wait." I don't know what he sees on my face because he smiles sadly and says, "I know you don't get it yet but you will. We've all accepted you into our hard-fought for family. We aren't letting you go now."

He disappears down the hall and into his room and I'm just left staring.

Am I really a part of that now? I'm a part of their family until they can't or don't want to handle my issues anymore. Despite the insecurities rearing their ugly heads, the happy tears come, silently.

My mom died just before I started college. It's been more years than I can stand to remember but I haven't felt a part of anyone or anything since then. Always an outsider. Until these men, I didn't realize how alone I'd made myself, how alone I'd been made to become. And not just because my mom was my closest friend, but also because of what my ass of an ex-roommate did to me. I closed myself off since then to avoid getting hurt again. Yes, it wasn't healthy and maybe I did miss out on some beautiful friendships, but I couldn't bring myself to open up again.

Until now. Until someone looked at me and decided they wanted to be in my life and made it happen. Until they took the choice away from me—no, took the choice away from my trauma, not me. I know that, with them, I always have a choice.

They snuck in when I wasn't paying attention and I know I want them there but I wonder if I can keep them? Time will tell, as it always does.

The lock turns, the front door opens and I wipe my face before they come into the living room and catch sight of me. I've already had a monumental breakdown in front of them and

162

I don't want to fall apart in front of them again but tell that to my tears.

The sight of them, looking as they do, exuding the energy that they carry like it's there just to warm me up, makes my heart lift and clench at the same time.

When Flynn sees me, his face morphs into a picture of concern. His steps halt and his arm shoots out to stop Owen from advancing. Owen gives him a sharp look but loses the look when he sees where Flynn's attention is.

"Nora," Flynn says. "Are you okay? Why are you crying?" When I can't speak through the hiccups, he sets the bag of food on the counter and drops to his knees. "I'm going to come to you now, slowly, and you can lean on me. Is that okay?"

I shake my head, trying to explain that this isn't a bad cry. I'm just so happy to be a part of their family and everything they've created together. But the words won't come.

He crawls to me and takes my hands in his callused, strong ones. Owen disappears into the hallway without a word, his long steps eating up the distance to Silas's room in seconds. The sound of them talking comes from the room, as Flynn holds my hand in silent support. I'm trying to control myself when they reappear at the mouth of the hallway, with Owen looking concerned and Silas, puzzled.

This is so fucking ridiculous but the tears keep coming.

"Nora, what happened, doll?" Silas asks me, then addresses Owen, "I swear she was fine when I went in to clean up. I told her you guys were coming over and I was going to wash up and to not freak out when you guys let yourselves in. Then you come in and tell me she's been crying."

If I wasn't crying, I'd be smiling at how adorably puzzled Silas looks.

Owen watches me and approaches when he comes to some sort of a conclusion. When he's a few steps away, I remove my hands from Flynn's and open my arms. Owen steps into them, curling me into himself and holding me close. I breathe in his orange and ginger scent and my tears return. As I cry, Owen rocks me, holding me tight and stroking my hair, telling me to let go of it all. I feel Silas by my feet and Flynn just behind the couch. I'm surrounded by almost everything I could need but there's two of them that aren't here.

When the tears turn to sniffles, I pull away from my good doctor and explain through a scratchy voice and receding hiccups. "I'm o-okay. I just s-so happy that I found you guys."

The tension from their body drains and they've all got soft looks of tenderness on their faces, except Silas's is one of the amused exasperation that I love so much. I smile shakily at him and shrug.

Owen places his hand on my right leg. "Let me take a look at your knee and we'll eat before the food gets cold, or hot in your case, Nora." He slides the pant leg up easily and quickly determines that I haven't injured it further.

With my left arm around his torso, Owen helps me up and to the table but stops. Flynn bursts out laughing.

"Nora," he says between bouts of laughter, "What the hell are you wearing, my little spitfire?"

I look down at my new sweats and the borrowed shirt and shrug.

"It's comfy."

Flynn, still laughing, twirls his finger in a circle for me to turn around. I roll my eyes but humor him by untangling myself from Owen and turning. Before I can do a full rotation, Flynn's hands are on my hips and he's kneeling behind me so his face is level with my ass.

Oh, lordy, I hope I don't rip one right now. I might just die of mortification.

"Nora," he says. I turn to look over my shoulder at his gleaming eyes and the great big Cheshire grin on his face. "Why do your pants say 'super' on the ass?"

I hold my hand up in a shrug and adopt a confused expression.

"Uh, because I'm a superstar?"

That gets him. His amusement is uncontrollable as he wraps his arms around my hips and nestles his cheek on my ass, laughing so hard that his shoulders shake and my hips with them. He holds me like that until he gets himself together. It feels so natural that I'm grinning along with him as Silas presses his lips together, trying to hold in his amusement, and *that's* when my eyes narrow, suspicious. I have a feeling I'm missing an inside joke here.

Flynn rises from my ass and sits down on one side of the table, placing me next to him. He pushes my chair and Owen props my foot up on the opposite chair. Silas gets the abandoned food from the countertop, plops onto a chair at the end of the table and claims a giant kahuna chicken cheese steak. Owen passes around water bottles from the fridge and sits at the other end, laying claim to a veggie wrap.

Once the food's passed out, and I have my turkey wrap in my hand and Flynn has a meatball-and-cheese sub, we all dig in. The conversation stays light and casual until Flynn asks about my family.

"So, Nora, where's your family? Any siblings?" He glances at me before taking a bite from his sub.

I take a drink of my water and clear my throat. *May as well,* I think before explaining. "I don't really remember my dad. He took off when I was around three. When my mom got pregnant with me, their already-strained relationship just got worse. She always said he wasn't a great man; just a charismatic one that knew how to lure people in. She never found anyone after him so I don't have siblings."

I focus back on my food and hope they catch the cue that I'm not inviting any more questions. But I should've known better. They're too engrossed in their food to observe and too curious for their own good. *Dogs with bones, all of them!*

"Where's your mom now?" Owen asks casually, like this topic change won't ruin the nice vibe we had set.

I play with the sandwich wrapping and whispers quietly, staring at the table, "She, uh, she died in a car accident just after I graduated high school."

Thud. And I smile a little at the sound of someone kicking someone else under the table and Owen's pained grunt. These guys are so funny.

"I'm sorry, Nora." He sounds it. "I didn't mean to ask an uncomfortable question."

I look him in his beautiful jade green eyes and give him a small, understanding smile.

"I know. There was no way you could've known. It's just difficult because she was my best friend and then, pretty much straight after her, all the stuff with my roommate happened so..." I trail off.

Flynn puts his arm around my shoulders, careful of my injured one, and whispers in my ear the three words every woman loves to hear.

"I brought brownies." I look up at him and into his mesmerizing eyes, alight with mischief, and give him a look of pure adoration, which he returns with a sly grin. We both burst out into laughter together, despite my bruised ribs.

"You sure know the way to a woman's heart, huh?" I tease.

Flynn gets up and grabs the other paper bag, brings it to me and opens the bag, wafting it under my nose. I close my eyes and inhale the delicious aroma like an addict on crack but my drug of choice is heaven in a paper bag. I grab at the bag with greedy hands and pull it into myself.

My sigh is one of pleasure. "If I die with a brownie in my mouth … I didn't imagine this is how I would go but I always hoped."

The guys just stare and burst out laughing as I bask in the beautiful sound. I take a snapshot of this precious moment in my mind and keep it for the good memories.

Pawing a great, big brownie from Flynn's hand, I shove it in my face for a huge bite, not caring that my lip protests the stretching. The guys, still chuckling, all take a piece too. Maybe renewed trauma craves chocolate because I swear that was the best damn brownie I've ever had. I smirk to myself at my private joke.

"Want to come with me this evening and have some fun?" Flynn asks me with a twinkle in his mismatched eyes.

Those always draw me in. Maybe some people might think they're weird or odd but I just think they're beautiful. They're so *him*. Hell, all the guys are beautiful, in their own ways.

I bite my lip, a little uneasy because, of all the guys, I've spent the least amount of time with Flynn. But I remind myself who he is. A member of my new family. My EMT rescuer. I might not have been here, if it wasn't for him.

I beam at him, forgetting for a moment that I'm injured, forgetting that's how I found them. Because all that matters is that I *did* find them.

So, I say 'yes' and mean it.

9 Abstract Art

Owen looks skeptical. "I'm not sure if that's the best idea. Your brand of fun might be a bit much for Nora right now."

Flynn gapes at Owen, a look of wounded disbelief on his face, and shoves away from the table.

"I would never do anything to put her at risk. You, of all people, know that." With that, he storms out to the garage.

For my part, I sit in a tense, awkward silence while Owen and Silas have a silent conversation. After what seems like forever, Silas pushes his food away and stands.

"I'll go talk to him." He kisses me on the cheek with soft lips, gives Owen another look that carries a thousand words, and heads out.

"He's right. I shouldn't have said that." Owen sighs and rubs the bridge of his nose with his thumb and forefinger. "Will you be okay for a minute until Silas comes back?"

I nod and shoo him out with a gesture of my hands. He gives me a sad smile, that I return with an encouraging one, and heads out the same way as the other two, giving my shoulder a squeeze as he passes by.

Instead of sitting and waiting, I gather the trash and slowly make my way into the kitchen. It takes me a few tries to find the trashcan but I finally do, hidden behind a cupboard panel. *Clever*. I turn and rest my backside against the counter waiting for someone to reappear.

Silas really does have a cute house. He hasn't mentioned a current girlfriend but I wonder if an ex-lover is responsible for it. That thought brings with it a surprising amount of jealousy. I almost groan. Like the situation with Kyle and Owen wasn't enough! I shake my head and decide that, *nope, not thinking about it*, and lock that thought away to be examined later.

Silas comes back through the garage door. When he doesn't see me at the table, a brief flash of panic sparks on his face before he spots me leaning on the counter by the sink. He comes over to me and boxes me in with a hand on either side of my hips on the counter. I feel surrounded, but not trapped.

"You didn't have to clean up."

"I know," I say, resting my hands on his shoulders and looking him in the eyes. "But—and this is something you should know about me—I don't like not pulling my weight and I'm not used to being tended to. It feels too much like a debt. So this healing period is going to be difficult for me. I know you guys don't see it like that but my brain is going to need some time to come around to that thought process."

He returns my look and relents. "Okay, doll."

That was easy. *Almost too easy.* Naturally, my suspicion's piqued but before I can call him on it, Flynn and Owen come back into the kitchen.

I look closely at them both and am relieved to see that they both seem better, more at ease.

Flynn holds his hand out to me, the devilish grin firmly back on his face. "Ready, little spitfire?"

That wicked gleam in his eyes makes me hesitate but I really do want to spend some more time with him and get to know him a bit better. So, I pull up my big girl undies, smile, and place my hand in his. Silas moves out of the way and Flynn helps me towards him. I give my company for the day a big smile and say, "The real question is, are you ready for me? I'm quite a handful."

We're almost to the door when Owen, the jerk, waits until the last moment to call out to us, an evil smirk on his face. "She needs shoes, Flynn."

I look down at my bare feet. Crap. I didn't even think about shoes.

"I'll go get them and some socks for you," Silas offers. I give him a grateful smile before he disappears into his bedroom, his broad back and tight ass moving fluidly as he disappears. I don't even try to pretend I'm not watching till he's out of sight.

Flynn leads me over to the couch, sits me down and takes a seat next to me, a contemplative look on his face. Silas comes back with the socks, shoes and a different shirt in his hand. He hands the footwear to Flynn, who lifts my feet onto his lap and puts the socks on for me.

I'm not really a foot person but there's an odd intimacy around us, as Flynn helps me with my socks and shoes. The sensation immediately goes into the box, to be examined later. It's getting rather full in there but I'm not in a rush to get to any of it. I'd rather just be in the moment.

Silas stands in front of me, careful not to tower over me, and holds up a shirt that matches the sweatpants I have on. The shirt is orange with a dark blue star on one sleeve. More importantly, it's stretchy enough to not aggravate my bad arm.

"I figured this would be better for you in public."

I smile. "Thanks, Si. How do you always know just what I need?"

The question was rhetorical but he replies, deadly serious, "Part of the job, doll."

Another brick of the wall chips away.

He shakes the shirt in his hands, making it ripple. "Let's get these switched out." He grabs the sleeve on my good arm, bends it at the elbow and pulls the rest of the shirt over my head and down my bad arm. Before I can process that I'm almost naked in front of all three of them, I'm already in the new shirt and he's tweaking my nose. "All set, doll." He plops down next to me on the couch as Flynn's pulling the last of the shoelaces tight.

Flynn pats my foot and I move it so he can stand.

"Need anything else before we go?"

"I should probably bring my phone and license, just in case. You know, since I don't know where we're going. Oh! Sunglasses! Because we might be outside. Maybe something warm? We might be out late and it could get cold. Do I need to wear different shoes?" I say, looking up at him from under my eyelashes, trying to be subtle about fishing for information, but he doesn't bite.

He just gets my phone, wallet, sunglasses and puts the first two in his pockets and slips the glasses on my head.

"Your shoes are fine and if you need something warm, I've got you. Anything else?"

I give him a glare, which he returns with a playful smile. I mentally roll my eyes. *Men.*

"Fine, I guess not."

He pulls me to standing and we head to the door. I shout out a 'bye' to both the guys as we step over the threshold and get a 'bye, gorgeous' and 'stay safe, doll' in return.

Flynn leads me to a sharp, sleek Dodge Challenger. It's gunmetal gray, except for the black hood and a flat, black stripe down the center.

"Did Silas customize this for you?"

Flynn grins and opens my door like a proper gentleman, helping me ease into the gray, leather seat.

"No, I just got her last week. He hasn't had a chance to get his claws in her yet but he's been pestering me the last few days." Once I'm buckled in, he shuts the door and climbs in through the driver's side.

With a loud roar, the car comes to life and the rumble of the engine vibrates under me as he turns it. I've always loved muscle cars. At the same time, he grabs a pair of black, aviator sunglasses from the dashboard and puts them on, sending his signature, playful smile my way and I'm not sure if it's the hot car or the hot guy but I am seriously turned on right now.

"Flynn, is it weird that I'm a bit turned on by your car?" He just gives me a knowing look and pulls onto the road, shifting gears. There's something about a man that can drive a stick. *Swoon*. "Too bad she's a girl..."

"Silas is going to love you."

My heart goes into overdrive at his choice of words and even more as he guns it down the nearly empty road. He handles it with such confidence. *I wonder if that extends to other parts of his life...*

"Well, Silas has already made his interest known, along with Owen and Kyle. Wanna be added to the list too?" I tease but I am interested in the answer, though I can't do anything about it yet. With all the flirting, I'm just not sure if that's his personality or if he really *is* into me.

"How about we get to know each other, as friends first, and we'll see where it goes once you're in a better place?" He's just so sweet and smooth, all rolled up tight in a burning-hot package.

I smile to myself at the answer, because it's so him, though a little disappointed that he doesn't confirm or deny any interest. Though my curiosity is piqued, I nod my agreement and watch the houses zoom by.

"So, my little spitfire, what do you like to do for fun?"

To him, it's such a simple question but I'm an oddball and how do I tell him that my only pastime is people watching? *Abort, abort!* I shrug, hoping he doesn't call me on the deflection. "I like different things than your average bear. You?"

He glances knowingly at me from the corner of his eye but lets it go. *Whew!* "I like music. How are you at karaoke?"

"Ummm ... say what now? I'm not good at all ... I mean, you've heard me sing! You were much better than I was. Besides, isn't that sort of thing done in bars?" I'm a little on edge. I'm not sure if I can handle a crowd right now.

"Good thing I own a bar then, huh? I can go in whenever I want." Giving me a playful smile, he glances at me before turning his attention back to the road. "But that's not what we're doing today. I thought something a little more relaxed would be more appropriate." I let out the breath I was holding. Thank God he understands. "I know you need time but you also need to have some fun and remember that there's beauty in life. So, how do you feel about art?"

I'm not sure what he means by that. Art is such a broad spectrum and encompasses so many different aspects.

"I like looking at different mediums of art: paintings, photography, sculptures, the like. As for if I like *creating art*, I'm not talented in that area. I have dabbled a bit in charcoal drawings, but my vision doesn't translate from my brain to the reality."

"Well," he says, pulling to a smooth stop at a red light and smiling at me, "Today, we're just going to a small, local art gallery I've been wanting to check out for a while. I was hoping it'd be easier on you because they don't have big crowds or loud noises. Does that work for you? We can swing by and see Heath afterwards so you can get a sense of the different type of programs he offers and set one up today, if you like anything. Sound good?"

I nod at him.

When he sees the light turn green, he turns to give me a cheeky grin and I brace myself with my hand on the 'oh shit' handle just in time for him to take off like a shot, shifting easily between gears, all the way to fourth. Laughter bubbles up from my belly and it's the first belly laugh since the attack. It lifts my heart with delight. I miss the look Flynn's giving me because I'm too focused on the exhilaration.

By the time he eases the car back down to a respectable speed, I'm coming down from the high but still smiling.

"The art gallery sounds fun. What kind of art do they display?" I'm curious to see what type of art Flynn is partial to.

He grins his Cheshire smile and says, "It's not typical art. It's more of an acquired taste, if you don't already have an affinity toward it."

Well, that was cryptic and unhelpful. That's more than once now that he's tried to pull the wool over my eyes so I call him on it. "You're very good at answering questions with non-answers, you know."

He smiles at me. "I knew you wouldn't be fooled. You're too observant. Sorry, Spitfire. Occupational hazard." At my probing look, he explains, "When I'm working behind the bar and people talk to me, they'll disperse questions into the conversation every now and then to make themselves feel better for talking so much, but they don't really want an answer. At the other end, some *do* want to know more about me, but it's more than is appropriate and more than I'm comfortable sharing. I'm not a fan of either extreme so I've learned how to answer without seeming like a dick and losing their business. Hence, the non-answer answers."

The glimpse into his life connects me to him a bit. He's a private person and so am I. It might be for different reasons but we're still the same, in a way.

We drive down winding roads until he pulls into a parking spot just in front of a small gallery with a gorgeous front window display on either side of the door. On one side, there are paintings and vases. But my eyes are immediately drawn to the other side, where a statue sits, with no adornments surrounding it.

It's *beautiful* and speaks to me in a way that nothing has for such a long time. A woman, petite with luscious curves, sits as the focal point, surrounded by three men. She's in a toga, seductively draped across her shoulder, standing with her hands on her ample hips. Her head is lifted high as she stares defiantly into the distance.

The men, all broad-shouldered and large, look like warriors of a different era, dressed in red capes and not much else. Two men are crouched on either side of her in a defensive position, ready to attack. The third man stands behind her, her back plastered to his front, as he looks into the distance, watching for danger.

They're a unit and that much is clear. And though she looks just as fierce as her men, they're surrounding her in a way that makes it clear that she's precious to all of them and they'd lay their lives down for her. But she'd just as quickly do the same.

I'm still staring at the sculptures when Flynn comes around to my door to help me out. I pull my eyes from the woman and her men and put my hand in his outstretched one. He places his other hand on my waist. He almost bends down in half, still supporting me, as I come to standing next to him.

I'm puzzled at his actions until I'm on the ground next to him and he rises to his full height, which is a good four or five inches taller than me. It hits me then that if he hadn't bent down, I probably would've had a panic attack but like always, these guys think of everything. They're far more spatially aware, always more conscious of their position relative to mine, than I am. It seems like it comes naturally to them.

He closes the car door with one hand and engages the locks. I place my arm around his slim waist and lean heavily on him as we walk to the gallery. His light arm around my back, with his hand gently on my hip, fits me right under his arm so I'm tucked into him nicely. The muscles along his back ripple against my arm and I might have pressed a little closer, but he'll never know why.

Without breaking our connection, he opens the door and walks us in.

I peer up at Flynn as he steers us toward the right side of the gallery. "What physical activity do you enjoy?"

He gives me a funny look before it's replaced by deviousness and his sly grin comes slow but certain. "My little spitfire, are you coming on to me?"

I reconsider my words and when it hits me, my face flushes a deep red all the way up to my ears. Flynn's laughter rings out in the otherwise-silent gallery and I narrow my eyes at him.

This means payback.

I wipe my face of all emption. "Nope, just wondering. I need to know that you can perform, if we ever have sex." The laughter cuts off immediately and he sobers up like I threw a bucket of ice-cold water at him.

Before I know what's happening, I'm in a corner with my back pressed against the wall and Flynn against me, chest-to-chest, hips-to-hips, and my funny attempt at pulling his leg doesn't seem so funny anymore. His hands are flat on the wall next to my head. One of his legs is between mine, pushing, upwards, upwards, until I'm lifting, high enough so I'm balancing on my toes and our eyes are level. I'm no longer sure if the heat in my body is because of his strength or because of the heat radiating from him. I place my hands on either side of his torso and grip his shirt, grasping for something to cling onto, because his eyes might just make me fall apart.

My eyes drift closed and my toes curl at the sound of his low, velvety voice as he lowers his face to mine. "Nora," he says, lengthening the vowels in my name, his lips brushing ever so lightly against mine, "*When* we do get there, I promise you'll have no questions about my … *performance*." I'm waiting for him to close the distance between us but he keeps himself there, our breaths mingling, his eyes holding mine. I'm not sure if I'm looking back at him or if I'm even still here because I'm still floating when he slowly pulls his mouth away and rests his forehead on mine.

Reality starts to slip back into place and, with it, awareness. I tense when I realize where we are and the position we're in. Flynn must feel it because not even a beat later, he's easing me down and helping me stand on my own two feet. I've still got my hands on his torso and it's like his skin is magnetic because I can't force them away.

He pulls back, just enough, so that all that is in front of me is him and those beautiful, mismatched eyes. "I didn't mean to do that, Nora, but I don't regret it."

"I don't regret it either but, Flynn I'm not comfortable with being moved like that yet. After reality came back, I started to panic." I hope the admission won't bite me in the ass and it's like he picks up on that uncertainty.

"Spitfire, you never have to worry about telling me the truth. In fact, I'll be pissed if you don't."

They keep telling me to be honest but I need to clarify something. "I won't lie to you and I'll be as forthcoming as possible, without breaking someone else's confidence."

He nods and gives me a look that says he didn't miss the diplomacy there and I just smirk back, a little proud of myself for the way I handled the situation.

We re-enter the land of the living and wander through the gallery but the visit is a blur. My mind wanders to his expression of interest. He didn't admit it in the car but I caught what he said: *'when'* we get to that point in our relationship. Naturally, my mind drifts to Kyle, Silas and Owen, how they've all expressed their interest in obvious or covert ways.

We come up in front of another painting and though I wandered through the last however-many in a fog, this one captures my attention immediately. It's a side-profile of a man and a woman in a sitting kneel, their thighs horizontal to the floor, butts to heels, heads bowed. They're completely naked. But that's not what has me bewitched though.

It's their hands, tied in intricate patterns of ropes behind their back, as a second man stands between them. Though he's facing us, his gaze is on the two at his feet, his hands on each of their shoulders. The love and affection that they share radiates in waves from the painting. It's an intimate depiction of the trust, the connection, between the triad.

Flynn steps behind me and wraps his arms loosely around me, resting his chin on my left shoulder.

"What do you like about this one?" he whispers in my ear, his peppermint breath caressing my cheek. "I like that the two kneeling are the ones that truly hold the power."

I consider that for a second and notice that he's right. At first glance, the power seems to be centered on the man facing us. After all, the two kneeling aren't even showing their faces and they're restrained. But at a closer glance, it's so completely obvious that the power flows through them all, that I'm surprised I missed it.

A chill runs down my spine, causing me to shiver as goose-bumps break out on my neck and arms.

I lean into Flynn's embrace and rest my head on his muscled shoulder. With him at my back, his arms tight around me—I've never felt this safe to be vulnerable.

I get lost in trying to express what emotions this piece awakens in me.

"I didn't realize in until now but that trust they have in the third person ... that's what drew me in. I've never been able to give my trust like that to someone ... but I've always wanted to." I didn't expect the turn this day would take, that I'd share a part of myself that I've never shared before but I don't feel like he'll abuse the gift I'm giving him.

He pulls me tighter and his lips find the shell of my ear again, as he whispers, "We'll work on making that desire come true, little spitfire."

I hate to break my connection with him or the painted triad but we can't stay here forever and I need to relieve myself. I take a breath and let it out before speaking, "Do you know if they have a public restroom?" I turn my face toward him but he's so close, *so* close, that I almost end up kissing his cheek. I turn sideways in his embrace and pull my face back. "Why are you so easy to open up to?" I muse to myself, searching his face for an answer, but not expecting one.

Flynn pauses, looking deeply into my eyes. I feel like he can see straight through me, right into my beaten, battered and broken soul. "I'd like to say I'm not usually but we both know that's not true. The difference is, Nora, that with you, I want to reciprocate." He turns me so we're standing side-by-side, his arm around me. "Let's go find you a ladies' room."

An employee directs us to the single-toilet restroom and, just outside the door, Flynn turns me to him. I can tell he's uncertain, not something I've seen from him yet.

"I know we don't know each other very well but do you need any help? I don't mind."

I smile at him, finding it funny that he said we don't know each other well, even though, right now, I feel the closest to him. "I should be just fine, thank you. It takes some weird wiggles to get things done but I manage."

I squeeze his arm and disappear into the room. After using the toilet and washing my hands, I'm drying my hands with the provided cloth towel when I catch my reflection in the mirror and the beaten woman staring back.

I close my eyes and wonder what I'm doing. Do I really want to go down this rabbit hole? I scoff. Can I even stop it from happening? Do I want to? It feels like all the events have already been set into motion. These guys have already weaved our lives together on so many fronts.

I have to at least be honest with myself, even if I'm not ready to admit the truth to anyone else. Yes, so far, I like them. *All of them.* Even Heath, who I've barely had time with.

But how can I convince my brain that we're just friends, nothing more? *I said I'd be honest with myself.*

God! I'm supposed to be focusing on healing. Maybe I need this whole situation to distract me from the attack? But that's not really a healthy way of recovering. I know I'll heal but it's just going to take time and these guys seem more than capable of helping along the process. I know, if I just give them a chance, give them a peek inside, they'll move things along faster than they moved after *him*.

When my roommate attacked me, I spiraled into a very dark place. Nowhere, no one, felt safe. I pulled further and further away and instead of pulling me closer, I was pushed farther than I intended to go. But I know, or I hope, it'll be different with them. I can already feel them pulling me in.

Resolved to have them as friends, I open the door and am surprised that I don't see Flynn immediately. I limp to the reception desk, where he's laughing with the woman behind the counter.

He glances at me and if I thought his smile was beautiful before, it blinds me when he turns towards me. He excuses himself to the saleswoman and heads straight to me.

He grabs my hand. "How about we go and visit Heath now?"

A genuine smile spreads across my face as we walk towards the front door. That sounds like a fantastic idea.

∞∞∞∞

We pull into a parking spot outside a very understated building. There are no signs with the gym's name or anything to indicate what the building is and, unless someone pointed it out, I wouldn't have known this was a gym just driving by.

The outside is an unassuming gray with average windows. But when we get inside, the contrast is striking. A long reception type desk, standing front and center of the lobby, accommodates a man and a woman. There's seating on either side of the lobby. Big, bold, MMA pictures dominate one wall with Heath in almost all of them. In fact, the whole thing screams *Heath*.

The walls are a soft dove grey and the floor is sealed concrete. Tucked into a corner along one of the walls is a trophy case, displaying over fifteen trophies but I'm not close enough to see what they are or for whom. On the other wall is a massive painting that's vibrant and evokes energy with its bright and bold brush strokes. Alternative music plays in the background, loud enough to electrify the place, but not so loud that a conversation can't be carried.

Upon our entrance, both the receptionists at the desk look up and smile wide. Flynn walks up to the man and gives his outstretched fist a bump.

"Walker!" the man says. "Hey man, how's it going?" When he catches sight of me, he does a quick sweep of my injuries and focuses back on Flynn. "What are we signing her up for?"

Flynn chuckles and gives a slight shake of his head, wrapping his arm around my waist and pulling me closer.

"It's good, Stan. Heath around? She's with us. We're not sure which programs just yet."

Stan watches Flynn's protective move and says, "Yeah, he's here. Let me page him up here for you." He's a good looking, well-built man, with brunette hair cut in a fade, a goatee in the same color and hazel eyes, but he doesn't hold a flame to any of my five guys.

Wait … what!

When did I start thinking of them as mine? No, *nope*, they're *not* mine. Not at all. *Get that thought out of your head, Molano.*

I look around the lobby, catching sight of the Flex logo behind the reception desk and unintentionally make eye contact with the woman.

She's dressed in similar clothes to Stan—a black polo shirt, with the *Flex* logo in vibrant red on their left pecs, khaki cargo pants and black tennis shoes—so I'm guessing they have a uniform. When she stands, I realize she might be the tiniest woman I've ever seen. If she's over five feet, I'll be surprised. Her long black hair, tied in a ponytail that falls to her ass, facial features and darker eyes hint that she might be of Persian descent. She puts her hand out for a handshake over the table and gives me a smile that's both welcoming and sad, like she's standing in comradery with me.

Like she's been where I am.

I take her offered hand and am surprised at the strength in her grip.

"Hi, I'm Jaz!" she says in a smooth voice.

182

"Nora," I return her greeting, "Hello."

Stan hangs up the phone, just as we unclasp our hands, and says, "Heath's on his way. He'll be down as soon as he can." After a warm smile for me, he gets back to his work.

"Come on, little spitfire, let's have a seat so you don't get too tired."

Flynn guides me over to the seating area that's to the side, furnished with black seats and a black coffee table. He helps me sit, takes the spot next to me and props my right leg up on his knees. I give him a grateful smile. I love when the guys are attentive and make sure to elevate my leg. I love it even more when they prop it on themselves. That small physical connection means the world to me.

After what seems like forever, I get the chance to do what I love: people watch.

I watch Stan and Jaz. They're great at their job, patient, friendly and approachable. When they're not greeting or talking to the people who come and go from the gym, they're efficiently answering the phone, scheduling appointments or laughing amongst themselves. I notice the people coming into the building. I thought it was a place only for women but a few men are here, as well.

Before long, Heath comes down the hall. He's in the company shirt and black tennis shoes, same as Jaz and Stan's, but instead of khakis, he's wearing a pair of blue jeans. He's pretty much dressed the same as the rest of the employees but this is his domain and it shows. Out in the world, he's confident and alert, just like now. But, here, he's confident and alert in a relaxed way. Here, it's like he knows that this is *his* territory. He knows who everyone is, where everyone is, and he's less vigilant as a result.

I move my leg off of Flynn's support and go to stand but before I can put any pressure on my feet, Heath is there, helping me up. I don't know how he crossed the remaining distance so quickly and silently in the seconds it took me to get my leg off of Flynn but he did.

"Nora," he says, pulling me into a firm hug, "Sweetheart, don't do that by yourself. Let us help you."

I mentally roll my eyes at his over-protective behavior but let it go. The next words come without thought. "Hey, G-man, you give really nice hugs." My face flames as soon as the words are out. *G-man?* We don't even know each other and I'm giving him nicknames and complimenting his hugging prowess! I swear, I've lost my filter around these guys.

He shakes with inaudible laughter against me and pulls back and looks down at me with a head tilt. "G-man?"

I decide I'm committed to this now so I give him a lopsided smile and elaborate. "Yep, G-man, because you're *ginormous*! And that's really saying something because I'm not a small woman by any means and you make me feel *tiny*."

"That's very fitting, since his surname is Griffin," Flynn supplies.

I beam at him at that. What a coincidence! I didn't even realize my spontaneous nickname for Heath was so perfect for him. Heath stills next to me and my face falls as I search his face for the reason. My panic immediately rises and my body gets tense. *What did I do?* "What? Did I do something wrong?" *He was happy a moment ago.*

Heath brings his hand up to the back of my head and strokes my hair, bending so our faces are level with each other. He whispers, "No, Nora, nothing is wrong. You just have a breathtaking smile."

The tension melts with my heart. Sure, people have complimented me before but when it comes from these guys, I know they mean them. I can hear it in their words, their voices, see it in their eyes.

And another one takes a hammer to the wall. It's disarming how quickly they're chipping away at the fortified parts of me.

"Come on, sweetheart," Heath says, oblivious to what he's done, "I'll show you around and we can set up a schedule that'll work for you." He slides me to his side with ease and Flynn falls in behind us. As we pass, Heath gives Stan and Jaz a two-finger wave.

One door on either side of the reception desk opens to two halls. The hall to the left is labeled *Flex,* while the other, to the right, is labeled *Flex Prep.* I'm not sure what Flex Prep is but I'm sure I'll find out.

Through the windows along the hallway, I can see the gym. It's well-equipped with the equipment ranging from novice to professional difficulty levels.

"This is the physical side of Flex," Heath informs me, gesturing to the hallway. "This is where we work on whatever you need to help in your recovery, that includes general physical fitness or learning defensive moves for protection. We do it all from A to Z and then some."

As we walk through the gym, Heath points out the various facilities offered: treadmills, free weights, barbells, pretty much every kind of strength training equipment. There's a mat area for ground work, a yoga section, machines I recognize and others I don't. The whole time, he keeps me tucked firmly into his side.

I look back to see Flynn's been stopped again. He keeps catching up and being held back. I grin. *The price of being popular.*

"Anything to do with water is in this area," Heath says, when we head through another doorway. It leads to the back of the gym area, where there's a large pool area, that spans a third of the entire back of the building. There's one Olympic-size pool, two medium-sized pools, a smaller, shallower pool and a jacuzzi. Along the front wall, there are therapy beds for normal massages and hydromassages.

The next door we go through brings us to the *Flex Prep* area. "The *Flex Prep* side is where we do work on the mental aspects of recovery. These are patient therapy rooms and we have several therapists on staff, with one psychologist overseeing all treatment cases. We're trying to add another due to our recent growth but haven't found the right fit yet." He points to another section of the gym and says, "My office is the room located in the front."

As Heath moves us to one of the two doors located on the right center, Flynn catches up to us but I'm too focused on the tour. I give him a cursory glance.

"The center island are locker rooms: the front is for women and the back is for the men." He pulls away from me to step into the men's locker room and, in a loud boom that makes me jump, he calls out, "Woman entering!" With an apologetic and reassuring smile, he brings me close once again and we take a quick glance inside the men's room. We don't go too far in but I get the picture. "The women's side is mirrored. All employees use these locker rooms too."

All three of us move out and head back to the front reception desk. By the time we get back, my knee's starting to throb from all the walking and I'm feeling the beginnings of a headache behind my eyes. When I put too much pressure on my knee at one point, I try to keep the pain off my face but it's really tender and I don't entirely succeed. Flynn notices and gives Heath a pointed look and they move into action.

Heath sweeps me up into his arms and Flynn holds the door, as they call their goodbyes. Heath gives me the kind of reprimanding look I'd expect he'd give a toddler and I duck my head in embarrassment. "You need to tell us when you're in pain, Nora."

He notices that I've averted my eyes because when we make it to Flynn's car, I'm set on my feet, with my back to the car, and Heath's pressed right up against me. "Nora, hear me right now. I'm not okay with you being in pain when you have the means to help it. I'm sorry if I hurt your feelings—I'll be more mindful of that in the future—but you need to communicate with us. We can't help you if you don't."

My brain hears the logic in his words but emotions are messy and don't always respond to reason and logic. As connected as I feel to these guys, they're still essentially strangers. Sometimes, opening up to them comes easily. Other times, it feels like a steeper hill to climb than physically healing right now.

Since he's requesting honest communication, I decide to give him just that. "Doing what you do, you must know that it's not always that easy. You're asking me to open up to you—and I have and I'm trying to—but you're basically strangers to me. I hardly know anything about any of you and you know more than I've revealed in years. So, I'll make you a deal: every time you want me to share something with you, you have to share something too. Deal?" This is the only way I can think of that might help me open up to them. And if I get to learn things about him in exchange, all the better for it.

"Done," he says without pause. "Now that's not saying I'm going to treat you with kid gloves. I'll just try and not be so harsh."

He pulls me into a really long, really tight hug that soothes me all the way down to my healing bones. I wrap my arms around him as much as I can.

"Thank you." Gratitude always comes easy to me around them.

I feel a kiss on the top of my head as he pulls back and looks into my eyes. I'm not sure what he's looking for but after a moment, he moves back so he can open the door for me and helps me in.

After he shuts the door, I'm buckling in while the guys have a brief conversation outside the car. With a back-slapping hug, they split up and Flynn comes to the driver's side and slips in.

"Hungry?" Flynn says with a smile, flashing his pearly whites at me, with smile lines appearing around his eyes.

It's been a while since we had lunch hours ago and I'm starting to feel some hunger pangs.

"Sure, what do you have in mind?"

Flynn glances at me from the corner of his eyes, assessing, as he pulls out of the parking lot onto the road. "Actually, Heath invited us to his house. Neither of us are spectacular cooks but Owen's taught us a thing or two. At least, enough to be sure we won't starve and don't have to live off of takeout."

Three cooks out of five? Sounds like a good deal to me.

"Sure. I've been craving some homemade food anyways."

10 Snip, Snip, Leave

As we drive to Heath's neighborhood, we pass boutiques, stores and office spaces. It's a nice part of town, nowhere near the rundown parts. His house is basically a bachelor pad, styled like a loft.

The bottom half is where the living room, with an incorporated dining area, and open kitchen are. The living area is minimally furnished with a big-screen TV, a light wood coffee table and a huge, tan, suede, three-seater couch. Two lazy boy recliners, in the same material and color, are on each end of the couch, at a slight angle. Behind the couch is the dining area.

The kitchen is just as simple with linoleum flooring, tan-and-brown speckled Formica countertops and generic wooden cabinets in the same color theme.

The dining table is tan around the edges with white tile laid in the center and about two-thirds as tall as the couch. A number of discarded items lay atop it. What looks like four matching, tan, wooden chairs sit around it. Off to the left of the table, a staircase leads up to, what I assume is, the bedroom, with a rail running along the overhang.

Flynn helps me to the couch and I sink into the fluffiest couch I've ever sat on. They'll have to lift me off of this—not that they don't already—because there's no way I'm leaving this cozy cloud. Why anyone would want to is beyond me. I have no idea how Heath leaves the house in the morning.

I take a look at the man in mind and realize he's already started prepping the food. He looks over to me and gives me a slick grin. "Fajita's okay?" At my enthusiastic nod, almost giving myself whiplash, he rumbles out a laugh. "Noted, fajitas are a good choice." With a wink, he turns back to his preparations.

Flynn takes a place next to Heath and they fall into a smooth rhythm, moving around each other like water.

I feel bad not contributing so I start to stand and say, "Can I help with anything?" Before I've even made it halfway up, they both glare at me with withering looks and I plop right back down. *Okie-dokie.* Message received.

Before I know it, I've dozed off and something warm and rough is stroking my cheek. I peek through one half-open eye at Flynn, perched on the coffee table, gently cajoling me awake with a smile.

"Come on, little spitfire. Dinner is ready, then I'll take you back to Silas."

I almost say I don't want to eat but the aroma of homemade fajitas penetrates my senses and I scrap that plan. With Flynn's help, I make it to the dining table and have a plate of heaven in front of me in quick succession. The food smells delicious and with the first bite, my taste buds sing. My jaw almost slackens with pleasure and it elicits a moan I really couldn't hold back if I tried. Which I didn't.

I'm beginning to wonder if there's anything they do poorly. With food still in my mouth, I mumble, "If this is you guys being able to *not* cook, I can't wait to see what Owen can really do." It's not good table manners but it feels like a crime if I don't tell them just how good their creation is right at this moment. It's *that* good.

They just grin. Heath replies for them both. "I'm glad it's to your liking." As he swallows another bite, he jumps right into planning and decision-making. "Now, let's go over what your focus will be while recovering. We can help in any way you're comfortable but one thing that I will suggest is meeting with one of our therapists. You can start with bi-weekly appointments at first to get into the habit of it."

Even knowing I need the counselling doesn't make the pill easier to swallow. I'm a private person—though, lately, all my dirty laundry has been aired to all the new men in my life. Now I have to open up to a complete stranger and bare my deepest, darkest insecurities? Logically, I know a therapist is a professional but again, emotions don't listen to logic.

It feels easier with the guys. Maybe it's because they've all been there from the start in one way or another—Flynn as the initial rescue, Owen as my doctor, Kyle as a friend and then Silas and Heath with their support in all its ways—or maybe it's them. Maybe it's just that they make my broken pieces feel a little less like damage and a little more like circumstance. I can show them my broken soul.

Flynn picks up on my unease. "If you want, Heath or I can do the therapy sessions. We're both licensed therapists. We don't work with clients so much anymore but we still practice. I'm sure either of us would be willing to take you on as a patient," Flynn says with a glance at Heath, who nods his agreement.

I think on that while I finish the last of my food and they let me ponder in silence.

In a way, knowing that I could see one of them would make this both easier and harder. Though they're easier to talk to, and they know a lot about my past already, some things, like the way I've processed and am still processing the trauma, are private to me. It might make the sessions less productive if I'm stepping on eggshells in fear of judgement. I also don't think it's an ethically-viable option.

"Thank you for the offer but I need to be able to talk to someone who I'm not trying to build a relationship with," I explain. Then I think about what I just said and my eyes bug out. "Not that I'm trying to have a relationship with you guys! I mean, I am, just not romantically!" I put my head in my left hand, trying to hide my mortification.

Could I be any more awkward?! Great, now I'm talking like Ross in my head.

At first, there's complete silence then chuckles sound and turn into body-shaking laughter. *Great, fan-freaking-tastic.*

"Nora," Heath says in a tone that asks me to look at him, a smile in his voice. I shake my head and he laughs a little. "*Sweetheart.*" I take a fortifying breath and lift my flushed face to look into his soulful, gray eyes. "We understand, sweetheart. Don't be embarrassed."

He grabs my dishes and stands and suddenly, he's massive, he's standing over me and my heart's beating faster, my arms are over my head, my shoulder's screaming and I yelp in pain while trying to duck away from the threat.

The hiss of a male cursing. "*Fuck.*"

You don't ever fucking do that to a man ever again, you worthless cunt.

Dishes clatter and crash to the floor, chairs scrape against concrete, including mine and I'm enfolded into an iron grip. Strong arms hold me gently, rocking me back and forth.

"Fuck, sweetheart. Fuck. I didn't know. I will never hurt you, Nora. I'd rather cut out my heart than hurt you. Fuck, come back to us, sweetheart, please."

I try to focus on my breathing. I know it's Heath holding me and I know Flynn is nearby. But my heart's still racing and my vision is still blurred.

"How'd you guys get her to come back last time?" Heath clips out to Flynn.

Instead of answering, Flynn starts singing. The melody is slow and smooth and sounds so familiar but I can't place it. It annoys me so I hold onto that feeling and try to let go of the panic. I try harder to place the song but it still eludes me and my focus shifts from the imagined threat to my surroundings.

I'm back in Heath's lap, where he's holding me on the floor. My breath is coming easier, my vision is clearer.

And I feel safe. Safer than I've ever felt since my life changed. Safer than I've ever felt before these men came into my fucked-up life. That terrifies me.

How long will they last? How long before it's too much? How long before they walk away?

Leave before they realize you're not worth staying for.

I shake the poison of that thought away but I resolve myself to fortify the walls of my heart.

I've gotten too complacent, too used to the idea of permanence. That stops now.

It took three days for them to climb inside me and try to claw everything I've built to pieces but I have to live a lifetime after them.

They'll get tired eventually. This will stop. My world will fall apart.

I have to be ready.

"You better now, sweetheart?" Heath asks and I almost fall into the rumble of his chest against my cheek but catch myself before I do.

I nod, disregarding the question as soon as it's said. I'll have panic attacks again and no one will ask if I'm feeling better. I can't get used to it.

Do what you need to do to heal. I can't heal if I'm falling apart after they leave.

"Can I use your bathroom?" I ask so I can gather myself for a few minutes in solitude.

He stands, with me still in his arms, and heads towards the stairs.

Let me down, let me down, let me down. I can walk! I scream at him in my mind but my lips stayed sealed.

Upstairs, we pass through a bedroom, painted in white.

The mattress protector is a deep shade of maroon and the dark hunter-green comforter is unmade. On the left is a mirrored room without a door. His closet, maybe? There are free weights along the wall but, other than that, the room is bare. The same concrete flooring as downstairs runs up here.

To the right is a smaller room with the door ajar, which Heath is heading towards, so it must be the bathroom. He turns on the light to a plain, white-tiled bathroom and sets me down. With an assessing glance at me, he backs out, pulling the door with him.

I take as deep a breath as I can to try and center myself and find some calm. I wish I could fall to my knees on the ground but I can't even fucking get back up without the guys. Instead, I lean against one of the walls and take slow, successive deep breaths.

When that helps a little, I look around, focusing on my surroundings, rather than my thoughts.

The bathroom is pretty standard, though it has a shower bath that looks really inviting. Other than that, there's only a toilet and a single sink. It's all very impersonal, very minimalistic.

When my heartrate has come down a little further, I turn toward the sink and lean on my left hand, examining my reflection in the mirror. My face is still a mess but what part of me isn't? I smile wryly at that thought.

At a closer glance, I notice the remaining swelling in my eyebrow and around my left eye. The split in my bottom lip isn't swollen anymore but I doubt I'll captivate a prince with the way it looks. I lean back, putting my weight on my left leg and drag my left hand through my hair. With my hair pulled back, I can still see the bruising along my hairline.

Overall, even though I look like a disaster, I hate to admit it, I've definitely had worse.

I pull my hand out of my hair and don't lean against the sink because I need to learn to stand without support. I make eye contact with myself in the mirror and try to give courage to my wilting soul. "I am strong. I *am* strong. I can get through this. With or without them, I can get through this. If I can survive J-J-Ja..." I take a deep breath and try again. "If I can survive J...J-Jason,"—*there, got it*—"I can survive this."

I'm saying all the right words but nothing's settling. Even to my own ears, it doesn't sound convincing. *God, I'm such a fucking coward!*

Fuck it. I'll put myself back together later. *Fake it till you make it.*

I wash my hands just to buy a few more seconds as I put a mask on my face. When I feel stronger or, when I *look* stronger, I open the door and step out.

Heath is just coming out of his closet at the same time. He's changed into a pair of navy-blue sweats and a plain, white shirt. His feet are bare but as he walks toward me, he slips on a pair of flip-flops, lying on the floor.

He approaches me cautiously but I harden my heart against it. "All set?"

I plaster a smile on my face and chirp, "Yep!"

Heath stares at me for a moment but doesn't say anything. He just carefully picks me up but this time, he picks me up so that my front is pressed tight to his front and I have to wrap my good arm and good leg around him for support, my right hand resting on his shoulder.

It takes the entire way down to get over the shock of his hard body against my soft, yielding one and I wonder if he saw something that made him seek out the contact. But by the time he's put me down and Flynn is helping me out the door with Heath on our heels, I put it out of my mind.

Once I'm in the front passenger seat of Flynn's car, Heath comes up and kneels on the balls of his feet. The look on his face is very serious and I don't think I'm going to like whatever it is he's about to say.

"Nora, I want you to hear me." *Well ... that isn't a promising start*. I just look at him but don't say anything. When it's clear I'm not going to respond, he sighs like I just confirmed something but I didn't. *Did I?* He continues, "I know what you're going to do and I'm going to try and save you some time and unnecessary distress. Don't. We won't let you. I told you that already. You can try and push us away but, in the end, it won't work. Not like this. If, no, *when* you're in a different frame of mind and you still decide you don't want to be a part of our family, that's a different story. Right now, that's not going to happen."

He stands and gently closes my door but doesn't move back right away, not before he shares a look with Flynn over the car. But I'm too caught up in my head to care much about their silent conversations.

Flynn gets in as Heath turns and moves back into his loft without looking back.

Flynn starts the car and pulls out without a word. There are some other cars on the road but nothing that makes traffic too heavy. I lean my head on the window and stare off into space. I start to formulate a plan in my head to create distance from all the guys.

He pulls into Silas's drive just as I'm finalizing the details I plan to put into motion. Flynn turns the engine off and just sits there for a beat.

With a deep breath, he turns in his seat to look at me. With a hand on my jaw, he turns my face toward his so I have to look at him. His eyes—I almost break and say, *fuck it, I'll deal with whatever pain comes when they walk away.*

Do what you need to do to heal. I can't heal if I'm fucking falling apart.

"Nora..."

I almost burst into tears at that. Did he lose the 'Spitfire' because I've lost *my* fire?

Leave before they realize you're not worth staying for.

"Nora ... Heath and Silas are going to be pissed at what you're about to do. Owen, Kyle, and me? We'll get it. Not because we don't care as much as the other two, but because our pasts aren't as fucked up as theirs and we have a little more patience for this kind of stuff. But Heath and Silas..." He shakes his head. "I know Heath told you not to pull away. Silas will too.

"But this is me telling you to do what you need to do to heal. We are here for you and this is part of the process. Do you hear me? We are *still* here for you. Don't you dare try and tell yourself that we aren't. Because nothing is going to piss me off but I promise you, that *will*."

Then he opens his door and steps out, coming around to my side as I sit in shock.

Fuck. Way to knock the wind out of my sails. I fight the tears back and Flynn just stands waiting so patiently, that I just want to fall apart in his arms but I can't.

Finally, I look up at him and immediately wish I hadn't. The hurt I see in his eyes, it's soul-crushing. He shouldn't have that hurt in his eyes. Why is it there? Is it for me? For himself? No, he said this would hurt Heath and Silas. Of course, he's hurting for them. They're family. Brothers by everything but blood.

But doesn't he know it's better this way? *Short-term pain, long-term benefit.*

Without saying anything, he holds his hand out to me and I take it and maybe it's me but I've never fit into like I do right now. His big, strong, calloused hands and my small, soft hands, they balance each other so well. They belong together.

I shake that thought from my mind.

Helping me from the car, Flynn keeps my hand in his as we head up Silas's walkway. Digging his keys from his pocket, his other hand goes to the small of my back and he guides me through the open door.

"Silas!" Flynn shouts into the quiet of the house. "I'm here with Nora!" There's no answer and I give Flynn a questioning look. Is Silas even here? "Sit on the couch. I'll go find him."

He lets me make the short distance on my own, which I'm grateful for. I'm just lowering myself down as he steps out of the door. I guess that's the logical place to look for a mechanic.

I rest my head on the back of the couch and close my eyes, steeling myself for what I'm about to do.

A door opens down the hall and Silas's voice carries. At first, my eyes are burning at the thought that I might never hear that voice again and then, it's for a different reason altogether.

"I don't give a fuck," he hisses, presumably into his phone. "I want her gone." Pause. "She doesn't belong with us, you know that. She's just trying to use us for what we give her access to." Pause. "Good, I better not see that parasitic cunt again." Another pause, I hold my breath, wondering what else he'll say to break my heart. "Yeah, Flynn should be here with her any minute. I gotta piss before they get here. Talk to ya later, brother." He ends his call and slips into the bathroom.

Flynn should be here with her any minute.

If my heart hadn't already shattered, that would have done it. It's all the confirmation I need that I'm the parasitic cunt.

I can't believe I was stupid enough to think they'd just accept me. Of course, they think I'm using them. I have nothing to offer them when they have so much to offer me.

I'm just a girl they took pity on and now that they realize how deep my issues go, they want to untangle themselves for me but I know they won't. They're too fucking noble for that.

It's okay. This makes things easier. They've already realized I'm not worth staying for.

So all I have to do now is leave.

Flynn comes back in from the garage. "He wasn't out there. He's probably in his home office or something. I'll check."

"Actually," I say, stopping him before he can disappear again. "Can you help me to a spare bathroom? He's in the one down the hall and I really have to go." I need to skip out before Silas realizes I heard every word.

Flynn looks at me with concern.

"You have to go again? Maybe we should have Owen check to make sure you don't have a UTI."

Shit! Quick, think of something, Nora!

"I just want to splash some water on my face. I'm feeling a bit feverish." Flynn's face morphs into one of a different type of concern. *Fuck!* That didn't work how I wanted.

Flynn doesn't ask any more questions. Well, guess it did work then. "Yeah, there's another just off the kitchen. I'll help you."

Flynn scoops me up from the couch and carries me to the other side of the kitchen, close to the garage, where there's a small half-bathroom.

He sets me down just outside the door and I give him a strained smile. "Thanks. I've got it from here."

I step in and close the door and immediately collapse onto the toilet lid, breathing through my nose.

I have to breathe deeper than the pain but it's so fucking deep.

How did this happen so quickly? For fuck's sake, it's only been a couple days.

I fight back the tears and chalk it off as a great accomplishment that not one drop of water made it out because I need some positivity in my life right now.

As I stand to splash some water on my face and wash my hands, I look at my reflection. *Shit.* My eyes look dead. There's no way they won't know something is wrong, not with how observant they all seem to be. Maybe I can write it off as fatigue?

With the whispered reassurance that these are the last few moments I'll have to endure this, I head out into the hallway with no Flynn.

There's an unexplainable ache in my chest as I limp my way to the kitchen. Silas is standing at the counter with a glass of ice water in his hand, and no hint of irritation when his eyes land on me. Flynn is opposite him, leaning on the island.

"Okay, do you want to relax on the couch or head to bed and rest there?" Silas asks.

I steel myself. "Actually, I'd like to go home ... like *my* home. I'm feeling a bit overwhelmed right now and I need something familiar. Along with time to get my thoughts in order." I can't look at Flynn as I make my excuses. I'm sure he knows what I'm doing.

But he already told me to do what I needed, so...

Silas stiffens up and his eyes narrow, scanning my every feature. What he's looking for, I have no clue. At least, that's what I tell myself.

"I don't think that's a good—"

Flynn cuts him off. "I'll take you, Nora." He gives Silas a look filled with a thousand words. Those damn looks are going to drive me insane—it's a good thing I won't have to endure them any longer. Silas's jaw clenches but he stays silent.

With an outstretched hand, Flynn approaches me slowly and when I take it, he leads me out of the front door. I don't bother to give any farewells to Silas, since he's the one who wants me gone so bad.

But his face when I look in through the window—it isn't in keeping with what I heard.

I try to reconcile that expression with his hard words and can't make them fit. Why did he look like his world has shattered? He's getting what he wanted, right?

Flynn helps me into the car and, other than me telling him my address, the ride is silent. I'm lost in thought of how I'm going to cut them off permanently because I'm under no delusions that I've seen the last of any of them.

We pull up to my crappy studio apartment and Flynn puts the car in park. He turns to me like last time and I can see the sadness in his eyes but I don't let myself process it. It exists and it's there but I shove it in my box of shit to deal with later. I'll get to the box before I die, I think.

I move to open my door but he stops me with a hand on my arm. When he speaks, his voice is heavy with a melancholy that doesn't fit with his exuberant personality. "I know you have to do this but don't be so stubborn that you don't ask for help from us when you really need it, Spitfire."

Spitfire. I don't let my heart lift at that.

I just nod my head and pull the door handle but Flynn pulls me to a stop. He gets out to help me from my side.

I give him a tight smile and wait for him to take my arm and lead me to my door. We stop and he gets my keys from his pocket and unlocks the door. He leads me in but instead of letting me in further, he guides me to the side and says, "Wait right here, I'm going to check everything out."

His concern stabs me right in my already-fracturing heart. *Shove that shit down.* I wait for him to check the small apartment. All he has to check is the bathroom and the few windows I have.

I try to not think about what he sees in my tiny apartment. It's not the best but it's mine and I've done what I can to make it feel like home. The wall behind my bed is filled with books of all kinds, all of them close to my heart. Some are romances, some are academic textbooks and there's a little bit of everything in between.

The bed itself is a queen but I don't need anything bigger. My bedding is gray and teal with white pillowcases. Beside the bed is a decorative square basket that I have turned on its side so it can double as a nightstand and still provide some storage for my clothes. Under my bed are flat, long rectangular totes for more storage with no wardrobe or closet. There's not enough space to justify it.

In the living area—because it can't be called a room— is a love seat couch that I got from Goodwill for seventy-five bucks. It was ratty and had ducks all over it so I gave it a surface clean and covered it with a charcoal-gray couch cover. The coffee table came from the same place but I redid it myself and now, it looks like it has life in it again with its deep cherry wood stain.

That's all I have for furniture in here. It's simple, not just because I don't have room for more, but also because I don't like a lot of clutter. It ratchets up my anxiety. My mind is usually so cluttered that if my living space was too, I wouldn't be able to concentrate on living.

Flynn tosses my keys and wallet on the coffee table then stops next to me. I don't let the pleading look in his eyes do anything to me. At least, I don't let him see how hard I'm fighting to keep my emotions in check. I could get lost in those if this doesn't end here.

When no response comes from me, he looks defeated but says, "You're good. You have all our numbers. Use them." He almost stops there but continues, "Don't let pride or fear stop you. I get that you're trying to keep us away as a misguided way to protect yourself. I get you have to go through this part to get to the next, but that doesn't mean this is easy for us, knowing you're suffering." He sighs and puts his hands on my shoulders, looking me dead in my dead eyes. "We won't bug you, Nora. You'll have to come back to us." Then he kisses my hair and he's gone before I can figure out how I feel about what he just said.

Shit, damn and fuck. He thinks he knows me but he has no clue. I'm not doing this for me. I'm doing it for them.

Lie.

Shut up, I tell myself.

Fuck, I think I've lost my marbles.

I turn my back to the door after I make sure the locks are engaged and close my eyes against the tears that want to be free. Rubbing my hand against my chest, I wonder why this hurts so damn much.

Unfortunately, my heart doesn't answer—or maybe it does and I can't hear anything anymore, not even myself.

I grab some painkillers from the medicine cabinet in the bathroom before moving to my bed so I can get lost in the oblivion that only sleep brings. My ribs are starting to throb so

I pop half a pill before I remove my leg brace. I leave my arm sling on.

Lying on my back and staring at the blank ceiling, I wait for sleep to claim me. It doesn't take long but it also doesn't last long or bring me any answers to the million questions tumbling through my head.

My last thought is what Heath said: 'You can try and push us away but, in the end, it won't work...'

Well, that was a fucking lie, wasn't it?

∞∞∞∞

I wake up with a scream in my raw throat. My pulse is pounding and I'm drenched in sweat. I can't catch my breath and it's making my ribs burn. The nightmare tries to drag me back down into the oblivion I thought would bring peace but I fight it.

Fuck, fuck, fuck. I'm not on my bed. I'm on the cold fucking floor, with his body pressing into mine and my face rubbing against the ground. I can't breathe. The pressure is building, building, building, the darkness closing in further.

I fist the ground beneath my hands, seeking something to pull me to the present, and come away with the familiar touch of my comforter. I take a deep breath. I'm not in his room. I'm in mine. I'm not in his bed. I'm in mine.

I fumble my way out of bed but I still can't see so I fall to the ground. My knee knocks on the hard floor and sings an ugly tune. My breath hisses out as tears flood down my cheeks. I cry out and try to hoist myself up from the fucking floor. It's a struggle and I strain my arm in the process.

Standing up is half the battle but when I manage, my steps are wobbly but I get it in the end. I hold onto the wall and stumble into the bathroom, feeling desperately and blindly for the light switch on the bathroom wall. Light floods from the ceiling and I have to shield my eyes for a moment but I'm finally free from the trickling tendrils that had a hold of me.

I grab the cup from the sink that I use to rinse my mouth when brushing my teeth and turn the faucet on as cold as it'll go. When it's halfway full, I gulp down the water and then shove it back under the tap, this time waiting for it to fill all the way. I turn off the water and drink this round much more slowly than the last.

Leaning against the door jamb, I wait for my breaths to even out and slow to a normal rate. It takes much longer than it should. I look at the clock above the toilet and see it's just after two in the damn morning. Guess I'm back to not sleeping through the night.

I feel fucking gross so I turn the shower on, strip down and leave my clothes and arm sling on the floor to deal with later. I stand under the hot spray until it runs cold. I just let the water run over my body because who has the strength to soap up? Not me.

Turning off the water, I swipe the shower curtain back and grab my towel from the towel rack. It's old and threadbare but it gets the job done. Once, it was a deep gray but now it's faded to a dingy, dirty water gray.

I dry as best I can and hobble out to the couch, leaving the light on in the bathroom until I can get a nightlight for in there. I never want to fucking deal with the dark alone again. I also don't want to deal with the wet bedding tonight so I say fuck it, grab the blanket from the end of the couch and lay down on the couch, my head on the armrest, the blanket draped haphazardly over me.

I close my eyes and try to shut off. I don't care that I'm still naked and my hair's soaking through the blanket and that I'm shivering. Future Nora can deal with that shit. This one's done.

It takes hours and the sun is just starting to brighten the sky before I finally, *finally*, nod off.

∞∞∞∞

I roll over and peel my eyes open. It feels like I just walked through a sandstorm without blinking once. My neck hurts from having it at such a high angle through half the night.

I sit up and grab my arm and leg brace, thankful that I had enough fore thought to bring them out here, putting the one on my leg first.

My stomach growls and I stand, wrapping the damp blanket around me and head over to the kitchen. *Future Nora's dealing with that and she's not enjoying it.* I snicker without humor.

Opening the fridge, I pull out the carton of eggs and scramble them up. I inspect the small contained of pre-cut vegetables that have been sitting in the fridge since before all this shit. Taking off the lid, I inspect them and when they pass the cursory glance, I give them a little sniff and throw them in the pan with the eggs. *If they've gone bad, future Nora can deal with that shit … emphasis on the 'shit.'* I snicker at the inside joke.

Moving back to the fridge, I grab the cheese and try to shred some for my eggs but since only one hand is in working condition, I discard that plan because I'm more likely to shred my hand than the cheese. I throw the grater in the sink and grab a fork, eating right from the pan once they're done. I burn my mouth as I eat but I don't really care. I'm eating on autopilot because I need it for my injured body, not because I fucking want it.

Out of nowhere, flashes of my most recent attack barrage my mind, flashing to the beat of imagined gunshots. The pan drops from my hand onto the stove and the remaining food flies out, making a huge mess. I can't seem to stop the images that race across my mind. Frozen in the middle of a panic attack, I can only endure it because who's going to sing to me now?

Helpless, I wait for it to pass. Once my mind clears, I feel empty but I don't care.

Actually, I prefer it. I know this place. Like Heath, I'm most confident in my territory. This is my territory. His is filled with barbells and yoga mats and mine's home to demons. But I know these demons. I know this despair and honestly, I'm almost numb to it now. Or I will be when I drive away the memory of caring men with promises of family falling from their lips.

It's the hope that brings me to my knees because it will fail and it fails, as it always does, and then how will I survive? Falling from the peak hurts more.

No. I'd rather fall into oblivion.

∞∞∞

I blinked and three days had passed.

I don't remember how they passed. I think I ate but I'm not sure. I'm certain I threw up in the toilet. Was that only once? The memory is hazy.

I touch my hair. Is that grease or is it wet from a shower? I run my hands over it. It's clumped in places and sticking out at others.

I look down at my hands and I notice they've paled. Were they always this bony?

My shirt is wrinkled and my pants are worse and I probably smell something awful. I wonder if the bruises have faded but I don't know because why the fuck would I look in the mirror? I'm not going anywhere.

I have to give it to the guys though. They've stayed true to their word. I haven't gotten any texts or calls and the notification bar on my phone is perfectly empty.

Why does that make me so sad?

I don't want to know or try and figure it out. I have to shove them all into my vault of things to avoid. The box was getting too small to hold the growing list so I upgraded.

Deep in my own depression, I'm jolted out with a knock on my door. I wander over to the door and open it without checking the peephole.

Owen stands in front of me with Kyle just behind him. The guys get a good, hard look at me and I must look a sight because the shutters fall down on their faces.

Owen curses under his breath and Kyle takes his phone out and makes a call, scooping up some envelopes on my doormat. When did those get there?

Owen lifts me up and settles me on the couch. What are they doing?

Owen gets my braces and puts them on me as Kyle moves around the room, doing God only-knows-what. I can hear him growling into the phone and I try to focus on his words but I'm so out of it. I drift off into my head, trying to understand why they're here. *Why* are they here?

They said they wouldn't come.

"Nora!" Owen says, his hands on my shoulders. I zone back in on him to him shaking me. Oops, guess he's been trying to get my attention for a bit.

I blink to clear my head and try to focus. He's so handsome. Why did I not want them to help me? His lips are moving but I can't understand what he's saying.

My vision starts to fade around the edges and my head feels dizzy.

Owen moves towards me quickly but I don't care enough to panic. The blackness is finally, *finally*, wrapping me in its comforting arms once again and this time, I know the nightmares won't come with it and numbed elation settles inside me.

I'm too fucking tired for this shit.

11 Hard Truths

I'm lying on the softest cloud I've ever felt. That's the first thing my brain registers.

The next is the pinch in my left arm.

My eyes try to open but only end up fluttering and then, fall closed. I drift back down into unconsciousness.

∞∞∞

When I float back up again, my mind is clearer. I'm still on the soft cloud but there's a wet washcloth running down my arm. It feels good, rough but refreshing.

I let those feelings wash over me for just a bit longer because I know that when I open my eyes, reality is going to crash like a tsunami trying to drown me. I'm just not ready to deal with it on my own again yet.

Slowly, it registers that I'm not in my bed and I certainly can't be alone if someone is wiping my arm down.

I force my eyes open and see Sara next to me with her big belly. She dips a washcloth into a bowl of water and turns back toward me.

When she sees my eyes open, she freezes for a beat. Once she recovers, she gives me a sad smile. "I'm going to get one of the guys, I'll be right back." That's all she says before she stands awkwardly, like all heavily pregnant women do, and slips out the bedroom door.

I'm in Kyle's room. Great, how did this happen? The last thing I remember is Owen and Kyle at my door. After that things got fuzzy, really quickly.

I look toward the pinch I felt in my arm and see an IV hooked up to me. That can't be good, can it? *Stupid question.* I sigh inwardly and wait for Sara to return. It's not long and, just my luck, she brought Kyle with her.

His gray t-shirt is wrinkled over a pair of dark gray sweatpants that have been DIY cut off at the knee. His feet are bare. All the hair on his head looks wild, like he's been pulling at it for hours.

But that's not what pulls me short. It's the anger on his face. He's *furious* and it looks like he's barely keeping it in control.

I avert my gaze from him because I can't stand to look at him right now. Instead, I watch Sara as she dips the washcloth in the bowl with my eyes tracking her until she leaves the bedroom altogether.

Fuck. There goes my break from reality.

Kyle just stands by the door with his arms crossed over his chest, making his pectorals bunch up and his biceps bulge. When I glance at his face, it's thunderous, and I flinch away from the anger there. My eyes fall in shame. *Fuck.*

"Yeah, I'd flinch too if I were your position." Kyle pushes out in a scary, deep voice that has the hairs on the back of my neck standing up. *Fuuuck.* "Owen will be here in a few minutes. He's just finishing up a call outside. He'll check you out, then we'll go from there."

It's hiding behind the anger but I can hear the emotion leaking into his words. Whatever the reason is for it, I don't want to know. I'm already seconds from falling apart and this might just break me.

I just stare at him and search for something, anything, to say. Everything sounds like shit in my head, so it'll taste like shit on my tongue, so I keep my mouth shut.

He just continues to look at me with his face unreadable, other than that barely-controlled rage.

After what seems like eons, Owen comes in. He's in the shirt he was wearing that first day at the hospital, the same slacks and shoes and I wonder how it is that we came back full circle. But he looks good. His hair is perfect, as always, and swept from his face. He doesn't look angry.

I see and ignore the dark circles under his eyes because I don't know why they're there and don't want to know.

You fucking know.

Shut up, brain, I tell myself.

Fuck, I really have lost my marbles.

"Nora, do you mind if I take some vitals and check over your injuries?" There's no hint of anything other than professionalism in his voice.

I nod my consent and he moves to my right side, where there's no IV in my arm. He grabs some latex gloves and snaps them on.

Kyle still hasn't moved a muscle, just standing to the left of the bedroom door, watching with those eyes that see everything and that anger on his face. It's unnerving and has me on edge.

Owen takes my blood pressure and listens to my heart and lungs. Then, he examines my head and shines a light in my eyes, watching for pupil response.

He puts the penlight to the side with the rest of the equipment. "Okay, Nora, I need to take a look at your shoulder, ribs, and knee. I'll need Kyle to help maneuver you, is that okay?"

I can't seem to find my voice. He's being so clinical and impersonal. Even when we were at the hospital, he was open and easy-going. And Kyle still hasn't fucking moved from his spot by the door!

It's starting to get under my skin and has me toeing the line on the edge of my control but I nod because *fuck*, I know I'm responsible for this.

Both men move instantly, approaching me with a slowness that I know is intended for me, to keep me from a looming panic attack. It helps but my nerves are already on the fritz and they're coming closer and closer. I tip over that edge.

Kyle notices and immediately halts his movements. "Owen, stop," he growls. "She's starting to panic." Owen freezes too and they both take a big step back.

Fuck, I can't do anything right. I throw my head back against the headboard and close my eyes.

Then Kyle starts to sing.

It's a slow, sad song that speaks of loss and breathlessness. It takes me a moment to place it as *Lung* by Vancouver Sleep Clinic. It sounds like shit, because Kyle really can't carry a tune, but the words penetrate my panic and break through. I open my eyes and find beautiful, chocolate-brown warmth staring back at me. I borrow from that comfort and cling to that warmth, urging it into my limbs.

He moves towards me again and I get a flash but he sees it immediately and steps back, carrying on the song. He stands there for a bit and my attention is solely on him. Nothing else exists.

Then he gets down on his hands and knees and crawls towards me. This time, I don't have any flashes and no seeds of panic take root.

Owen stands still, close but just out of touching distance, as Kyle climbs on the bed and slowly kneels next to me. He moves on to *It's Alright* by Fractures. It's quiet but I get lost in his awful voice and soon, I'm wrapped up in Kyle and all I can smell is the burnt metal scent that reminds me of home. That, with his God-awful singing, blocks out the rest of the noise in my head.

I don't know how it happened but when I focus back in on myself, I'm flat on my back with Kyle next to me, his head propped up on his bent elbow, resting on his hand.

"Okay, gorgeous," Owen says, a caution in his voice, "I'm going to lift your shirt and check your ribs now." As he feels his way along my ribs, the pressure of his featherlight touch falls on a particularly tender spot and I groan in pain. "Just breathe, gorgeous. I'm almost done." Somehow, he says it and my body instantly obeys.

Damn. How did he do that?

Once he's done at my ribs, Kyle helps to turn me on my good side and Owen seamlessly moves to my shoulder. They're both so gentle that tears spring to my eyes and start to leak out before I knew they were going to come.

"Are you okay, Nora honey? Are we hurting you?" The concern in Kyle's voice is so genuine that it only makes my tears come faster. My breathing increases and *that* makes my ribs hurt, but I don't feel any pain from what they're doing.

"No." I choke out, my voice cracking, "You're not hurting me." I seal my lips tight, trying to fight off the tears and Kyle gets this soft look in his eyes that nearly undoes all my hard work.

"It's okay, Nora honey," he coaxes in a gentle voice, his finger tracing along my jawline, "You don't have to be strong all the time. Let them go. You'll feel so much better after you do."

I only fight the hurt, fear and pain for another moment before I forget why I was fighting at all and just let go.

There's something so cathartic in letting someone comfort you. I haven't had this in so long. Not since my mom passed away years ago.

Kyle holds me while I weep against him. And I realize that I'm not just crying for today or yesterday or the past week. I'm crying for my entire life.

I weep for the loss of my mom, for what Jason did to me. I weep for my old "friends" leaving me to deal with that shit on my own. For my life being so lonely. I weep for the recent violence done against me and then when I'm all cried out from all that shit, I sob because I want these men in my life so fucking bad, but I'm scared shitless to let them in.

So, in short, it takes a long fucking time for me to stem the flow of tears. By the time I do, it's dusk and my body is achy and stiff.

My eyes feel puffy and I'm sure I look like a good mess.

Kyle keeps his arms wrapped around me, holding me securely in his safety. They've all made me feel safe in their own way and I need that so desperately right now. I felt the same safety in Heath's arms and then I'm crying again because, fuck, Flynn said I would hurt Heath if I left and I left anyway.

I decide, then and there, that I'm willing to go through any pain that may come but I'm going to let them in, even just a little. I can only let them in so far though because, otherwise, when they leave, it'll destroy me.

And they will leave but the goal has changed to short-term comfort in exchange for long-term pain, I suppose. I don't want to hurt them anymore and I can't find the comfort they offer anywhere else. So, fuck it.

I'll deal with it when it comes.

"Feel better now?" Kyle rumbles and I feel it against my face which is against his chest.

I take a slow breath in as deeply as I can before my ribs twinge, then, slowly, let it out, letting go of the last vestiges of my worry and helplessness, at least for now.

"Actually, yeah," I whisper into his chest. "Thank you, Kyle."

He gives me a gentle squeeze and slides out from under me without jostling me. Really, how do these guys move me so effortlessly? Internally, I smile because I've missed being amazed by the fluidity of their movements.

Kyle stops near the door, careful not to stand by the bed and over me. "I'm going to get you some water and have Owen come back in here to finish looking you over." He walks out of the bedroom door, leaving it cracked, and I wonder when Owen left. I was so consumed by the emotions that I don't remember him leaving.

I try to gather my wits and compose myself. I'm not sure how well I do but I do feel so much better now. Who knew letting go would be so freeing?

I try and stretch my limbs, stiff from the tension. That just means that it feels oh-so-good as I stretch that I let out a moan.

Kyle and Owen both enter the room as I do.

"Hey, gorgeous. How are you feeling now? Any better?"

I give him a small smile. It's not necessarily a happy one but it's not sad either. "Yes, better."

He gives me an assessing look and moves toward me, while Kyle sits back down on the bed. "Okay, ready to have me finish looking you over?"

"Yep," I chirp.

A lopsided grin appears on his face. He starts at the top, checking my face where the bruising is. The swelling has gone down and my face doesn't feel nearly as tight anymore.

"Much better," he says, talking mostly to himself. "Though your eyes are a bit puffy but I suppose that's from your recent crying session."

"Good to know I'm not the only crazy one that talks to myself around here." I slap my hand over my mouth and my eyes bug out in embarrassment.

Oh, shit. I just said that out loud.

Kyle chuckles from the end of the bed and Owen gets this huge dazzling smile on his face. It's so bright, I'm left to wonder how the sun left the solar system and found a place on his face.

"I'm glad you're in a more uplifting mood," Owen coos. The words are sweet but I don't want to remember the worst depression I've ever been through just yet, so the ensuing silence is awkward. After an uncomfortable pause, he tries to redirect the focus. "Let's try and focus on your body for the moment, shall we?" He turns to Kyle. "Kyle, can you help me so I can get a look at her shoulder again? I didn't get to really look at it before."

Kyle stands up and I flinch back from both of them. Again, they freeze and Kyle steps back.

"Nor?" Kyle questions me.

"I don't know why I do that. I'm sorry—"

"Don't," Owen holds up a hand, stopping me. "Never apologize to anyone for honest reactions like that. Right now, you feel how you feel and you have just suffered a serious trauma. Don't hide from us. We can deal with it. In fact, I'd rather we did so we can help you move past them."

I let a breath out. "Okay."

"Kyle, down on the ground like last time, please." Owen isn't really asking, even if he phrased it like a request.

Surprisingly, Kyle does as he's told and falls to his hands and knees.

"You don't have to do that!" I panic. This cannot be happening. I mean, what the hell?! He's a grown-ass man and he's crawling on the ground, just so I don't freak the fuck out! So, naturally, I almost choke on my tongue.

"Nora, if this is what you need, I'll gladly do it." Kyle reassures me as he crawls.

I'm not sure if I should swoon or scream or both but *come on!* How *hot* is this? Can these guys get any sweeter?

I look to Owen for help, for all the good that does me. He's the one that told Kyle to do it and right now, he just has this shit-eating grin on his perfect fucking face with his eyes dancing with amusement. He just shrugs. *Shrugs.*

Jerk.

Kyle makes it to the bed and kneels on the floor with the top half of his body resting on the bed. He's got a sexy smirk on his face that says so many things and I don't know where to start with him.

These guys...

I can't hold my smile in any longer and the giggle comes unbidden with it. For fuck's sake, I've been reduced to a giggling teenager. *Goodness, get a hold of yourself, Molano,* I mentally chastise myself.

The bedroom door slams open and my giggles cut short at the sight of the three hulking figures standing just out of the light so I can't see any details. I shrink back at the sight as both Owen and Kyle look toward the door, completely at ease.

Through the darkness, Silas emerges, rolling his eyes, following by a scowling Heath and a very concerned-looking Flynn. The last two looks I can understand but Silas's is confusing, to say the least.

Until I remember the conversation I overheard him having on the phone.

Yep, he's done with my shit already. I wonder what this means for me working for him? Probably not good things. I sigh and avoid his gaze.

Kyle settles next to me on the bed, putting his arm behind my back and supporting me against him. Owen sits on the edge of the bed, on my other side. Silas takes a spot along the wall across from the bed, crossing his massive arms across his body and making them bulge. His dark, black shirt stretches across his wide chest and he kicks up a black-booted foot along the wall. Out of all the men, he's the furthest one away and that speaks volumes to me.

Heath and Flynn both move toward the bed simultaneously and I tense up. Kyle feels it and barks out an order, "Stop!"

The two do and look at Kyle, Heath with steel in his gray eyes and Flynn with confusion.

"Nora is having a bit of trouble right now, being approached," Kyle explains. "So, until she can overcome her panic in that situation, we all need to get down on our hands and knees to move close to her."

Ohhh, shit! A-fucking-gain! They are not going to go for this.

A fire lights in Heath's gray eyes and his fists clench at his sides, but regardless he drops to his knees, his massive

219

shoulders following. It's the most humbling thing I've seen to date and my mouth falls open. I stare in shock as he crawls to the end of the bed. He straightens at the waist, his knees still on the ground.

Once he comes to a standstill, Flynn waits until I turn my attention to him and looks me dead in the eyes, before he melts to his knees. He keeps eye contact with me the entire time, challenging me with his gaze. I don't know what that look means; I just know that it's incredibly empowering. It makes me feel like I won something and that something is his submission, only for me. I'm reminded of the triad in the painting from the art gallery.

I feel the spark of a fire light inside me as Flynn stalks like a panther on his hands and knees, his eyes never breaking contact. He crawls up the bed and lays along the end, cupping my feet in his warm hands and rubbing them. That knowing smirk says that even though I feel like I've won something, he's won something too.

I decide to examine it later and relax more into Kyle's side. Owen slides further up the bed, stopping with his back against the headboard next to me, his long leg pressed along mine, sitting hip-to-hip. I'm sure the rest of his body would be pressed to me too if I wasn't leaning into Kyle.

I chance a glance at Silas's face and see a mask of nothing. Yeah, I bet he's only here because the others are. A pain pierces my chest and hurts so deeply that if I wasn't trying so hard to keep it from showing, I'd be in a ball right now.

Where's the man who teased me about clinging like a monkey to him as we cuddled in sleep? *Oh, yeah, he got lost behind the one who thinks I'm a parasitic cunt.*

When everyone is settled, Owen speaks up for the first time since everyone arrived. "Okay, so now that we all know about this new development with Nora, I think we should touch on a few other important topics."

"You mean like her trying to starve herself or not fucking asking one of us for help when she goddamn needed it?" Silas's voice slithers out, chilling my skin from across the room. He couldn't be further away if he was across the Atlantic.

"Geez, King, way to be sensitive," Flynn admonishes him.

The remark has no effect on Silas. He still has that cold look in his icy eyes. They definitely go with his mood right now.

"She doesn't need me to coddle her," he snaps. "You're doing it enough for all of us."

Ouch. He really knows how to hit where it'll hurt the most.

Kyle's body tightens next to me and Flynn's jaw goes hard as he glares at Silas. Owen and Heath don't seem to have a reaction or, if they do, they're very good at masking them.

"Silas, cut the shit." Kyle grinds out through his clenched teeth. His body is coiled so tight, he might snap like an elastic band if I move. How he keeps his touch so light on me when he's so full of tension is beyond me to understand.

"No, she needs to know that we see her, that her actions affect others. You can sugarcoat shit all you want, Walker, but it still tastes like shit to me. It may make me a dick but I won't lie to her." He addresses me, "I'll always give it to you straight, doll."

Though the words are harsh, maybe I need a little bit more of that honesty. If I had gotten it earlier, I might not have fallen into such a deep place while I was alone in my apartment.

I know the others want to make things as easy as possible and I respect them for it but I also need some of Silas's brutal honesty. I'm thankful that he's willing to be the dick and give me the hard truths, even when he knows they'll hurt. It's almost like he trusts me to be strong enough to handle them and that's the most empowering thing that he can do for me.

I look at him anew and wonder, not for the first time, about the conversation I overheard. Maybe my opinion of him wasn't accurate. Other than that one conversation, every evidence points to the contrary. But if he wasn't talking about me, who else could he have been talking about? They haven't mentioned any other women in their lives.

But, then again, I haven't known them for long at all, so it's kind of conceited of me to assume he was talking about me. They have other family, other friends, a past.

Was I just hearing what I wanted to hear to justify pulling further away?

"You can tell her things without being a dick, you know," Heath drawls. Silas just rolls his eyes but doesn't otherwise respond. Heath turns to me. "But he is right, sweetheart. We can't just sweep those things under the rug. We need to know the reasons why this happened so we can help you make sure it doesn't happen again. Deal?" The same thing Silas said, just in a much gentler way.

It's nice knowing that he's also willing to give me the hard truths, while still making an effort to watch how they make me feel.

"Regardless of how we go about it, the point is we need to address them," Owen says, putting a stop to the back-and-forth. "Nora, would you like to talk about what happened when you were alone at your apartment?"

He frames the question so gently that I do share.

I tell them about the overwhelming fear that suffocated me, about how, after leaning on them for such a short amount of time, I couldn't deal with everything on my own anymore. I tell them that, in my despair, the old feelings from my past resurfaced and I was no longer able to separate any of it from the present.

For the most part, they just listen, with occasional questions but that's it. They let me get it all out and when I'm done, I feel oddly cleaner. Not spotless but like the grime that was weighing me down has been washed away and only the debris remains. Like my skin isn't so irritated from it all.

Everyone is silent for several minutes after, until Flynn asks if anyone is thirsty. Heath, Kyle, and I all give some form of an answer in the affirmative and Flynn leaves to get us some water. When he comes back, he stops at the door and tosses a bottle to each of us, keeping one for himself. Then, he lowers himself back to the floor and I want to smack my head against the wall and groan.

By the time he's back in his spot, my cheeks are aflame. They shouldn't have to crawl for anyone, especially not me.

"You guys don't have to do that, really," I start, then rush on when Owen opens his mouth to speak, "It makes me feel uncomfortable for all of you and me. You shouldn't have to crawl for anyone. You're all better than that." That was a lame finish.

They all exchange those looks that speak to each other without saying a word and I have a feeling it's not going to go in my favor. None of them say a word against me though so I allow myself to be hopeful, even though I know I'm deluding myself.

"Alright," Owen says. "So Nora is going to stay with one of us. We won't leave her alone for the time being. That means someone is always at the same location as she is, until she can overcome her fears." All the guys nod in agreement, including Silas, then Owen turns to me. "What that means for you is that we won't be up your ass but you can't stay by yourself. We will take you anywhere you need to go, because I don't want you driving just yet. It's also a good idea for you to go to *Flex* and start the recovery program there. That means talk therapy and physical therapy."

He's right. I know I need to go. Though it's hard for me to admit that I need help, I just have to swallow my pride and do it, if I want to get better.

I look to each man in turn and make my decision. "Okay, I'll go on one condition ... None of you can be my therapist and you don't get to have any access to my sessions. I'll share with you in my own time. Deal?"

"Deal," they chorus in unison.

"Now, let's talk about all the bullshit in your head," Silas, ever-tactful, says. Heath rolls his eyes at Silas's bluntness.

"Fine but can we get something to eat while we do? I'm starving," I say. All the guys glare at me. "What did I say?" I ask, horrified.

"Don't make jokes about you starving for a while, sweetheart," Heath responds.

"You have to have lost at least ten pounds in three days, Nora. Did you eat at all?" Kyle prods.

"Yes, but I couldn't stomach much because of the anxiety," I admit shamefully.

I know I should've taken better care of myself. I just couldn't get past the panic and fear that consumed me.

"There's nothing we can do about the past but from now on, you'll be on a strict diet to help you gain back the weight you lost and to help your body heal." Heath orders, sounding a lot like Owen.

"I'm not going to argue with you."

I have to say, there's something for owning up to your mistakes and taking the steps to correcting them. I've always believed that if you can do that, then you're an alright person in my book, and I think I'm on my way to becoming that person.

12 Wet Dogs

"Push it out!" Stan pushes me to dig deep for the last rep.

Fuck, who knew butterflies with a five-pound weight could be so damn hard? Before I got hurt, I could easily do fifteen, but with my shoulder only just healing, along with the rest of the bullshit, it's like I'm starting back at the beginning. I guess essentially, I am. None of the guys will let me overexert myself more than *they* think is safe.

I get it but sometimes it can be a bit much. Like the other day, I was moving laundry from the washer to the dryer and Kyle took over for me. I mean, it's just fucking laundry. I guess it's too taxing for me though because he made some lame-ass excuse about not wanting me to see his boxers. I've seen him in them every damn day I've stayed with him but, *sure*, he doesn't want me to see them all soft and warm from the dryer.

Fuck's sake! Now I'm imagining the view I enjoy every time I stay with him and multiply that by five because good God, these guys are a sexy sight.

Not that any of them are doing it to tempt me. *Oh no.* Heaven forbid, that line is crossed.

I can't prove it but I'm pretty sure they all came to some sort of mutual agreement that I'm romantically off-limits. Not that I'm in any position to date right now but shouldn't I have been consulted? Nope. *Men*.

Flynn doesn't even flirt like he used to! I miss it, surprisingly, that feeling of being desired. Not that they don't often have hard-ons when I'm around.

God, mornings are a favorite of mine. I always wake with one of the guys next to me; sometimes, more than one, if they end up crashing at whichever place I'm staying at that night. Which happens more than you'd think it would with five grown men.

I've lived a while and nothing compares to the feeling of waking up, safe, in a strong pair of arms, all warm and snuggly from cuddling all night.

The added hard-ons are just a bonus. Although, I'm sure that any one of them would wreck me with the heat they all seem to be packing below their belts. And some of them have some serious ink and metal happening.

Flynn's an obvious contender, with his full sleeves, but he also has a tattoo running along the side of his ribs that isn't visible unless he's shirtless. The words 'Bent but not Broken' are inked in black. It makes me wonder what the significance of it is, or if there even is any. He has a tongue piercing that he hardly ever wears.

Heath has a chest tattoo that reads 'Discouraged doesn't mean Defeated' and a wicked-looking dragon scales tattoo that wraps around his upper calf. They go along well with a nipple piercing. The day I saw the full metal and ink package—also the day I saw him shirtless for the first time and learned he was an animal whisperer—was a beautiful one. It was his day off, just him and me, and we sat on the couch in his bachelor pad as he told me all about the pets in their odd, little family.

Apparently, the rough-looking gym owner helped train all of Owen's horses and dogs, as well as training his own dogs. Owen and Flynn share a house and even though Flynn, like Kyle, doesn't have a pet, he cares for all the dogs at their house—both Owen's and Heath's.

Silas's dog, a beautiful Beauceron breed, was rescued from the animal shelter by Flynn. He called Silas, aware that Silas's dog had passed away from old age and he wanted a new one, and the second Silas got a look at Greta, that was it. He adopted her on the spot. Even though I didn't get to meet her the first time I stayed there, since she was outside, we quickly got introduced to each other and bonded. She's the sweetest thing! I can't believe her original owners gave her away. Apparently, they hadn't realized that she'd have such a dominant personality when they got her.

Surprisingly, and this is the most shocking thing, Silas doesn't have any tattoos or piercings, at least, none that I can see. With his rough exterior and often-winning personality, I would not have guessed that.

I also wouldn't have guessed that Owen would have piercings but, though he's inkless, he has at least two piercings, both in his nipples, and I suspect a third. It's below the belt though so I can't confirm it, yet. But I have my reasons for suspicion.

Kyle has a tattoo that runs along his forearm that reads, 'Shaken but not Shattered,' but no visible metal.

These guys must have some serious stuff in their pasts to be sporting these kinds of tattoos.

"Nora, focus." Stan brings me back to reality and a blush spreads across my cheeks. I duck my head in embarrassment and Stan gives me a knowing smirk. "I think someone has a certain redheaded giant on their mind."

I shoot back, "I'm taller than Sara so she's not a giant." Then, I stick my tongue out at him in a nanny-nanny-foo-foo way.

"Real mature, Molano." He smiles, shaking his head at my antics. "Get that back in your mouth before a fly lands on it."

"I wouldn't mind her sticking her tongue out, especially if she was doing it to stick it in someone else's mouth." Flynn interjects, making me jump. My mouth falls open from shock. That's the most he's flirted with me in ages!

"Flies can go in there too, Molano." Stan says, grinning at my open-mouthed gape.

I shut my mouth with a snap of my teeth and give Stan a glare that seems to just bounce off of him with no effect. I've never met a group of guys that are this unaffected by a woman's glare. "We're almost done here. You on after?" Stan asks Flynn.

"Yeah, I'm taking her to the house. It's bath night for the dogs so I need her help." Flynn flashes me a smile and a wink. I grab my towel and wipe my face, trying to hide my flaming cheeks, but I doubt I've fooled either of them.

Stan directs me. "Okay, time for a cool down, stretch, then you're free to go."

"I'll come find you when you're done." Flynn waves us away as he moves over to another member and starts talking about.

Stan and I move to the floor and he helps me stretch out my body. It's been a slow process in healing but my body, at least, is past the worst of it.

Once I'm done, I make my way to the women's locker room and grab my bag from my locker. I head to a changing room and switch out my workout clothes for some dark purply, comfy sweats and a sky-blue pullover hoodie. Then, I shove my feet into a pair of white Toms and throw my bag over my good shoulder. I redo my hair into a high, messy bun. After splashing some water on my face, I give it a good pat down. The swelling is gone but there's still a significant amount of bruising. There's not much I can do but wait for it to heal on its own.

Giving up on making any more improvements to my appearance, I give myself a last look in the mirror and swing out into the hall. Flynn is waiting to the side of the women's locker room door.

"All set, Spitfire?" Flynn slips my bag from my shoulder and onto his. I roll my eyes in exasperation. "You know, most women would think that's gallant," he says pointedly.

"Maybe I'm not a normal woman. It's sweet but it's just a bit much. I mean, I carried it in here and did an entire workout without hurting myself. It's not like I can't make it to the car without causing myself injury from just holding a damn bag."

Flynn chuckles next to me and it spikes my ire. I narrow my eyes at him but he's too busy laughing at me to pay attention. Slipping my bag back onto my shoulder, he apologizes with a smile. "You're right. I'm sorry. I wasn't trying to coddle you."

Did I just win a round?

He's still smiling and so am I. Which means I *did* just win a round. So, we're just two loons standing in the hallway, smiling at each other.

I try to break the odd situation. "Don't we have some dogs to wash?"

"Nope." Flynn pauses. "*I* have dogs to wash. You're going to mostly sit and watch. Not because I'm trying to coddle you, but because some of them get riled up at bath time."

I haven't met their dogs yet, or been to their house, so I'll have to take his word on the dogs' excitement.

Before we step out into the parking lot, I wave 'bye' to Jaz and dig my sunglasses out of my bag's side pocket, shoving them on my face.

"What is it about you in a nice pair of sunglasses that amps up your sex appeal?" Flynn fires off that bomb.

The *screech* of a record scratching sounds in my head and my brain freezes to a halt.

"What...?" I breathe out as all the air in my lungs is sucked out from shock. What just happened? That was blatant flirting, wasn't it? Holy hell!

Flynn just continues on, like I didn't just get metaphorically get punched in the gut. The car unlocks and once I've climbed in, he keeps the door open and gives me a smile that scares me a bit in its sexuality.

"Let's just say I'm taking my kid gloves off."

I practically melt into the front passenger seat and pull my legs in, trying to make sense of that. He slams the door shut and strides around to the driver's side. His sculpted ass makes contact with his seat and he closes the door, firing up the engine in quick succession.

It roars to life as I get my brain to work. I'm starting to freak out in an excited kind of way right now. "What do you mean, you're taking your kid gloves off? I didn't even know you had kid gloves on!"

Flynn gives me a long look before he answers. "It means I'm not going to hold back on my interest in you any longer. I don't suspect any of the others will be either. So, be prepared for a lot more attention in an intimate way."

Oh shit! Now I'm starting to panic for a different reason. I know I was just complaining about them not showing any interest in me romantically but now that whatever was stopping them is gone, I'm not so sure I can handle it.

"Nora, look at me and listen," Flynn commands. My head snaps towards him and I focus on his beautiful, mismatched eyes. "We will never pressure you to go farther than you want to or do anything you're not ready for. If you don't want our attention, speak up. We'll get it. So I'm going to ask you right now, Nora. Are you interested in me on a more personal level? If you say no, it won't change anything currently between us."

I am interested. *Oh boy, am I!* But the problem isn't that I'm interested in him. The problem is that I'm also interested in four other guys. They're all dominant males and, with the exception of Owen, I seriously doubt that they'd be willing to share me. Not that I'm an object to be shared.

There are so many complications to this whole situation and so many things to consider.

I realize that I haven't answered Flynn yet and I've just left him hanging. To my surprise, I blurt out, "Yes!" I almost regret the snap decision but then the look on his face is so soft, so filled with caring, that I can't regret it, even if I wanted to.

"Come here." Flynn wraps me up in a tight hug over the middle console. It's a bit awkward but I'm always up for a hug from one of them because no one hugs like them. "I don't want you to be worried about things like sex or other intimate acts. I know you're not ready for that yet. I'm in no rush, Nora. We'll take things at your pace, okay?"

I nod my agreement, suitably reassured, which I know was his intention, and sit back in my seat and buckle up. Flynn does the same and gets the car in gear, easing out of the parking spot.

After a while of driving past places that I see but don't process, he pulls into a long, gravel driveway, lined with tall trees on each side. The house is further along the property with a circular drive in front. An Adobe style house, with an attached three-car garage, sits proudly in a clearing.

Flynn hits the button on the garage door opener and, immediately, the door rolls up for him to back his car in, next to a bright, candy apple red Jeep Wrangler with black side flares and a hard top. It's lifted and looks like a rock crawler. Since I haven't seen Owen's car yet, I wonder if it's his but there is a third empty space in here.

I look to the man next to me and then back to the Jeep. Seems to fit him more. "Yours?" I ask, when he comes around to my side and opens the door for me.

"Yeah, I like to do four wheeling. She's all tricked out for it. Silas is constantly fixing whatever I break on her when the season hits. He takes his truck out too." I'm imagining what

Silas's ride is when my brain hits the proverbial gutter. "You could come once you're fully healed. It'd be rough on your ribs right now, with your injuries."

I give him a small smile, pretending like I'm not imagining coming for Flynn, as he helps me out. "Sounds like fun."

"Come on, Spitfire. Let's go get wet."

He's so stuffed full of inuendoes and they all make my body come alive. He gives me a playful smile and grasps my hand to lead me inside. When we enter the house from the garage, he steps in front of me and I'm left wondering why until four very excited dogs round the corner and start jumping with such enthusiasm, they should be blurring. Though they range in size, from medium to large, the one thing they all share is that they're all muscular and fit.

"Calm," Flynn commands over their barking, in a firm, modulated voice. "Sit." Immediately, the dogs obey, sitting in a hodge-podge arrangement. He eyes them to make sure they're listening before turning to me.

"The big guy in the back is Bishop. He's a Boerboel and he's one of Heath's." He points to the biggest one, sitting right at the back. He's a fawn color with a black muzzle and black around his eyes. He probably outweighs me by fifty pounds.

"Owen has two dogs. The one next to Bishop is Loki"—he points to the red chocolate Doberman, who does a cute spin on his hind legs and then sits back on his haunches with his front paws in the air—"and he's one of Owen's. I can already tell he's a troublemaker and a show off—the best kind. "In front of Loki, we have Asia and she's a Catahoula leopard dog. She's also Owen's and the only girl here." Asia is a light grey color, with black and brown spots that remind me of a leopard, which is probably where part of the breed's name comes from.

"Lastly, this big guy on the left is Cain, a Perro de Canario, Heath's other mongrel. Don't let him scare you. He's actually a big teddy bear." Cain looks fierce and, to be frank, he does scare me a bit. He's a dark brindle color with clipped ears. A deep, low woof comes out of him and I wonder how *this* guy is the teddy bear?

Flynn points to the side and says, "Stand there and I'll let each one come up and greet you individually so I can keep an eye on them. They all have strong guard dog personalities. I don't think they'd hurt you but they can get pushy when they're all together and worked up, which tends to happen when meeting someone new." I'm thankful he's looking out for me because I don't want to even consider dealing with this pack when they're worked up. "You have nothing to worry about, Nora. They're all well-trained and great at listening."

"Got it." I nod and go take my place where he indicated. "Who's first?"

Flynn looks over the group and calls Asia. "Asia, come easy." She does, taking one step at a time. Once she's in reaching distance, Flynn takes my hand and holds it up for her to scent. Her nose twitches as she does and, after one final sniff and another look at me, she gives my fingers a quick lick. "Asia," Flynn warns her, before explaining to me. "We don't let them lick, unless they know we're okay with it. Some people don't like it so we've *tried* to teach them not to. But apparently it didn't take with this brat, did it, you sly little fox?" Flynn lovingly gives Asia a brisk rub on the sides of her neck. It's amazing how he interacts with them, completely dominant with no traces of playfulness. Just as he stops petting Asia, Loki tries to sneak up for his turn but Flynn stops him with a sharp order. "Loki, back, down." Loki promptly moves back and lays on his belly with his head on his paws in front of him.

"Asia, back, girl," he says in a gentle tone, sending her back before calling the next one. "Cain, come easy." Cain is the one that makes me the most nervous. He looks the most vicious and even though I know I shouldn't judge based on his looks, tell that to my hippocampus. Cain gets up and *saunters* up to me

233

and stops directly in front of me. "Cain, scent." I give Flynn a look of confusion because he didn't tell Asia to scent. "Cain's looks give most people the wrong impression of him when they first meet him. We've found that it's best to give him commands in any preliminary meetings with anyone."

Though that sounds logical, I know I'm more than just nervous.

Cain gives me a good sniff before his tail starts to wag. Flynn says, "You can pet him if you want to. I promise he won't hurt you."

After a brief moment of hesitation, I do and am amazed at how soft he is.

"Cain, back." When Cain falls into line, he calls for the next. "Bishop, come easy." He turns to me as Bishop comes. "Usually, I would have Bishop go last, since he's the most reserved of them all but since Loki"—he directs this at the dog with narrowed eyes and I melt with how adorable that is—"didn't want to wait his turn, he'll be going last."

Bishop lugs his big body up and hesitantly moves toward us. Flynn goes down on one knee and gives him a nice long pet, encouraging him in a soothing voice as he walks closer towards me.

"Okay. Hold your hand out for him, Nora. He's good."

I extend a slightly shaking hand at the big dog. I feel like this is some sort of test and if I pass this, then it will amount to something huge. Bishop sniffs me, once, twice, and I hold my breath for his reaction. But all he does is give me his ass and walk back to the rest of the pack. *Well ... that was a bit anti-climactic.* But for all I know, that could be really good for him.

"Loki," Flynn says, an edge to his tone, "Come easy." Loki stands to his full height, an inch or so taller than the rest, with the most diva attitude I've ever seen in a dog and literally prances up to me like a show dog. I know they didn't teach him that and it's just his personality. I laugh at the silly dog and smile as he smells my hand, petting himself on it with no contribution from me. Flynn smiles fondly at Loki's antics. "He's the friendliest of the bunch but if we're not careful, he's likely to get into mischief." In that instant, Loki pushes up into my legs, nearly knocking me over in his show of affection. "Loki, back," Flynn barks at him. Loki scoots back and looks thoroughly chastised. "Alright, bath." Flynn orders the dogs and all four of them pivot and scramble, rushing to the back door.

He reaches back for my hand and I tuck mine in his.

"We're going outside?"

"Yep, we've got a wash station for the dogs and horses out the back." He winks at me, then slides open the glass back-door.

I step out behind him and into a 'backyard' that's too freaking huge to be called that. A massive area of grassland leads from the back porch to a gravel trail, where there's a concrete slab that's designed into a wash station for the animals. There are poles at the sides with attached D-rings to cross tie the horses and about a foot of chain at the top. About seventeen yards past that is a big, white structure that looks like it's made from wood.

All of the dogs, except for Bishop, are running around, barking and playing with each other, racing and jumping from one place to the next. Bishop, however, is walking right next Flynn and I as we make our way to the concrete slab. I notice a bottle of soap and a rubber glove in his hands that I didn't see him grab on our way here.

Next to the concrete slab, there's a waterspout with a hose attached to it, which he turns to let the water run a bit. In Arizona during the summer months, the water has to run or you'll get burned. Not that it ever runs cold in the summer. Even in September, like now, the water can still burn.

"What's that building?" I ask Flynn.

Without looking to see where I'm indicating, he replies, "Stables for the horses. You can't see from here but behind it is a paddock for them for when the weather's not too hot. The stables are air-conditioned for the hot summers."

I whistle out loud. *Wow.* That's some serious set up for a new doctor and a bar owner. That's really impressive.

"Okay, since he's here, I'll do Bishop first. Just let me get the leashes so they don't run off and roll in the dirt when we're done." Flynn heads back to the house and Bishop sits on the toe of my sneaker. Asia and Loki are in a tug of war battle with a long, thick rope that has knots placed in it at equal intervals. Cain bounds up to Bishop and I tense up. Bishop must have sensed my unease because he lets loose a low growl that has Cain skidding to a halt and cowering to Bishop.

"I'm okay." I reassure Bishop with a pet on his head. "I'm just not so good with sudden moves like that." *Great.* I really have lost my damn mind. I'm talking to a dog like he's a real person. But then I remember how Flynn scolded Loki like he's a toddler and I decide that I'm okay.

As soon as he comes to mind, Flynn closes the door to the house and walks back to where I'm standing, a few leashes in hand. He fastens them to the chains along the poles, which are used to cross tie the horses. There's enough concrete that the leashes won't reach the dirt.

"Ready?" He looks to me while rubbing his hands together.

"Yep, what do you need from me?" I'm not all too sure how much help I'll be but I'll do what I can.

"Hold the shampoo. Loki likes to run off with it and we're out after that bottle." Flynn's smile is easy, like he finds Loki hilarious. He lets out a sharp whistle that makes me jump and Bishop growls low again, while Cain lays at my feet with his tongue lolling out.

I take the bottle from Flynn as Loki and Asia bound over, but they too pull to a stop a few feet away at Bishop's low growl. Flynn cocks his head at him with a quizzical look on his face.

"What is it? Is he okay?" I hope I'm not upsetting their normal routine.

"He's guarding you."

"Is that bad? I didn't tell him to do anything. He just came and sat on my foot." My words rush out, trying to explain the situation.

"No, it's not bad at all, Nora. Just unexpected. He wasn't commanded to guard you and, unless he knows someone and is attached to them, he doesn't do this. I mean, I've never seen him guard anyone but Heath without a command."

I bite my bottom lip and peer down at Bishop. He looks up to me with soulful brown eyes and gives a soft woof, then headbutts my thigh. I smile and scratch him behind the ears and fall a little bit in love with him in that moment.

I keep my hand on Bishop's head as Flynn starts giving baths. I handed him the shampoo and watched Loki closely after he tried to steal the bottle from me. If it weren't for Bishop, he would've succeeded. Meanwhile, I was so distracted by Flynn taking his shirt off that I felt like a cartoon character.

Once it's Bishop's turn, Flynn calls him over and he goes, albeit reluctantly. While he's getting washed, Cain stretches his leash as far as it goes to reach me and I help him out by going to stand next to him. He lays down with his front paws and his head on my shoe, watching Flynn and Bishop. With the late-afternoon heat, the rest of the dogs are almost completely dry by the time Flynn is done washing up Bishop.

He grabs a towel and starts rubbing Bishop down briskly.

Turning off the water so they don't get themselves wet again, he unhooks all the leashes and leads the dogs back toward the house and I follow, marveled at how well-behaved they are. None of them pull on their leashes and they all let Flynn lead, like he's their alpha. I've never seen human-animal interactions like this and it's fascinating.

We make it inside and I take a better look at the main living space. The back wall of the house has picture windows that let in plenty of natural light. On the wall farthest from where we entered, there's a big screen TV mounted with a taupe, three-seat couch, matching love seat and a big lazy boy chair facing it.

Like Kyle's house, there's a high counter with four high bar stools with teal cushions on the seats. The legs are metal and the stools are all backed. The counter separates the kitchen from the living room but throughout the place, the flooring is the same light gray tile, that's designed to look like wood. The counters in the kitchen are slate with white speckled throughout and all the appliances are brushed stainless steel, top-of-the-line. Of course, they have to be with Owen's hobbies.

"Hungry?" Flynn says, pulling me out of my perusal. "I can make us some breakfast for dinner if you want something."

Mmm, eggs and bacon. "When am I not hungry? You guys make me burn more calories than I can eat in a day. I could eat a horse!" Flynn looks at me, mortified, then in the direction of the stables and I start laughing my head off. "No! That's not what I meant." He smirks at me and I stick my tongue out at him.

"Watch it. You're no longer off limits, Spitfire. I can do what I want with that thing now," he says with a wink and turns toward the fridge, pulling out the ingredients for our breakfast/dinner.

13 A Thousand Words

Flynn is working on the food when the dogs start to go crazy, barking and racing to the front door, right before the doorbell chimes in the house. Surprisingly, Cain stays glued to me, while the other three rush toward the front door.

"Can you get that Nora?" he says, focused on the meal prep. "It's probably one of the guys and they might have their hands full."

He's busy and I know how to open a door so I head that way with Cain almost glued to my heels. He's pressed so close to my side, I almost trip over him. A sharp whistle from Flynn has them all sit just far enough away from the door that I can open it without hitting one of them. When I do, there's no one there.

"Odd." I step closer and peek my head out, just in case they're walking away but no, the place is empty. A manila envelope, with my name in big, black, bold letters, is sitting on the doormat and catches my attention. But I don't live here so why would someone leave something here for me? None of the guys would. They'd just give me whatever they wanted me to have.

Hesitantly, I pick up the envelope and turn it over, taking one more look around just to be sure I didn't miss whoever rang the bell. Still no sign, so I move back and shut the door firmly, a little unsettled.

"Who is it?" Flynn calls to me from the kitchen stove, where he's got the bacon sizzling now.

"I have no idea but this was on the doormat." I move to one of the barstools by the stove and hold up the envelope so he can see my name on the front.

The dogs disperse and find their own things to do as I tear the end of the envelope open and pull out sheets and sheets of pictures. They're all of me from the last few weeks since the attack behind Flynn's bar. Some of them have the guys in them but the camera focus is on me. There's pictures of everywhere, I've been, almost everything I've done and my brain starts to freak out as I spread the pictures all along the countertop. There are so many, they're overlapping.

Flynn clicks off the stove and moves the bacon off the hot burner, coming around to my side. Holding the envelope up, Flynn shakes it and a piece of paper, folded in half, falls out. He lifts it up, unfolds it and my heart stops when I see what it says. In big, black, block writing, it says:

NO MEANS NO!

WITH THE EXCEPTION OF ME.

SEE YOU SOON...

Flynn whips out his phone out and has it up to his ear but I'm frozen in fear, helpless to move, as the night replays again and again in my mind. That's what I said to the man who attacked me at the bar. How did he find me? There's a boulder on my chest and my breathing gets fast. The first tendrils of panic swirl in my eyes when Bishop and Cain, without prompting, are plastered to the side of my legs and that's when I notice I'm shaking.

"Detective Daron, this is Flynn Walker, the EMT that found and brought in Nora Molano. You're working her case." He pauses as the detective says something I can't hear. "That's right. Look, she just got an envelope with a shit ton of pictures of her and a threatening note." Another pause as he listens to Detective Daron's response. I catch his eye and he gives me a tight smile and I just look back at him with dead eyes. I don't have it in me to do anything else.

How can this be happening to me? What did I ever do that was so wrong?

"Got it. See you shortly, Detective. Thank you." Flynn rings off but after pressing a few more buttons, it goes right back to his ear.

"Heath, Nora just got a suspicious envelope with pictures of her and a note. Can you get Kyle and head over here?"

Heath must be losing his shit right now. His raised voice carries through the phone and Flynn pulls it away from his ear with a wince at the volume. "I don't know. She hasn't said anything since we found the note tucked inside." Pause. "Yeah, I called him first." Heath keeps shooting off questions and Flynn answers them all in a brisk, hard voice. "We should let them know but they don't need to rush over if they're busy. The three of us should be able to cover this." Another pause but shorter. "Okay, you should get here about the same time as the detective."

Flynn hangs up and ducks his head so he's got my attention. He eases up to me and runs a comforting hand along my back.

"Nora, I need to know why the note has you so freaked. You weren't this freaked when it was just the pictures. Talk to me, please."

I feel like I've done nothing but have one freak-out after another since I met the guys. How my life got so filled with drama in just a few weeks, I can't fathom. Everything is a mess and I feel like I have no control over it. Like I'm getting tossed around and beaten when I haven't even recovered from the first attack.

On autopilot, I answer him, "That's what I said to that guy from the bar before he attacked me." Baffled, I look into Flynn's eyes and I shatter, once again. The volume of my voice raises as I yell through the panic, "How did he find me?! How have the police not found him yet but *he's* found *me?*" Flynn rounds up the agitated dogs and shuts them in a room down the hall.

When he gets back to my side, I've got big, fat tears rolling down my cheeks. He gathers me into his arms and rocks us back and forth. But he has no answer for me and isn't that saying something? *Fuck, this sucks.*

Gravel crunches as a car pulls into the driveway. I pull away from Flynn to wipe my face on my sleeve. Two car doors slam shut and then the front door opens with so much force, it bangs off and against the wall, right into Heath's hand who was prepared for the return swing.

Heath and Kyle come close but when they're about six feet from me, they both pause to check that I'm okay and not getting triggered.

"You both better get the fuck over here right the fuck now," I croak out.

They do, albeit slowly, and Heath wraps me up in his steel bands for arms while Kyle looks over the pictures without touching them.

"Oh, sweetheart, I've got you." He stands me up and takes my place on the stool, then hauls me in his lap, stroking my hair and rocking us like Flynn did. I cry softly into his broad chest and try not to jerk too much when I take in a breath. My ribs are better but they haven't fully healed yet.

"What'd you two touch?" Kyle questions Flynn.

"We both touched the envelope, she touched the pictures, I touched the note." Flynn responds, his voice tight.

The doorbell rings and Flynn moves to answer it. The dogs bark like they're going nuts inside the room and Heath growls and passes me to Kyle, who just sat on the stool next to him.

"I'm gonna go take care of the dogs so they don't tear up that room or distract any of us while the detective is here. Be right back, sweetheart." With a kiss on my temple, he disappears towards the dogs and opens the door and all four rush out. When Heath gives them a command to follow, all but Bishop obey. Heath eyes him for a moment before saying, "Good boy," and leading the other three out the back door.

Flynn leads Detective Daron inside the house and moves to the stove, continuing with the cooking. We all shake hands with the detective, who then takes a seat on one of the three remaining stools.

The detective faces me. "Can I have these for evidence? We can dust them to see if we can lift any fingerprints, aside from yours."

"And mine," Flynn interjects. "I touched the envelope and the note."

Detective Daron gives him a nod of acknowledgement before turning to me. "Okay, Nora, let me get your statement and I'll bag these. Then, we can go from there."

I recount every last detail of the past half an hour, starting from when the doorbell rang, up until he got here. Heath comes back and sits next to me in Kyle's lap, as I'm explaining the significance of the words in the note. I'm thankful for the strength that Kyle shares with me—my forever rock, my foundation to stand on when I'm feeling shaky. It's just what I need right now, to be close to them.

When I'm finished talking, Flynn puts the plated food in front of us all.

"Please, stay and have some eggs and bacon if you'd like, Detective."

"No, thank you. I should be going. I'm sorry this happened, Miss Molano. Once we have more information, we'll get in touch." Then, he gets up and heads toward the door.

"Here, honey, go to Heath real quick. I'll walk Detective Daron out," Kyle says cryptically, placing me back in Heath's lap, who I cuddle for warmth. I feel like I'm playing musical men at this point.

Kyle heads out with the detective, both talking together in hushed voices.

"Why did Kyle go with Detective Daron?" I ask the remaining two men.

Flynn and Heath have a silent conversation before Heath answers me. "Kyle is a consultant for them sometimes," is his very short retort.

Right now, half-answers aren't good enough for me, not when it's my safety on the line. "Yeah, no. I'm going to need more information than that, G-Man."

His chest expands beneath me before he exhales, reluctant to reveal more than I already know. "Before Kyle got his firearms business going, he would help the police with difficult cases that couldn't be solved with regular resources. He has some recon skills that technically aren't illegal, but they'd be frowned upon if a law enforcement officer used them. By having Kyle gather the information for them, everyone gets a nice tidy case and a win."

Wow, how did I not know this? Kyle is a real badass. I mean, I was always suspected he was badass, but nothing to this extent.

I look at Heath with a questioning, suspicious look.

"What, sweetheart?"

"So that's why Flynn had Kyle come over. I want to know why he called you and not one of the others."

"I helped train and set up the training program for the K-9's, so having us both here was logical."

He thinks he did a good enough job at evading my question and I don't have my suspicions but I do. I'm just too tired to deal with that can of worms right now.

"Fine, keep your reasons, for now. Just know, I'm onto you all."

I slip off of Heath's lap in favor of my own stool and dig into Flynn's creation. Surprisingly, Flynn pulled off some delicious eggs and bacon. To be fair, it's kind of hard to fuck those up though.

Kyle comes back and makes himself a plate, piled high with extra bacon.

"Don't let Owen catch you with all that," Heath warns him.

"Worry about your own food," is Kyle's reply.

"How did he get all those pictures of me, of us, without at least one of us spotting him?" I feel violated in a way I've never felt before but it's no less intrusive. "What if he's out there right now watching us?" The panic builds again and I drop my fork with a clatter on my half-eaten plate, resisting the urge to run to the window and search for this man—or go hide in the basement, as far away from him as possible.

Kyle and Flynn rub my back as Heath stands abruptly.

"I'll go get the dogs and do a sweep. Kyle?" Kyle returns Heath's question with a nod and they both head out through the back door, with Bishop close behind while Flynn stays with me. Soon after, I hear the dogs barking as they enter and race around the house.

Heath leads Cain to me. "Cain is going to be in here for you, Nora. He won't leave your side until I tell him it's okay. Cain, guard Nora." Cain comes directly to me and stands guard, his back to me, standing as close to the stool as he can, as Heath leaves for the other dogs.

Flynn gently prods me into action. "Finish up, Spitfire, then we can put in a movie."

Turning back to my plate, I shove some bacon in my mouth. Bacon can make anything better, right? *Mmmm*, bacon.

"Cain," I call to him softly. When he turns his head towards me, I hold out my last piece of bacon for him and he gently takes it from my hands. So mannered for a dog. I smile slightly and move on to my eggs, as Cain crunches on the bacon, wagging his tail as he does.

Melancholy falls over Flynn and I as we silently finish up our food but I know he's trying to hide it from me. Once we're finished, he takes our plates to the sink, rinses them and puts them in the dishwasher. The whole time, Cain doesn't move from my side.

After around fifteen minutes, Kyle comes back in through the front door and heads straight for me, slowing his pace the closer he gets, to help avoid another panic attack. He frames my face with his hands on my cheeks.

"The dogs didn't find anything. Heath has them searching the stables right now. No one is out there, at least not anymore." His thumbs stroke my cheeks just under my eyes. "You're safe here, Nora honey. We'll make sure of it. Heath is going to have Cain with you and teach you how to handle him." Kyle's eyes are so soft with compassion, that tears spring into my eyes. Seeing them, he soothes me. "No, honey, please don't cry. The guys and I will break our backs to make sure you're safe and feel it."

How do I explain that the reason for my tears is not because I'm afraid of not being safe, but because I'm afraid of what's happening to my heart? Each of them has taken a spot in it and I don't know what to do.

I sniffle to hold them back. "These are not frightened tears."

"What kind are they then, honey?" Kyle's deep voice always slides over me so beautifully, that it's ironic he can't carry a tune. This man's beauty runs so much deeper than his looks, the same as all of them.

"I'm not sure exactly but I know they aren't because I'm afraid. I've never felt safer than when I'm with you guys."

He looks pleased at that and says, "Okay, honey." He sits and digs into the plate of his barely touched food.

"What movie do you want, Nora?" Flynn asks me.

"Suicide Squad, please." I love movies where the villains are really the heroes.

Flynn smirks at the request and goes to put the movie on.

"Where's the bathroom?" It hits me like a shot that I have to pee something fierce. I guess with the recent events I hadn't noticed but now I've got to go.

"Just past the living room at the end of the hall," Kyle says, before going back to demolishing his massive pile of bacon. I stand and with me, Cain, who's ready to follow me. Flynn is busy pulling out blankets and some fluffy pillows when I meet him in the hallway.

"Almost ready. What do you need, Spitfire?" he enquires over the stack of bedding he's got in his arms.

"Just need to use the restroom. Wanna help?" I think I'm being cheeky but it backfires quickly.

"Not my kink but if it's yours, I'll oblige," he quips.

My mouth falls open and I just shake my head and walk off because I have no response to that. He laughs with his head thrown back as I scoot past him with Cain right behind me, pretending to stay as far away from him as I can. Good goodness, I stepped right into that one.

Reaching the door, I push it open and flick on the light then move farther in. Cain enters too, laying down on the mint-green bath rug in front of the shower bath. The bathroom is mostly white, with pops of mint-green here and there, matching towels and soap dispenser. There's another door between the sink and a third door where the toilet is in its own little room.

Curiosity gets to me and I crack open the mystery door to find that it leads to a bedroom. I take a quick peek before shutting the door completely. Closing the main bathroom door to the hallway, I enter the small toilet room and close that one too. Thankfully, Cain doesn't try and come in because I'm not sure he would've fit. After finishing, I go to wash my hands, where Cain is still laying patiently on the rug. His tail starts wagging at the sight of me.

I stare at my reflection in the ornate silver and filigree-edged mirror, shaking my hands of the excess water. Geez, all the guys have nice homes. Sure, Heath's is a loft but it's still nice. How do they afford them? It makes me wonder, not for the first time, if they aren't all moderately rich but I don't want to ask such an invasive question. I dry my hands on the incredibly fluffy, soft towel. See! It's little things like this that I know cost a whack, that make me wonder. I know four of them own their own businesses and Owen is a doctor but those things all have a lot of overhead expenses.

All done, I head back out into the living room where Cain lays in front of the three-seater couch and lets out a tired, doggy groan. I'm beginning to wonder how I found him scary at all because he really *is* a big baby. Of course, I haven't seen him actually guard or get pissed off, so there's that.

Flynn and Kyle are sat on the love seat and the lazy boy, with me on the couch, when Heath comes in with Loki and Asia. Loki goes straight to the water bowl in the kitchen, while Asia bounds over to Flynn on the love seat and plops right on top of him. He doesn't seem to mind and gives her a rub down, before tucking her under his arm next to him on the couch. *Me thinks someone has a favorite,* I think in a weird, villain voice. God, I amuse myself.

"I left Bishop in the stables, in case the guy comes back." I'm concerned for Bishop but he's massive and I know he can hold his own. Knowing he's out there, protecting us, has the tightness I didn't know I was holding in my body release. "Wait for me, I'm going to get some water. Sweetheart, you want some?"

"Please," we all answer. My laugh comes hard and fast. Heath smirks and shakes his head but grabs a bottle for everyone, setting them down on the coffee table. Then, he grabs me by the hands and helps me stand up. While I watch confused, he kicks his shoes off and takes a seat on the couch, leaning his upper torso and head on one armrest and sprawling out with his feet hanging off the armrest at the other end. He snags one of the blankets that Flynn brought out and motions for me to come to him. I do, wondering what his game is, and just stand in front of him because I'm unsure where I can fit. He's taking up the entire couch and then some.

Using my hips to guide me, he lays me right on top of him, on my stomach, and tucks me in under the blanket so I'm warm and using him as a bed. I conclude that I like this game and I hope he plays it again.

"Relax, sweetheart." His voice rumbles through my entire body. I rest my hand on his shoulder and wrap my arm around his body. It's way more comfortable than I thought it would be so I do as he says. Flynn starts the movie, Heath drapes his arm over my waist to give himself some more room and Kyle sips on his water bottle. I wish Owen and Silas were here too.

Before long, I fall asleep to the steady sound of his heartbeat.

14 Gloves Come Off

Since Flynn broke the seal on the no-romance-with-Nora ban, all five of the guys let me know that they're interested, in their own way. Not just *their* interest, but also how they feel about each other's interest.

The next morning, I wake in Owen's bed with his arm pinning me tight against him, which is the usual position that I'm in when I'm sleeping with the guys.

I blink my eyes open and turn my head to look at Owen, fast asleep, exhausted from another long shift. He hadn't made it home by the time the guys put me in his bed, with Cain on the floor next to the bed, close to the door. I try to slide out from under Owen's arm but when I make it halfway, he tightens it and pulls me back into him.

"Owen," I whisper against him, stroking my hand along his arm. All I get in response is a sleepy grunt so I try again. "Owen," I call softly.

"Gorgeous," is his rough, sleepy response. I smile to myself and run my hand up his shoulder to the back of his neck for a gentle squeeze.

"Good morning, Doctor," I playfully tease him. "Do you think you could let me up? I have needs that have to be met."

I didn't mean that in a sexual manner but that's exactly how Owen takes it.

"I'd be happy to meet your needs, gorgeous," he whispers in a scandalous tone, nuzzling my neck with his nose and making goose bumps erupt on my body. I freeze, not sure what to do about this unexpected advance. "Nora?" Owen lifts his head and studies my face. "Forgive me. I should've asked first. That was presumptuous of me."

"No, it's not that. It's just unexpected, not unwanted, Owen." *Oh God, I wish I could throw those words back in my mouth and swallow them.* Closing my eyes and turning my head away in an attempt to hide, I wait to see what he'll do. The tension builds inside me for several moments as he stays silent, to my mortification. Just when I think I can't take it anymore, he moves above me, pinning me to the bed.

"Gorgeous, look at me, please." Owen coaxes me in a light tone of voice, completely at odds with the dominant position. When I look into his sleepy green, gem-like eyes, I catch fire from the heat in them. "You know I want you, Nora. I said as much at Kyle's. You seem better but if this isn't something you're ready for, tell me and I can wait. I'd wait an infinite amount of time for you."

He'd wait forever for me. Those words completely demolish my brain-to-mouth filter and my tongue can't stop wagging. "Flynn told me last night, before all the stuff with the pictures, that he was interested in taking things farther between us too."

Owen and I stare at each other for a bit, as we both process the word vomit, before he responds.

"I'm not surprised. In fact, I suspect that most of the others will make their interest known, sooner rather than later." He doesn't seem the least bit upset about that.

"That doesn't bother you?" I ask in astonishment and his chuckle is my response.

"Not in the slightest, Nora."

Ummm … okay, that's not enough. "Care to elaborate on that, doctor?"

"I'm not selfish enough to want to keep you all to myself. I'm a doctor, which means long hours and little time to devote to a relationship. I know that a partner needs more time and attention than I can often provide, especially currently, with where I am with my life. That's not to say I'll be okay with you seeing just anyone but, within the five of us, I'm more than accepting of it."

That was a lot of information but oddly, it all makes sense.

During breakfast, after our separate showers, Owen and I are sitting at the bar with Flynn, after the good doctor made us all pancakes, with homemade strawberry syrup, topped with fresh strawberries and whipped cream and a side of turkey bacon. I shove a mouthful of pancakes in when Owen casually— though I'm sure he timed it because he's more observant than that—brings up our conversation from earlier.

"Nora told me that you've made a move toward her, romantically." He pauses to see if Flynn would say anything. When he doesn't, Owen continues. "I've also done the same."

Boom. Bomb drop, right there at the breakfast table. Motherdicks!

It's way too early for this heavy, serious shit already. I place both my hands on either side of my face, using them like blinders for horses. *This isn't happening*, I cringe inside, wondering why Flynn hasn't said anything yet. I peek at him and see him giving Owen a hard look.

Shit, he's not okay with this arrangement. Of course, he isn't! What guy would be?

"While I appreciate being told, Owen, I'm sure Nora would've told me when she was ready." Flynn scolds Owen.

"I'm sure. However, she has concerns about all of us pursuing her at the same time," Owen reveals.

Flynn looks to me, studying me. "I understand that, Nora," he soothes, taking my hand closest to him between both of his. "I'm fine with it. I'm well aware of how the others feel about you, even if they don't all know it yet. I would never deny them a happiness that I myself want to have with you."

God, that was so very thoughtful, not just for me and him, but the rest of the guys too. There. Two-fifths of the weight is lifted off of me. *The rest* ... I still need to see how the others will accept this news.

∞∞∞∞

The next day, Heath brings me to Owen and Flynn's again, as it's his day to spend with me. He's helping me learn how to handle Cain and the other dogs, though Cain is the one he wants with me, because of his natural protective tendencies towards me, his aggressive nature, how ferocious he gets when his charge is threatened and how freaking scary he looks. It helps as well that, when he's got a bone in his mouth, this dog does *not* let go until it's destroyed.

"Okay, sweetheart, give him the command," Heath says for, what feels like, the millionth time. I can hear the frustration in his voice. I know I'm disappointing him but it's not as easy as he makes it seem to have control over the damn stubborn dog.

"Cain, search." I put as much authority into the order as I can but Cain remains relaxed, though still alert, and doesn't get up from his sitting position. He cocks his head at me like he doesn't understand what's happening. Well, he's not the only one!

My goal is to get Cain to find the dong that Heath hid somewhere in the backyard. In a growl of frustration, I throw my hands up in exasperation. "What am I doing wrong?!"

"You have to believe in yourself and have confidence in your ability to command him. He won't listen if you don't believe that you can *make* him listen. I know you can do this, Nora. I have no doubt about that. What I don't know is why you don't have the same faith in yourself?" *Okay, did not expect the deep turn this conversation would take.* "Nora, what's holding you back?"

Shit, how do I answer him? This is the same issue my therapist and I were working on earlier in the day. She thinks I need to rebuild the trust that I have in myself, in order to trust that the guys aren't going anywhere.

I look at him and his open, searching, gray eyes and take a chance on him, trying to trust that my heart knows what it's doing.

"Flynn and Owen have both told me they want to take our relationship to another level, in a romantic sense."

Heath's body gets visibly tight, as he goes statue still. It's better to rip a band aid off quickly, rather than prolong the suffering, right?

"They did what?" Heath whispers. That's not good at all. That usually means he's trying hard to keep from yelling and only trusts himself at a whisper to prevent it. Cain starts to get antsy at my side.

"You heard what I said, G man," I retort softly to help ease the hit, as Cain and I both eye the unpredictable giant.

"Nora." He swallows and wets his lips with his tongue, drawing my eyes to his lush mouth, then tries again, "Is that what you want? Those two?"

"Yes and no." With my hand on Cain's head, I sigh. "I don't only want them. I also want Kyle and Silas *and* you. I want all of you, Heath. I know it's not normal or fair of me but it's how I feel."

Heath hangs his head, like it's much too heavy for him to hold up. *Damn it, did I break him?* I worry my bottom lip between my teeth before I try to get a reaction from him, be it good or bad.

"Heath?" I question.

"If this is what you truly want, sweetheart..." *I'm still his sweetheart.* "Then I'll do my best to always give you what you want." He says those magic words that release a part of my soul I didn't know was locked tight. *Three-fifths down.* "I trust you to know what you want and be able to make it work for all of us. That's not to say it won't be an adjustment but I'm in."

I step into his arms and kiss him. It's filled with such sweetness that I'm surprised I don't get a toothache.

∞∞∞∞

Two days later, I find myself at King's garage, working the reception desk and completing a parts order when Silas strides up to the opposite side, leaning his forearms on the top. I glance up at him and give him a quick smile.

"Give me just a second to finish up this order then you can have my undivided attention, Si." I go through the final process of entering the shipping address and paying. "All done," I say, pressing the 'enter' bar and turning to him. "What's up?" I quip.

"I'm making a lunch run for the boys in the shop. Wanna tag along?"

"Sure, let me grab my purse, just in case." I haven't paid for food since that first day at the Mexican restaurant, not for lack of trying though. They just won't leave any opening unmanned!

"Nora," Silas warns on a growl, knowing exactly what I'm getting my purse for. I just give him an innocent look that says I have absolutely no clue what he's growling about.

He just shakes his head in disbelief and I grab my purse and pull my sunglasses out, slipping them up my nose, as we exit into the parking lot. Cain trots along behind us. I don't worry about him wandering off, because he hardly leaves my side unless Heath relieves him.

Silas unlocks his Tundra and opens my door, then helps me into the high seat. I buckle up as he comes around to his side, holding the door open for Cain to jump in and move to the back. He climbs into the driver's seat, clicks his belt buckle into place and turns the truck on, backing out of the space and pulling out onto the road. *Play With Fire* by Sam Tinnesz is on the radio and Silas turns it down to just background noise.

"Where are we going for food?" I ask, after some time of driving, but Silas doesn't answer. When he pulls into my favorite Chinese restaurant, my eyes light up.

"I'll be right back. Keep the doors locked and don't open them for anyone but me."

I roll my eyes at his overprotectiveness and give him some sass. "You know I'm a grown woman, right? I'm pretty sure I know not to open the door to strangers. Well, unless they're offering candy of course."

He leans over and wraps his hand around the back of my neck, pressing his forehead to mine. "I'm more than aware that you're a grown woman, doll. I'm so aware that I have to remind myself daily to have patience and give you more time before I can act on my desire for you." *Holy shit.* His warm, minty breath fans over my face, heating me up and cooling me down at the same time, and a shiver runs over my body.

Keeping with the honesty train I've boarded, I tell him the truth. "You're not alone in that desire, Si. I catch myself daily wondering what your lips would feel like on mine. You're also not the only one who has a romantic interest in me." I don't want to keep any details from him but I'm also apprehensive to how he'll react.

Drawing in a big breath through his nose, he holds it for about thirty seconds before slowly letting it out.

"Do you return those affections, for the other person?" he asks in a gruff voice. I see the apprehension etched in his eyes.

256

I don't want to make it worse but I can't lie to him either, so my voice is tight with anxiety when I say, "People. And, yes, I do."

"Fuck. I knew I waited too fucking long." He pulls in another breath and blows it out. "I won't tell you it's me or them. That's not who I am. However, I can't say that I won't get jealous and possibly act like a fucking caveman at times. Just try to keep me from seeing too much, at least for now."

Astonished at how well that went, I instantly agree, as he pulls my mouth to his and knocks my socks off with a kiss straight from my dreams, full of demand and want.

Four-fifths. And the last one's the scariest.

∞∞∞

I'm just rinsing off the conditioner in my hair when a knock sounds on the door. It's just Kyle and I tonight, which is rare, since there's always at least two guys where I'm staying.

"Nora," he calls through the door. His voice is muffled because of the wood and the sound of the water falling. "Can I come in? I forgot my razor in this bathroom."

"Yeah but heads up, I'm in the shower!" I call back. It's not the first time he's been in here while I'm washing up.

The door opens and I can't see him because his bathroom has a walk-in with the showerheads at the very back to prevent the water from crossing the threshold.

"Sorry, I forgot to put it in the other bathroom again."

I laugh. "I don't know why you're apologizing to me. This is your house! You might as well just shave in here, instead of walking all the way to the other bathroom, then coming back to get dressed." It all seems so silly. I mean, we're both adults, for Pete's sake.

"Are you sure? If you're not comfortable..." Kyle trails off.

I roll my eyes, though he can't see me. "It really is fine. It's a natural thing when two adults basically live together." When there's no response, I frown.

"Kyle?" Did he leave without me noticing?

All of a sudden, his muscular frame, in only low-slung, gray pajama pants, is filling the doorway. His eyes are glued to mine and don't wander, as he stays frozen in the doorway.

"What are you saying, Nora?"

I still turn my back to him. At least then it's just my ass on display.

"I'm saying that we're both adults and should be able to share a bathroom. I'm comfortable enough with you that it doesn't bother me." The intensity of his gaze amplifies with those words so I whisper the next words low enough for him to miss them, "Though, not so much right now."

Kyle takes a few steps closer, just out of the spray's reach, his hands clenched in fists. "Does that mean you want to date?"

I look back at him over my shoulder, wondering how we got here but I'm glad we finally did. At least, it will finally all be out in the open. "I'd very much like to date you, Kyle." *Whew, that was harder than I expected.*

He closes his eyes and tilts his head back so his face is pointed at the ceiling.

"Honey, I am coming to you right now. I'm warning you, brace." His voice is rough with emotion and then he rushes me, gathering me up in his arms, before I have a second to think. The water soaks into his pajama pants, along with the rest of him, but he doesn't notice or doesn't care. His eyes just stare into mine. They're the clearest I've ever seen them. "We can get your stuff from the other houses tonight, after I'm done with work."

Wait ... what? "Why? Won't I need my stuff there, for when I stay with the other guys?"

"Nora, you don't need to stay with them overnight," he says, astonished at the suggestion. "You'll come home with me at night. I don't want my girlfriend staying with other guys, even if they are my best friends."

Oh shit. Oh. Shit! I went about this the wrong way!

"Kyle," I begin, unsure how to explain when I've screwed up so monumentally. Either he doesn't realize that the others have expressed their interest in me or he doesn't realize that I share it or he wouldn't have come to this conclusion. "Kyle ... we wouldn't be exclusive." His body stills against me and the shutters go up until all that remains in his eyes is a thunderous storm. But I've come this far and I need to go further because this needs to be cleared up right now. "Owen, Silas, Flynn and Heath all want to date me too ... and ... I want to date them."

"You want to date them, *all* of them, *and* me?" he repeats and though I can't understand the tone of his voice, I know what I see in his eyes. When I nod my head, he starts to pull away. "Nora," his tone is hard. "I don't share my women. Not even with them."

Fuck.

"I realize this isn't conventional and I may not even want this arrangement permanently, but right now, I can't leave anyone out. I like you all for different reasons. I like how you all fill different parts of my broken soul." I try to help him see why I want what I want but my heart is already falling, little cracks forming. "Please don't ask me to choose just you."

"I'd never give you an ultimatum, Nora honey. But I'm just not built to share like that," There's a long pause where all that fills the room is silence and the sound of the water meeting the ground. He looks over my head at the water falling and says, "I might consider it." But when his eyes meet mine again, the hurt in them nearly brings me to my knees. "Give me some time with this." Then he walks out of the shower and leaves the bathroom altogether, leaving behind a wet trail.

I wrap my arms around my stomach and try to hold myself together but I fail. I've already lost. The tears stream down my face and get lost in the water flowing from the showerhead above.

Lost on the final one.

15 Bricks Hurt

Two weeks have passed with no updates about my attacker and no more packages appearing but that's not how I'm counting the days anymore. I'm counting in how long it's been since I've seen Kyle. Since the conversation in the shower, he hasn't been around much and the only time I talk to him is over text but even that is minimal and impersonal. The rest of the guys and I are getting closer and closer but every time I bring up my missing piece, the guys get aggravated so I try not to talk about him much.

It's been forty-five minutes since Silas left for work when the doorbell rings. I feel awkward answering his door so I continue with my schoolwork. It's probably someone soliciting or making sure we've found Jesus. I don't need anything and I already have my own spiritual beliefs. Now if it's girls selling cookies, I'm going to be disappointed that I missed them.

I quickly forget the possibility of missing some delicious cookies and get engrossed in my work again. Since the attack, I haven't been back to school. I've been taking all my classes online because I still have issues with getting triggered, sometimes in the most ridiculous situations. My therapist says it's normal and I know it but, apparently, one of the things we need to work on is my high expectations of myself.

I'm almost done when a crash and the sound of glass shattering echoes through the empty house. In the backyard, Bishop is going nuts, where he went out for a run a little while ago. I place my laptop on the table and cautiously get up, heading in the direction of the front door, where I think the sound came from.

When I get there, the floor is covered in tiny and big shards of glass. In the midst of the chaos, is what appears to be a brick thrown through the front side window of the door. There's a paper wrapped around the brick, attached by a rubber band. Making sure I'm careful of the glass, I go to pick up the brick and unwrap the band from it to remove the paper. It's crinkled like someone balled it up several times, then changed their mind and tried to flatten it out again. I turn it over and freeze in shock.

No. No. There's no way.

I drop the paper and rush to my phone, no longer caring about the state of my feet as they bleed all over the ground.

I dial the first number that comes up in my 'recent calls' list, which happens to be Kyle's. I went to call him last night because I missed him but hung up before the first ring went through.

Now, it's been so long since we've had a proper conversation that I'm not sure if he'll answer but I let the call go through anyway. As the phone rings, I start to panic and my breathing escalates until I'm almost hyperventilating. It takes three rings and a certainty in my chest that he won't pick up before he does.

"Hey, honey, I thought you were doing schoolwork today?" Kyle greets me.

"I need you to come here right now!" I try to modulate my voice but I don't even come close.

Kyle's voice shifts as I hear the sound of his closing down his workplace as he fires question after question at me. "What's wrong? Are you hurt? Tell me what's happening, Nor."

I'm for sure hyperventilating now and my head is starting to get light from the lack of oxygen. "Brick," I gasp. "Someone ... someone threw a brick ... in the window. It's— I can't, Ky. I'm scared. I'm so fucking scared. Please, get here!" By the end, I'm sobbing and I'm not sure how much he understood of anything I just said but I know he'll come.

"Okay, honey, this is what I want you to do. Put me on speaker." Immediately, I do and the sound of Kyle's voice in the empty house brings me down a little bit. "Go sit on the couch and put your head between your knees for me. Let's use some of the techniques you've been working on with your therapist, okay?"

I'm not sure I can function with the amount of adrenaline coursing through my system right now so I follow the instructions to the letter. How he knows my current therapy techniques is something I can't dwell on right now so I just put the information in my newly downsized 'deal with later' box.

"Okay, done." I'm barely keeping my head above the surface right now. I squeeze my eyes shut, trying to find some relief from it.

"Good, Nora. Now, I want you to tell me how your feet feel on the floor. Is it cold or do you have socks on?"

I try and focus on how they feel and that's when I notice that they hurt. I don't dare open my eyes or I might lose the very weak grasp that I have on my sanity.

"They hurt. I think I stepped on some of the broken glass, Kyle." My voice breaks and I have to take some deep breaths.

"It's okay, honey. We'll deal with that once I get there. I'll make sure you're okay. Keep going. Move up to your calves."

I refocus and flex my calves.

"They feel normal. My sweats are laying against them. My ass is in the soft cushion of the couch. I can feel my hair on my lower back." He urges me on with his soothing voice so I try to focus on the physical, rather than the internal. "My stomach is in knots of fear..."

"No, Nora, don't talk about your fear. Tell me how your body feels. How things feel against it. I'm almost there. Just hang on for five more minutes, honey. Then I'll be there and we'll work it out together."

"Okay, okay, I can do this. My arms are over my thighs, my palms flat on the cold tile." I notice my breathing is almost back to normal, which is making my head feel normal again. "Kyle, I think I'm good until you get here. I won't move. I'll be waiting on the couch for you. The guys should probably know what's happening. I'm sure they'll want to be here too. *Fuck*, we need to call the cops."

"Okay, honey, I'm going to let you go. I'm going to call Detective Daron, then I'll text the guys." There's a pause before he adds, "If you need to call me again, don't hesitate, okay?" I know he's worried but I'm confident that I'll be able to keep my shit together until he gets here.

"I'll call, but I really think I'll be okay until you get here. How far out are you?"

"Four minutes." Shit, that means he's speeding.

"Don't get a ticket, Kyle Harper!" I scold him. They all speed but I'm sure he was even worse than normal to get to me as quickly as he can. I hear a small chuckle from his end and I know he's satisfied that I won't slip into a panic attack before he gets here.

"They'll have to catch me first. Bye!" He hangs up before I can formulate a proper response so, instead of falling back into fear, I distract myself with coming up with sassy comebacks to him when he shows up, talking to someone. "I don't know. I just got here. Daron is on his way, along with Silas and Heath. Can you call Owen? I tried but he didn't answer. She's got Bishop out back." Pause. "Okay, I'm going to take care of her. Hurry and get here, man." He makes it to me as he hangs up.

I lift my head and see Kyle on all fours crawling toward me. They don't have to do it as much lately, only when I'm having a panic attack or just coming out of one. At first, it felt ridiculous to me so I told them to stop. But that just made them start crawling around me all the time. They turned it into a game and I laughed so much that it started feeling normal.

They really have no shame when it comes to doing what I need for help.

Once he makes it right near me, he waits a beat until I nod that I'm okay for him to sit next to me on the couch.

He pulls me into his lap and I put my head on his shoulder as he wraps his arms around me. "The guys are on their way. Well, all but Owen. I couldn't get ahold of him but Flynn's on it. Detective Daron will be here with his partner shortly and asked us not to touch anything we don't have to." I prop my feet up on the cushion next to Kyle and that's when I see the blood.

Shit!

"I'm bleeding all over everything. I need to clean it up!" I move to stand but Kyle locks his arms around me, keeping my ass in his lap.

"Don't worry about it. We don't want to accidently destroy any evidence. Besides, I'm sure Silas doesn't give a fuck about you staining his fucking couch cushions, other than the fact that you're bleeding, of course. That's going to piss him off but only because it means you're fucking hurt." *Uh oh, that was a lot of cuss words.* That's never good. Out of all the guys, Kyle curses the least and it only comes out when he's pissed or upset. Plus, his voice is on super-growl mode, which means his emotions are running on high right now.

I hate that he's upset but I needed him. And he'd be way more pissed if I didn't call him when I needed him. That's true for all the guys.

"Okay, I won't worry about it, Ironman. Cross my heart." I try my best to calm the beast just under the surface of his control. He glares at the saying I chose but kisses the top of my head, gently rocking us from side to side. I lay my head on his chest and listen to his heartbeat. The rhythm calms me, though it's justifiably a little fast, but it begins to slow the longer we hug. I don't know how long we sit there but it's likely not long before the front door slams open and I jump from the noise.

"We're in the living room. Be careful. She's still not all the way down from her panic attack." Kyle calls out a warning so whoever it is doesn't come barreling into the room. Moments later, Silas and Heath round the wall with fire in their eyes. It's directed at me but I know it's not for me. It's for whoever threw the fucking brick. "Easy, guys, slow. She's lucid but not talking much."

They both come to a halt immediately and I see them take deep breaths that have their shoulders rising, then they let them out in unison. They repeat that until they visibly calm and I gesture at them to come to me. Slowly, they come forward, like they're approaching a feral animal. It still pierces my heart every time they have to do this. I wish I wasn't so broken still but I just can't seem to push past these lingering feelings. With how perfect they all are, it makes me feel even worse about my failures.

They're so strong and I'm so weak and damaged that I often question what they get from our friendship. Whatever it is, I can't seem to give them up so I just go with it but the question is always in the back of my mind. I don't ask them because I don't know if I'll be able to handle the answer.

Silas sits next to Kyle and me on the couch, grabbing my hand in his, which engulfs mine. His hand feels so warm against mine. I don't feel particularly warm in this moment. In fact, the numbness is starting to creep in around the edges of my mind, though I'm fighting it. I don't want to shut off and go into zombie mode. I want to feel, to be able to deal with this. I don't want to keep hiding. Having the guys helps but I know that until they all get here, it's going to be a struggle for me to stay in the present.

Heath stands with his back to us, his arms crossed over his massive chest. I know it's because he's fighting his rage down. It still sends me into a cower any time he gets angry near me and he's been working so hard on controlling that but, again, I wish he didn't have to. I wish I didn't freak out any time one of them gets a little too angry or a little too loud. Those are the triggers that persist the most.

I reach up behind Kyle and place my hand just below Heath's ass on his upper hamstring. His muscles tense for a quick second, then he reaches back and moves my hand into his. It's rough and calloused and it feels so good against mine. Even though it makes me feel small and fragile, I know he's got me. I know he's here. Just having him there means I'm strong.

Silas pulls his phone from his front pocket and looks at the screen. "Flynn is six minutes out. He got through to Owen. He's just wrapping up a small procedure, then he'll be on his way." Just knowing they're on their way helps release some of the tension I was holding in my body.

I snuggle deeper into Kyle and he rests his cheekbone on the top of my head. His arms relax around me and cross at the wrists in front of my stomach. Silas starts massaging my hand, moving his way up slowly. Heath, though still tense and silent, holds my other hand the entire time. I'm not alone and haven't been since that first night that Flynn found me in the alley all those weeks ago, except for the short stint in my now perpetually-empty apartment.

We wait in silence until the door opens again and Flynn's voice carries through to us.

"I appreciate your quick response, Detective Daron. They should be in the living room." He leads the detective towards us but stops several feet away and holds an arm out to stop the detective as well. I look into his beautiful mismatched eyes. They hit me right in my stomach and start to soothe the knots instantly.

"I'm good, Picasso. You can come closer."

The relief in his eyes is immediate and he comes around to sit in front of me on the coffee table. I started calling him Picasso after I found out that he designed all his tattoos, even though he didn't ink them.

Flynn doesn't touch me, much to my disappointment and though I try to hide it, I'm not sure I do a good job because his mouth goes tight at the corners.

Detective Daron greets me with a sad smile on his face. "I'm sorry to be seeing you under these conditions again, Nora." I lift my eyes to his and return his smile with a tight one of my own.

"Thank you for coming." I offer. What else is there? I'm not happy about the reason he's here either.

I move to sit up and Kyle helps me off of his lap and next to him so I'm between him and Silas. Flynn moves to the floor between my legs and Heath turns so his hands rest on my shoulders. They each offer support and bring me a feeling of strength. I'm just missing my steady Dr. Baker, who is always there, always observing, but knowing he's on his way soothes me. He'll be here, as he always is.

Detective Daron observes how we're positioned around each other but doesn't say anything.

I look up to Heath and see the fire still swirling in his gray eyes. Yeah, he's pissed. He tends to not talk or just whispers when he's mad; otherwise, he'll explode. "G-Man, can you get a seat for Detective Daron, please?" I'm hoping giving him a purpose and some time to walk it off will help a little. He squeezes my shoulders and moves off to get one without a word before returning and placing the chair on the opposite side of the coffee table, directly across from us.

"Thank you, Heath," Detective Daron says as he sits. Heath's already back to me, behind me, always watching my back. This isn't just now. He always takes that spot when I'm panicked, no matter what, no matter where the others are. "Okay, Nora, I'd like to start from the beginning, if that's alright with you?" Detective Daron asks before I'm ready to start.

"Actually, we'd prefer to wait until Owen gets here." Flynn responds before I can. The detective looks to me and I nod my confirmation.

"Okay, no problem. Would you like to be updated on your case while we wait?" He volleys back. I was wondering about it so I agree to that. The guys are silent as he tells us that they have a few suspects in custody and that they want me to come to check out the lineup. My body tightens and all the guys must feel it because they go on alert and look to me. "You'd be protected, of course, and none of the suspects would know you were there. They will be in a line up behind a one-way window. You'll look at them from the front and side angles. Then we will have them say a phrase and you'll have as long as you need to make a decision about if you recognize any of them as your attacker. It's all completely anonymous." Detective Daron tries to reassure me.

"It's not that..." I hedge. "It's just that I don't want to go alone. Can they all, plus Owen, be with me?" I'm not sure if they'll allow all of them to accompany me but the thought of facing my attacker without any of them starts to raise my anxiety.

"Nora won't be going unless we can all accompany her," Owen states clearly on his way in, leaving no room for argument. I was so lost in my worry of going without all of them, I didn't even hear the door open. Detective Daron's eyes travel up to Owen as he takes a seat in one of the lazy boy chairs off to the side of the couch.

My good and proper doctor is in his dominant persona now. When he gets like this, he takes control of whatever situation we're in and all the guys allow it. I suspect it's his way of dealing with difficult circumstances, almost like a coping mechanism.

The detective doesn't appear to bothered by Owen's proclamation. "That's no problem," he concedes with no fuss. "Okay, Nora, are you good to start now?"

I'm not, not really, but I'll never get any closer than I am in this moment with all my guys here. I start from the doorbell ringing as I did my schoolwork and follow the events from there up until Kyle got here. The entire time, Detective Daron is taking notes on a tablet only intervening with a few follow-up questions.

Once I'm done, he stands to leave. "I'll call you to set up a time for all of you to come into the station tomorrow." Just then, his partner comes into the living room. I had no idea she was here at all.

"All possible evidence is collected and bagged," she states.

"Good, we just need to get pictures of her feet and the blood trail." He looks at me quickly before looking at the guys. "Then we can go and you are free to clean her up and get the window replaced."

She's taking pictures of my bloody footprints from the door to where I am. They look so much more horrifying than I thought they'd be. I sit frozen in place as she comes around to me and starts clicking away.

"Can you stand so I can get full front and back pictures after I get the bottoms of your feet?"

I'm still stuck in horror, so the guys help me. Flynn moves in front of me and lifts my feet so she can get the shots she needs. Then Silas and Kyle gently help me up and I wince from the pain when they do. Kyle supports me at my waist and Silas lets me lean my upper torso on him, taking as much weight as he can. She takes her pictures and the guys effortlessly turn us so she can get my backside. "All done. Sorry to see you in less than happy circumstances again, Nora." Then they're out the door and I'm back on the couch with Owen in front of me, inspecting the bottoms of my feet, while all the other guys are dispersed around the house. I can hear Silas on the phone about the window replacement and the sound of broken glass being swept up filters through to us.

"Flynn, can you go and get me the med kit from the garage, please?" Owen requests.

"Got it." Flynn retorts before I hear the garage door open and close. Kyle's voice reaches me from wherever he is talking about upgrading the security system on all of their properties. They're all doing things to move us past this and into a better, more protected future.

Me? I'm useless. Under the overwhelming sense of being a burden, tears build and build and race down my cheeks, even though I'm fighting them.

"It's okay, Nora. You can let it all out. We'll keep you safe. This won't—"

Owen doesn't get any more out because I completely lose it. "I'm not fucking worried about me! I'm worried about all of you and the burden I put on all of you! The money I cost you! The fucking sleep you lose because of me and my fucking nightmares! The time I take away from your jobs! Don't you dare tell me I don't! You had to leave early from a procedure you were in the middle of, just to come and deal with me and my shit!" my voice cracks from the yelling and the emotion leaking in at the end. All activity has stopped and I close my eyes in embarrassment. My voice comes out broken and soft. "I take and take from all of you in one way or another and give nothing in return. How do I balance the scales and make all of this right? How do I pay any of this back?" My whisper sounds even louder than my yelling in the prevailing silence.

I open my eyes and stare into Owen's jade green ones and expect to see compassion or sympathy. Instead, all that stares back is a hardened stare. "Stop it," Owen commands, I don't know how he does it but I want to obey him—I just don't know how to get over my guilt and selfishness. "Nora, listen to me. Don't just hear me. I want you to *actually listen* to me. We are not the type of men that do things for people we don't care about. We don't let others into our lives on whims and help them. We absolutely don't let our lives revolve around a woman. Yet, we do all of these things with you. Do you think we'd do that if you didn't mean a great deal to us? If you didn't make us more, better, *whole?* You give us so much more than we give you but you just don't see it because it's always easier to see the negative in things, than the positive. We all want you in our lives. You wouldn't be here if we didn't."

I just sit there, tears streaming down my face, blood on my feet, in utter shock. Nothing has gotten through to me like this moment. When I focus on the room again, they're all standing behind Owen watching me, waiting.

"You all want me in your lives. I add value to each of your lives." I smile an unknowingly megawatt smile and they all tense up more than they were. Shit, I said something wrong.

"You do, Nora," Flynn responds.

Kyle goes next. "You give more than we can ever give back."

"I've never been able to control my anger," Heath reveals. "Never wanted to. You help make that possible. Please don't take it away. It's so freeing to be able to let it go and not have to hang on to it."

Shit, I'm going to cry if they keep this up.

"I don't ever want to hear that shit come out of your mouth again. You give us plenty." *Okay, note to self, Silas really doesn't like how I see some things.*

"I won't," I try and reassure him. "I get it now. I was just so wrapped up in me that I couldn't see past my own selfish views and see how I gave to all of you." I look each of them in the eye as I try and convey to them how much I get and what I want to offer to them.

272

Slowly, they all begin to relax. I can feel the tension leaving us, as a peace I've never known settles deep in my heart.

Oh fuck, I'm gone. I'm done. The realization that I love them hits me like a jackhammer. When did this happen? *How* did this fucking happen! Now what am I going to do with this shit? How am I going to get through this and make it out the other side unscathed?

Fuckity, fuck, fuck, mother dicks! Through my inner freak-out, Owen cleans my feet and applies a triple antibiotic ointment then bandages them up.

And instead of dwelling further, I sit back, relax on the couch and grin at them. "I'm pretty fucking awesome." They all burst out laughing and the last of the tension leaves us.

16 Suspect Pool

Owen set everything up so the next day, for the police lineup, my anxiety is kept at a minimal level.

Silas and I arrive together to everyone else already there, including Kyle. I hope I'll have a chance to talk to him more after this. I don't like how things have become between us but I know that I'll respect his decision if he doesn't want to get involved with me. If he says it's not something he can do, I don't know where we'll go from there but I hope it's somewhere better than where we are right now.

I grab Silas's hand to draw strength from him.

I wanted to be comfortable today but still look put together, so I picked a pair of dark wash jeans and a long-sleeved black top, that hugs my torso and arms but is loose around the chest and falls off one shoulder. I didn't know if I'd be doing a lot of standing so I went with flats and, for maximum comfort and minimal effort, I threw my hair in a ponytail. A long, silver necklace and matching, dangling earrings complete the outfit so I don't look like I rolled out of bed without even washing my face. Dressing like I'm put together makes me feel more confident when I walk to the station with Silas by my side.

"He can't see you, doll," he says, squeezing my hand as he leads us to the rest of the guys, waiting outside the police station. "He can't hurt you again. Not that any of us are going to let you out of our sight while you do this."

We come up to the rest of the men who I consider mine and I look at each one of them in turn, holding Kyle for last. I search his face but he's not looking at me any differently than he ever has. I hope that's a good thing.

"Ready, gorgeous?" Owen checks with me. He's dressed in what I like to call his 'doctor clothes,' back in the dominant persona that places him in charge. The only tell that he's nervous is that he keeps glancing at his watch.

"As I'll ever be," I chirp with false cheer.

"It's okay to be nervous or afraid," Heath interjects, moving to me. His big hands on my shoulder heat up my skin, all the way to my bones. I appreciate the sentiment but I'm already done with this day. Dragging this out is only adding to my anxiety levels.

"I'd really just like to get this over with."

"Okay, let's go then." Owen takes charge and heads inside with Kyle close behind him.

Flynn gives me a wink that makes me smile, which is what I expect he wanted. With the response he wanted to elicit, he gives me a small smile and follows the other two inside.

Heath slides his hands down my arms and catches my right one in his, lacing our fingers together. I reach back for Silas's hand and clasp his in a tight grip. He applies a small amount of extra pressure then releases back to a normal hold.

We enter in a linked line and pass through the metal detectors one-by-one. By the time we make it through security, Owen and Kyle have checked in at the reception desk and Detective Daron is coming out of a big room that's home to a lot of desks, behind a wall of glass windows.

The detective shakes hands with Kyle, then Owen, before moving down the line. When he shakes hands with Flynn, my Picasso is ahead of us by a couple of feet and he says something to the detective that I don't catch. Detective Daron nods his head in response and then looks at me with a sad sympathy that I don't understand. Heath and Silas position themselves next to me, one on each side, still holding my hands.

"Nora, we're all set up and ready to go. If you'd all like to follow me please?" Detective Daron leads and turns us down a long hallway with doors on each side, opposite each other. Though I have Silas and Heath behind me, I need Kyle right now. I look towards him, trying to convey to him without words that I need him by my side but I can't catch his eyes. Owen leans in to him and whispers something in his ear. Kyle's mouth gets tight but he comes to me regardless, and holds his hand out, waiting for me to take it. I look up to Silas and Heath and they both give me encouraging looks, letting go of my hands and guiding me towards Kyle's outstretched one. I step forward, unsure where things are between us, but glad that he's here for me now anyway.

"I've got you, honey." That's all he gives me before tucking my hand in the crook of his elbow, but it's just what I needed.

We follow Detective Daron down the long hallway, the others trailing behind us. I peer over my shoulder and give them a quick smile and get four, soft, encouraging looks back.

We're ushered into a room with a big, blacked-out window taking up most of the wall to our right. There are several folding chairs and a small table with a coffee pot and paper cups, creamer and sugar on the wall opposite the window.

Owen and Kyle stand next to me as I step up to the window, wondering if he's behind there already or if he's even here at all.

The others move to the back wall and Flynn and Silas sit in the chairs. Flynn looks relaxed, like he's stopped in for a chat with an old friend, while Silas has a tension in his shoulders, his arms crossed over his chest, legs stretched out in front of him, crossed at the ankles. Heath stands with his back toward the wall, arms crossed, much like Silas, and his feet just over shoulder-width apart. Regardless of how they're standing or looking, I know they're ready to jump into action at the drop of a hat.

Detective Daron clears his throat, grabbing my attention. "Okay, Nora, let's go over how things are going to happen, shall we?" I nod as butterflies take off in my stomach and he continues. "Once you're ready, before the suspects are brought in, I'll hit this button and the lights will come on. Then, in a single file line, they'll be led in and turned to face forward. Take a good look and let us know once you're ready to view them from side angles. They'll turn to each side again. You can take as long as you need on each side. Once you're done with that part, we'll have them face forward again and we will have them say the phrase you told us he said in your statement. If you need any of them to repeat it, we can make that happen. You have no time limit in here. They can't see or hear you and when we're done, they're led out and placed back in their holding cells, while you all stay here. If you do identify one of them as your attacker, we will pull him out of the lineup and you can formally press charges against him. He'll then be taken to a different section of the station and booked. All of the suspects match the description you gave in your statement. Any questions so far?" He's done a good job of explaining things and knowing was half the help. It eases the knots in my stomach.

I shake my head at his question. Then, looking to the guys, we all give the go-ahead to get started.

Detective Daron hits the button signaling for the suspects to be brought in. The lights flicker on, like all fluorescent lights do, accompanied with a low electrical hum. Behind the window, the door opens and suspects start entering one by one, single-file, just like Detective Daron said. They all turn to face the window.

In total, there are five men that enter the room, all of them facing forward and staring at the window. I start with the first man and my eyes take in every detail. None of the men have any hair on their heads, as my attacker was bald, but this first guy is too thin.

I move on to the second. He's built more like the man from the bar but his eyes are too light. I don't think I'd be able to forget how his eyes froze me from the inside out. It's odd

277

because Kyle's eyes are a warm dark but they bring a calming ease. Nothing at all like my attacker.

I step in front of the third man. My blood drains from my face and I get lightheaded. I involuntarily take a step back and bump right into Owen.

"That's him. Number three. That's the guy from the bar who grabbed me inside, then beat me in the alley later." I'm so fucking light-headed, I feel like I might pass out.

"Are you sure, gorgeous?" Owen whispers in my ear.

I vehemently nod my head, exacerbating the lightheadedness and making myself dizzy so that I can't stand on my own anymore. Luckily, Owen already has his arms loosely around my stomach, but tightens them when he feels me start to go down.

"Get her a chair! Easy, Gorgeous, easy." Owen soothes as Heath pulls a chair over and I plant my ass in the seat.

One of the guys hands me a cup of water and I take big gulps of it to help wash away the terror of seeing my attacker, essentially, face-to-face again. Owen is crouched in front of me with his hands on my knees warming them through my dark wash jeans.

"Nora, look at me," Owen tries to grab my focus. "Nora, come on, we're all right here. Look at me." I still don't lift my eyes, that dark, evil gaze front and center in my head. With a hand on my chin, Owen turns me to look at Silas and Heath, one in front of the only door and one in front of the window holding the suspects. They both have their arms crossed over their chests and danger in their eyes. "There's no way in hell these two are going to let him get anywhere near you, Gorgeous." I turn to look at him and come back a bit. "That's right, there you are. Do you want to continue now?"

278

I do. I just want this part behind me so I can move on and not be so afraid anymore that the man is going to jump out from under a rock and get me.

"I want to get this over with." My voice is shaky and sounds weak to my ears but I can't turn back now. Owen stares into my eyes and once he's satisfied with what he sees, he moves back and stands with his back to the window. Heath has taken his place behind me with his hands resting gently on my shoulders. I'm not sure where the others have gone off to. I can't devote the energy into knowing right now either.

Detective Daron moves into my line of sight. "Number three is the man who attacked you?" I nod my affirmation and he pushes, "You're sure? Do you need him to say the phrase we talked about?"

"You can have them all say it but it's not going to change the fact that number three is my attacker, Detective." I look him in the eye and hope my resolve shows through. It must have, because he gives me a brisk nod, then exits the room.

Soon after he does, the lineup of suspects is taken away to, I presume, their holding cells. Detective Daron returns with some papers after a short time.

"Alright, I've got his processing papers here and your official forms to file charges. If you'll come with me, we can get this taken care of." All the guys go to move with the Detective and I but Detective Daron stops them with his hand in the air. "I only have two chairs for civilians at my desk. You'll have to decide which one of you is coming with because you can't all come to this part."

Well, shit. Now what? How am I going to choose which of the guys is going to come with me? But before I can even begin to eliminate anyone, Kyle steps up and takes my hand.

"I'll be the one going with her." His voice is firm and doesn't leave room for argument.

Warmth suffuses through me and my body releases more unknown tension. He doesn't look at me, just the detective, as we head out and make our way towards Detective Daron's desk. We go over the paperwork, sheet by never-ending sheet, and oddly enough, Kyle does most of the explaining over what everything means. Once all the t's are crossed and i's are dotted, Kyle and I shake hands with Detective Daron and then he leads me out to where the other four have been waiting in the lobby.

They all look up as we enter the lobby and the door closes behind us, sealing off all the noise with it. I'm not sure I want to deal with the looks they're giving me. Silas looks ready to rip my attacker's head off. Flynn has a slight grin on his face like he's proud of me and can't contain it all. Then there's Owen, who has his serious 'I'm taking everything in and making mental notes of the tiniest detail' look. Heath looks about as done with it all as I am. I look up to Kyle and see that he has a blank mask in place and my heart deflates at the sight.

I was hoping that him being here for me today, like he has been, meant that he was going to come around. That look doesn't say that, though.

"Who's hungry?" Heath breaks the growing tension as I search Kyle's face for any clue as to where he is with his decision making.

My growling stomach tattles on me and Flynn comes up to me, throwing his arm over my shoulder, pulling me into his side and away from Kyle. With a chuckle, he kisses the top of my hair.

"I think that means my little spitfire is!" he exclaims to the others, turning me toward the front exit and the rest of the guys fall behind us.

Before the door has a chance to close, a debate about where we're going to eat has broken out with three wanting a place that serves breakfast and the others wanting Mexican food.

They all look to me and I shrug, because honestly, it all sounds good to me.

I hold my hands up in surrender and back away towards Silas's truck. "You guys decide amongst each other. I'm good with either choice."

After we have breakfast at a Mexican restaurant, we head to Owen and Flynn's house, because Owen is going to finally show me his horses! Kyle excuses himself. Apparently, there's some last-minute work on a rifle order for a high-paying client that he needs to finish up and it's going to take all day. It sounds like an excuse to my ears but I know nothing about what his job entails.

We load up, with Silas, Heath and I in Silas's truck and Flynn and Owen in Flynn's car.

Pulling into the driveway while Flynn parks his car in the garage, we all get out and head toward the front door. Flynn and Owen just walked inside the house. Heath is walking with me and Silas is ahead by a few steps. I feel like a huge weight has been lifted from my shoulders, knowing that the man that attacked me is behind bars and won't be getting out soon, hopefully.

"Heath!" Owen shouts from inside the house in an urgent tone. I snap my head up and notice the front door isn't fully closed. It's slightly ajar. Silas takes off running through the door and seconds later, he also calls out to Heath. Heath grabs my hand and pulls me quickly behind him. Something is very, very wrong.

Before we make it into the house, Silas slips out and places his hands on my shoulders, moving me to the side of the door so I can't see inside. I can hear Owen and Flynn's urgent voices from inside but not enough to make out what's happening.

"Nora, doll, stay out here with me for a minute until Heath says it's okay for you to go in." Silas uses a soft voice that I only ever heard from him the first time we met when I was at his garage. They both share a look and Heath goes in while Silas keeps me outside.

"What happened? Why don't you want me going inside, Si?" The look on his face is grave and filled with sorrow.

A loud roar echoes from inside and makes me jump.

Panic is starting to bubble up inside me and I don't even know anything right now. "Silas what happened! Why is Heath freaking out right now?" Why the fuck is Heath falling apart!

Crashing comes from in the house and I try to bypass Silas but he's got a firm grip on my shoulders. I stare up at him and see the sorrow, the pain, the need to protect me and I know then that I don't want to know but I have to. More crashing comes from inside and it sounds like Heath is tearing the place apart.

"Nora, doll." Silas is trying to be gentle. He's never watched his words or tried to soften things with me before. Fuck, fuck, fuck. This really isn't good. "One of the dogs, they..." He swallows and I see tears brim in his eyes.

No. No. No. *Please don't tell me something happened to a dog.* I'm shaking my head before Silas can get any more out. He gathers me close and continues. "Bishop was killed and Cain and Loki are injured."

NO! Hot tears start streaking down my face and Silas becomes blurry. I can't fucking breathe. I can't fucking breathe!

"No, Silas, no. They're fine. Bishop must just be sleeping. Maybe they had a small fight but they'll all be okay. He's not dead!" My sobs make my words hard to understand and I don't know what he understood but I know he got the gist when he elaborates.

"No, doll. There's no way Bishop is sleeping. Someone did this. Someone broke in and got to him. It looks like the others tried to defend him but they were no match for whoever did this."

I hear sirens in the distance but I can't keep from replaying Silas's words in my head.

Someone did this. Someone broke in and killed Bishop.

** TO BE CONTINUED **

Made in the USA
Las Vegas, NV
22 May 2022